THE UNIQUE MAGAZINE
Fall 1990

ISSN 0898-5073
Cover by Frank Kelly Freas

Weird Tales® is published quarterly by the Terminus Publishing Company, Inc., P.O. Box 13418, Philadelphia PA 19101-3418. (4426
Larchwood Ave., Philadelphia, PA 19104-3916). Second class postage paid at Philadelphia PA and additional mailing offices. Single copies,
$4.95 (plus $1.00 postage if ordered by mail). Subscription rates: One year (4 issues) for $24.00 in the United States and its possessions,
for $30.00 in Canada, and for $33.00 elsewhere. The publishers are not responsible for the loss of manuscripts, although reasonable
care will be taken of such material while in their possession. Copyright© 1990 by the Terminus Publishing Company, Inc.; all rights
reserved. Reproduction prohibited without prior permission. *Weird Tales*® is a registered trade mark owned by Weird Tales, Limited.
Typeset, printed, and bound in the United States of America.

THE EYRIE

Old vs. New. Welcome to another issue of the new *Weird Tales®*, celebrating a *new* writer of horror and fantasy, Chet Williamson, and proving once again that a writer doesn't have to have been famous in 1925 to make the cover of the present incarnation of *Weird Tales®*. It has always been our intention that our *Weird Tales®* should duplicate the *experience* the original pulp magazine offered to readers of its own time. *Weird Tales®* in the 1930s was not primarily a reprint magazine. It was offering *new* material by such contemporary writers as H.P. Lovecraft, Robert E. Howard, Clark Ashton Smith, C.L. Moore, and so on . . . even the first efforts of such new kids as Robert Bloch.

That is why our *Weird Tales®* is not filled with reprints of stories *from* the 1930s. It would be as if the old *Weird Tales®* consisted mostly of reprints from 1880 and a few scraps from writers who died around 1910. It wouldn't have succeeded then and it won't now. We have no intention of following that course.

Certainly there have been successful reprint magazines in the past. Robert A.W. Lowndes was a master at editing them. His *Magazine of Horror* and his *Startling Mystery Stories* lasted many years, and made quite an entertaining

mix of reprints from the pulps — mostly *Weird Tales®* — and an occasional new story, such as one by, say, another new kid just breaking into print — Stephen King. But the appeal of such a magazine is inherently limited, and surely cannot contribute as much to the field as a magazine which provides a showcase for *new* material by contemporary authors.

So why, you may well ask, are we reprinting a Stephen King story from *Startling Mystery*, in this very issue of *Weird Tales®*?

We will admit that we've been re-thinking the no-reprints policy a bit. We will *not*, we assure you, try to save money and effort by using lots of reprints. But we think there are extraordinary cases where a story *isn't* available in any reasonable way and is of *great* interest.

We're willing to make exceptions. In fact, there have been more exceptions all along than we've actively pointed to. Gene Wolfe's "The Dead Man" in our first (Spring 1988) issue was a slightly revised reprint of Gene's very first story, which had never been published anywhere outside of a 1965 issue of *Sir!*, a men's magazine. Who saves old men's-magazines, other than *Playboy*? Not even Gene owned a copy of the issue. Certainly the story was completely un-

known to current readers. On this same rationale we will soon be reprinting Jonathan Carroll's first story, from a 1978 *Penthouse*.

We have also freely used stories which have appeared overseas but never in the United States. Mervyn Wall's "Cloonaturk," which we published in #296, was written in the 1940s and published in Britain. It had not been reprinted anywhere since 1974, when it appeared in Wall's collection, *A Flutter of Wings* (Talbot Press, Dublin). Considering that it tied for first place in the reader vote, we would have been foolish to have refused it in the name of a "no reprints" policy. We have also used several stories from the British magazine, *Interzone*.

The King story is a very special case indeed. The interest in anything King does is, naturally, enormous. Are we doing this because it will sell extra issues? Of course. We would be liars to say the thought had not crossed our collective editorial mind. Selling issues is our job. Anything which sells a few extra copies helps hurry up the day when we can make *Weird Tales*® bimonthly and publish *more* new fiction than ever.

"The Glass Floor" has previously appeared only in an issue of *Startling Mystery*, which was never widely distributed. It has not been anthologized. It does not appear in any of King's collections. On the collectors' market, issues of *Startling Mystery* usually go for about $5.00 apiece. *That* issue can command prices close to $200.00, which is a ridiculous amount to pay for a short story, we think. So we've decided to make it available to all the people who aren't willing to pay $200.00 a copy.

So, while we have not repealed our present reprint policy, we are willing to bend it occasionally. For example, our upcoming Robert Bloch issue (#300) does contain one outright reprint from an old issue of *Weird Tales*®, Bloch's classic short story "Beetles." The story

Editors & Publishers:
George H. Scithers
Darrell Schweitzer
John Betancourt
Assistant Editors:
Leslie Smith
Dainis Bisenieks
Diane Weinman
Michael W. Betancourt
Don Keller
Carol Adams
Circulation Manager:
Richard Kabakjian
Computer Consultant:
David J. Williams III
Of Counsel:
Yale F. Edeiken
Photographer:
Advanced Litho, Inc.
Typesetter:
Campus Copy Center
Printer:
Malloy Lithographing, Inc.
Hard-cover Binder
Hoster Bindery, Inc.

SUBMISSIONS?

Like most editors, we get unsolicited manuscripts, *lots* of them. We survive, as do other editors, only by imposing Rules.

Yes, we read unsolicited manuscripts — *if* they are in proper manuscript format. Each must arrive with a self-addressed, stamped return envelope big enough to take that manuscript back to you, or with a stamped, addressed, business-letter-sized envelope *and* instructions to dispose of the manuscript if not bought. And no, we will not read manuscripts in unacceptable format.

This proper format is described in numerous reference works. One of them is *On Writing Science Fiction: The Editors Strike Back!*, by George H. Scithers, Darrell Schweitzer, and John M. Ford — which also goes into the whole art and practice of writing and selling fantastic literature. *On Writing* is available for $19.50, postpaid, from Owlswick Press, PO Box 8243, Philadelphia, PA 19101 (if you live in Pennsylvania, add $1.17 for sales tax).

is accompanied by the new *screenplay* of the same story. The two provide an interesting illustration of how the print-to-screen process works.

Coming soon will be two or three never-before-reprinted Lord Dunsany stories, part of a huge lode discovered by S.T. Joshi and Darrell Schweitzer in the course of work on a Dunsany bibliography. They found close to *three hundred* previously unknown items by this master fantasist, a few of which might be of interest to *Weird Tales*® readers.

Thoughts on Fantastic Poetry. Verse has always been a part of the Unique Magazine, although never a central part. Verse is used in many magazines as a form of filler when there's no cartoon or ad available. 19th century magazines used a lot more short poems than modern magazines do, possibly because the technology for reproducing cartoons wasn't as readily available.

All of which sounds very cynical, and tends to trivialize the verse. Indeed, much filler-verse has always been trivial. There is no denying that any magazine, even this one, is *laid out* with the poetry used as filler. A magazine goes together like a jigsaw puzzle. Once the stories and major non-fiction pieces are in place, we fill in the available holes with poetry, ads, and art fillers.

But we don't *buy* poems like so many links of sausage. We buy them like stories. That is, each poem must be actually worth reading, even as the best verse from the old *Weird Tales*® still is. It's less easy to compile a list of classic poems from the old days than classic stories, but one does think of the "Fungi from Yuggoth" sonnet sequence of Lovecraft, and much verse by Clark Ashton Smith, Robert E. Howard, and perhaps Leah Bodine Drake.

This raises the whole question of what precisely we mean by fantastic — or even "horror" — poetry. At the lowest level, this can mean doggerel about ghosts and bloody bones, that is, a few trite images presented in a manner which vaguely resembles verse. Certainly we reject a lot that fits that description.

But the whole subject of poetry itself is a thorny one. We once knew a literature professor who was convinced that poetry had died in our culture at least fifty years ago. Certainly it is, as the phrase goes, "not at all well." An issue of *Publisher's Weekly* devoted to poetry publishing once quoted a publisher as saying, "The problem is, poets don't buy enough books."

Indeed that is the problem in more ways than one. The implication is that no one else *ever* would. Gone are the days when the general reader read poetry at all or even expected to. The reasons for this are too complicated to go into in detail, but we have found ourselves able to glance through whole issues of, say, *American Poetry Review* without encountering anything we would recognize as a poem, much less anything memorable. It is easy to blame academia, or Ezra Pound and/or T.S. Eliot and/or their followers, and certainly they must all share some of the blame. But poetry in English is in a fallen state. Poets are allowed to be completely obscure. We are expected to not so much *feel* a poem as puzzle it out. Amateur writers who admit they can't write prose turn to what they think is poetry, rather the way that, at any art school, you will encounter art students who admit they do abstracts because they can't draw; and no one seems the wiser, save for the audience, who have walked away long ago. Ezra Pound, for all he was quite an obscurantist himself sometimes, did utter words of wisdom on the subject when he said, "Poetry should be at least as well written as prose."

So, the malaise is in poetry generally, not specifically in fantastic verse.

The problem is that anybody,
just ANYBODY
can string a bunch
of words together
in short lines like this
even cutting the
words off
for
effect
and call the result poetry.
But nobody wants to read it.

So, how can we discuss the nature of fantastic verse when no one is quite sure what a poem is anymore, not even the practising poets?

Certainly we don't want doggerel about bloody bones. Anything we buy as a poem must *be* a poem first and fantastic just as essentially, but secondarily. We call to mind some of our own favorites in fantastic/horrific verse, much of Poe, Keats' "La Belle Dame Sans Merci," Coleridge's "The Rhyme of the Ancient Mariner," Yeats' "The Second Coming" — and we realize that only one of these was written in the 20th century. We admit that the only contemporary poet whose work we follow with any enthusiasm, to the extent of buying his new books as they come out, is Tom Disch. Possibly this makes us terrible reactionaries. We tend to gravitate toward traditional forms, even very exact ones like the sonnet.

Are there any rules of poetry? Yes, in *Weird Tales®* at least, there are.

First, a poem should be clear. In a college literature course it seems okay to say, "Well, I don't understand that, so it must be too deep." Not here. If a single line doesn't quite make sense, we will send the poem back for revision. We have done so. Sometimes we've been able to buy the result. The purpose of any kind of writing, after all, is to communicate. If we read a poem, then don't know what we've read, we judge that poem, as a piece of writing, a failure. We think you would too.

If a fixed form is to be followed, it is to be followed correctly. No thirteen-line sonnets, no limericks that aren't anapestic. If a poem is going to attempt rhyme, it should achieve it without too much straining to make "Polish" (of Poland) sound like "polish" (as in shoe-polish).

We do not insist on fixed forms, by any means. Certainly much fine poetry has been written in blank or free verse. (If you're going to try one or the other, you should know the difference.) But poetry must be something more than muddy prose chopped up into short lines.

For *Weird Tales®*, a poem should have some sort of fantastic content or imagery, but, returning to the requirement that it should be a real poem first, fantastic second, the poem should also have *something to say*. Like a story, it should be *about something*, and present something the reader hasn't read before. Certain fantastic images and moods can best be presented in verse. A poem is *not* simply a story in rhyme, even if it is a narrative.

A poem should have emotional content. It should be horrific, beautiful, eerie, sad, funny, or whatever. All literature is, at its most basic level, emotional, moving rather than clever. If you can grab the reader emotionally, much else will be forgiven.

We don't think, as one practising poet we know believes, that poetry has to be *re-invented* from the oral level up before it can have any meaning for 20th century Americans, but we do think that a lot of the standard ideas and much of the mystique of 20th century poetry are dead limbs which need to be chopped off so that something new can sprout from the living trunk. Here at *Weird Tales®* we prune, in our own small way.

About this issue's cover. For once we have tried an experiment of having many artists illustrate an issue rather than just one. We'd like to hear your

reactions.

This issue's cover is by that great master of fantastic illustration, **Frank Kelly Freas**, and it marks the 40th anniversary of his work in the field. Kelly sent along the following "origin story" about this particular cover:

Spring 1950. Artschool. Illustration class. Project: Magazine cover; two colors, no black. Any subject. Classmate, now pro, back from New York:

"Hey Kelly! That's a Weird Tales *cover!"*

"It's not finished. Right now I got the satyr playing a nothing horn and I want a Benny Goodman-style clarinet in there and . . ."

"It's done! Send it NOW! It's just what Miss McIlwraith wants . . . etc. etc. . . ."

"But it's not . . . etc. . . ."

So I sent it in and she grabbed it and ran it as her November 1950 cover, nothing horn and all.

Of course I was ecstatic. . . . That was my first cover for a national magazine. . . . But still . . .

Forty years I have agonized over that damned horn. The original painting, of course, was sold long ago — somewhat accidentally and without any pay (or my knowledge for that matter) — but definitely gone.

Then along came the fortieth anniversary of that cover — which represented the birth of my career as an illustrator.

George said, "Do it." — and I was overjoyed.

I did it. My way. At last — long last.

I won't say it's necessarily better than the original, and I don't think it's any worse — but four decades of a nagging Heart's Desire have finally been fulfilled.

What finer gift to celebrate my fortieth anniversary as a science-fiction and fantasy illustrator?!

Thank you, George.

We now start the letter column proper with a rather puzzling letter from **Phillip Fuller** of Catskill, New Hampshire, who seems to agree with us on some points, but does so angrily:

I would like to show my displeasure with your handling of the Weird Tales® *magazine. I expected some gore and adventure that would stir the blood, but all I get is the use of past glory to promote the magazine. Get rid of those references to Lovecraft and Bloch. They overshadow the featured stories and set a standard not even a resurrected Lord Dunsany could compete against. I know a kid in my school who reads* Weird Tales® *for its present writers, not because of is old glory. I demand more ghouls, the author of* The Monster Club, *and some characters we can relate to. That is the reason why Stephen King is so popular and Poe is a legend. Relativity!*

Puzzling, yes, because we do not regard this as a magazine that lives off its

past. The whole thrust of our *Weird Tales®* from the beginning has been to keep the magazine current. That is why we do not fill our pages with reprints from the mouldering pulps, but instead use living, contemporary authors. (The great irony is that the one dead author likely to make it into these pages soon is, in fact, Lord Dunsany.) So we are completely in agreement that the magazine should be contemporary. We think it *is*. But we hasten to point out that *Robert Bloch* is alive and well and decidedly contemporary himself. His most recent novels, published within the year, are *Psycho House* and *Lori* (both from Tor Books). We've mentioned Lovecraft, but hardly set up him as an Ineffable Standard to which all must aspire, except perhaps in the area of Cthulhu Mythos stories. Ghouls? Specifically stories about corpse-eating critters? Well the Arabian vampire in Tad Williams's "Child of an Ancient City" (#292) may not have been, strictly speaking, a *ghoul*, but it was one of the most impressive monsters we've seen in a long while. As for adventure, we think the recent long stories by Gerald Pearce and Michael Rutherford are decidedly adventurous. (And Rutherford offers authentic ghouls.) Author of *The Monster Club*? Maybe we are dessicated old relics ourselves, because we don't understand this reference. P.S.: We still like Poe, but have no plans to reprint him.

Greg Koster, a frequent correspondent, writes:
Issue 296 received, read, and enjoyed. Best part of the issue was the artwork. I know it is impolitic to dissent too nastily from the editorial verdict (you might print it, and expose my 'logic' to the readers!), but I have to say that Janet Aulisio has done the best job for you of all your artists, particularly on the cover. Whew, what a jolt that gave me. The interior illos were equally effective. One difference of note: for me at least Janet

SLAB'S TAVERN
& Other Uncanny Places

by John Gregory Betancourt
(Author of *Johnny Zed* and *The Blind Archer*)
Illustrated by George Barr

Betancourt's first short story collection assembles all of his fantastic 'Zelloque' stories, originally published in *Amazing Stories, Dragon Magazine, Fantasy Book, Marion Zimmer Bradley's Fantasy Magazine*, etc. A treat for all lovers of dark fantasy and sword & sorcery!

"Moody, brutal fantasy."
-- Orson Scott Card
Science Fiction Review

$15.00 (trade hardcover)
$35.00 (signed/limited edition)
Add $1.60 postage and handling
(In New York, add 4% Sales Tax.)

W. Paul Ganley: Publisher
P.O. Box 149
Buffalo, NY 14226-0149

Aulisio has always had a distinctive style. Even a complete ignoramus like me can often recognize her work, though it be unsigned. But there were a few pieces (pp. 125, 84, 73, 67) that I wouldn't have guessed were hers. I haven't noticed this happening in other mags, so you may have a chrysalis in your artist's showcase. Who knows what will come of this? But we saw it in WT first.

The featured author was not as effective as, say, Lee or Wolfe. I am easily annoyed by stories such as "Night Bloomer" or "Monster Movies" that have the too-ambitious junior executive gouging his way to the top — without actually showing what she or he does. Cavanaugh & Fairchild are thin characters compared to Cruz, and at least part of this thinness is caused by their lack of

anything to do. *Granting there are executives who do nothing, the bulk are sixty-hour-a-week workers, most weekends spoken for too. Whatever Michael Milken's sins (I have a ten-foot thick roll of paper for the abstract, if you're interested), lack of energy and purpose are not among them. Mr. Schow seems to know (or at least can imagine) drug-dealing better than high-level executive work.*

Seabury Quinn: I concur with your opinion of the Jules de Grandin tales, but I think your reasoning a bit shaky. Critical consensus: Which critical consensus? You say H.P. Lovecraft is a great horror writer? Not if you listen to, say, Edmund Wilson, for whom Gogol is the last word in horror. Too many critical consensuses are attempts to give some poor writer the works. Influence? This road leads to the Sam Moskowitz style of criticism, with post hoc ergo propter hoc being the sole God and Prophet. It is true that Influence isn't to be ignored (ask Mr. Hemingway), but the lack of Influence is scarcely proof of anything. Who imitates Tom Reamy these days? But who would try to say that he wasn't a substantial talent? Lasting Influence: This critter can be tamed, or enraged with a little manipulation of dates. Where was William Hope Hodgson in 1938? Or Robert E. Howard in 1950? Ergo, they are no damn good. No, I don't really believe either one of these arguments.

I don't know why I have gone on so at such length, unless it is to denounce all theories of criticism. It seems to me that the one thing they have in common is a desire to exclude, to shut out. But this shutting out is little more than an attempt to rationalize personal reactions, or to impose a party line on writers. The previously-mentioned Edmund Wilson is a swell example of the first, and the literary journals of the '30s and '60s will give you tons and tons of examples of the second. (Remember when H. Rap Brown was an important writer?) I guess my real objection is to the (in my mind) increasing trend in which writing about fiction becomes more important than the fiction itself.

You folks put out a fine magazine. Thank you.

Well . . . we could write a whole essay out of your next-to-last paragraph. Maybe we will someday. But the thing to remember about Edmund Wilson is that he does *not* represent a consensus. His opinion has been completely overwhelmed in the past forty years or so by pro-Lovecraft sentiment from around the world. His infamous essay "Tales of the Marvellous and Ridiculous," may now be found in S.T. Joshi's *H.P. Lovecraft: Four Decades of Criticism* as an historical curiosity, the sole example of *dissent* from the consensus. Only time tells these things. There *was* a brief period toward the end of the 17th century when William Shakespeare wasn't regarded as particularly important, but about two hundred and fifty years of criticism suggest that he is. More importantly, his work is still performed, read, and enjoyed by people other than critics — which is what really matters in the end. Any critic should acquire a certain measure of humility, realizing that anything he or she says may prove wrong in a hundred years. Who knows? Someday Seabury Quinn may be a great writer — but we rather doubt it. As you so neatly put it, critics are seldom at their best when they try to exclude or enforce a party line. Edmund Wilson, for all his other virtues, was too prone to tell us we should not read Tolkien or Lovecraft because they're unliterary, trashy, and bad for us. But millions went on to read them. Thousands of critics found merit in their work. (Both have spawned sizeable critical cottage industries.) And Edmund Wilson is remembered as a narrow-minded freak. His opinions on imaginative literature, by and large, have proven worthless.

Kenneth W. Meyer of Oxnard, California, writes:

At the risk of beating a dead horse, I'd like to comment on Seabury Quinn. "Pastiche" is certainly not the right term for Jules de Grandin. Derleth's Solar Pons is a pastiche of Sherlock Holmes; de Grandin is not, even though he has a Watson-type stooge. So did Hercule Poirot, after all, and nobody calls that a pastiche.

I'd say that Quinn was as original as Robert E. Howard. At the time when Howard was inventing "swords and sorcery," Quinn was inventing "guns and sorcery." Lovecraft's "heroes" mostly react, and don't believe in the supernatural visitations until they're clobbered by them. De Grandin, by contrast, is always in control.

Personally, I enjoyed the de Grandin stories Popular Library published. I wish they'd come out with more.

Agreed, "pastiche" isn't the way to describe the de Grandin tales. The *character* is original within certain (very narrow) limitations, and the stories do not replicate the plots or manner of work by someone else. But the character was of an already familiar type, even back in the 1920s. Quinn was an innovator in neither form nor content. And it is precisely *because* his detective is always in control that the stories have so little power compared to Lovecraft's. His menaces were never menacing. We never believed de Grandin was actually in danger. This limitation turned up again in TV's *Night Stalker* series: after Carl Kolchak had laid several dozen spooks of various kinds to rest, one more here or there hardly seemed impressive. De Grandin went through the same ritual *ninety-three* times. Possibly the stories can still be enjoyed, but only in small doses.

Now that we've aroused so much reader curiosity, we might mention where the Jules de Grandin stories can be found: 1) in the Popular Library paperbacks you mention, from about ten years ago. 2) In virtually every issue of Robert Lowndes' *Startling Mystery Stories*, circa 1966–71. 3) in *The Phantom Fighter* by Seabury Quinn, Mycroft and Moran (a companion imprint to Arkham House), 1966. 4) And of course old issues of *Weird Tales®* itself, not all of which, the later ones especially, are particularly expensive or rare.

Lawrence V. Conley of Davis, California, writes in praise of Michael Rutherford:

The Spring 1990 issue of your honorable magazine was excellent. The look, the feel, the art, superb.

I would especially like to comment on the story "Knight of Darkness, Knight of Light."

Quite simply, for sheer enjoyment and "whiskawayment," it was perfectly wonderful.

If I wished to read a traditional axe-&-buckler, doom-&-lost-city story, it would be one written by none other than the master R.E. Howard. His is a unique style that for the most part, in his Conan tales, grips the reader and pulls him or her into the pages and puts you right there in the middle of another world. Never, with the exception of Moorcock, have I found another writer in this genre that can hold me like Howard; not even Leiber or Wagner; but this story by Michael Rutherford grabbed me with the first line and held on like a champion bronc-buster. I felt for the demon. I thrilled for Ragnack. I was in the forest. I hunted the King boar. I saw the valley of bones and the cavern of darkness. I could empathize for both worlds.

Bang. Bang. Bang. Rutherford can tell a Goddamned story.

Simply put, "Knight of Darkness, Knight of Light" gave me hope that good adventure may still be found.

Although I consider myself literate and well-read, I am ashamed to admit that I have never heard of Michael

Rutherford. So tomorrow I will go down to my favorite bookstore and look for more of his writing.

Please, in the name of old granddad adventure, print more stories like this one!

Alas, the only thing by Michael Rutherford you might find in your favorite bookstore is the novella, "The Tale and Its Master," in the 1988 *Year's Best Fantasy* volume edited by Art Saha (DAW Books). "Tale" was Rutherford's first published story, originally a booklet from Spring Harbor Press (1987). It was a superb, amazing debut. Of course, on the strength of that, we eagerly sought Rutherford out. "Knight of Darkness, Knight of Light," was, to the best of our knowledge, only his second published story. A third, "Wager of Dreams," will be in our 300th issue.

David A. Smidt of Lakewood, Colorado, writes in praise of the Featured Author:

Thank you *for giving us the fantastic stories by David J. Schow! (Issue 296). Mr. Schow's style of writing is among the most palatable I've encountered since subscribing to the new* Weird Tales®. *"The Shaft" was so packed with humorous lines mingled with eerily foreshadowed scenes that I am an instant Schow fan. "Monster Movies" and "Night Bloomer" were also close favorites, followed by Michael Rutherford's "Knight of Darkness, Knight of Light." Please bring back Janet Aulisio in future editions!* Weird Tales'® *excellent print and paper seem to be the perfect format for her stunning artwork.*

But Schow proved somewhat controversial, as is demonstrated by this letter from **Margaret Frastley** of Duluth, Minnesota:

As an avid horror fan (and contributor to several small press publications), I was delighted to have finally gotten hold of a copy of Weird Tales®. I retired to my chambers that evening relishing the prospect of a good read — unfortunately I was to be partly disappointed, having the ill fortune to have gotten the SPECIAL DAVID J. SCHOW ISSUE. Not having heard of him before, I did not realize, you understand, what I was in for. Having read (and enjoyed) your letter column, I'm happy to know you're open to reading irate letters from disgruntled consumers. So, if you will, a word about "splatterpunks."

I am strongly of the opinion that this type of writing is (a) ineffably puerile, (b) subversive and decadent, and (c) a guise adopted by sophomoric goons who lack the skill to scare readers without bludgeoning them to death. Granted that WT was never intended to be a font of good taste, I still think you should exercise some discretion with material that might offend some readers. For one thing, these stories aren't even scary because they're too outrageously crude to amount to anything but sensationalist sleaze that appeals to immature minds.

As one well-known writer wrote, the point of macabre fiction is to disturb, not disgust. I dislike "slasher" films for the same reason I dislike this rubbish which the editors of this publication evidently consider worthy of devoting a large segment of the magazine to. The people who write this stuff must do it because they're too lazy and insensitive to produce anything of real artistic value. Also, if these twits want to broadcast their immature sexual fantasies, they should write for the skin magazines; there are readers, you know, who have a really low opinion of this type of written fecal matter and would rather be spared the bilious effusions of scatophagous blowflies who make the filth they feed on.

P.S. I appreciated Mr. Schweitzer's story, by the way — that's the sort of thing I DO want to read.

Whew. We can't help but feel that most of the "splatterpunk" writers would take your epithet "subversive and

decadent" as a very high compliment. We're surprised you'd not heard of David Schow, since he was so prominently featured in *Twilight Zone* magazine and has won a World Fantasy Award for "Red Light." We suppose you'll want to avoid his work in the future. Also, we don't think you'll like anything by John Skip and Craig Spector, and you will *definitely* not want to read John Shirley's horror novels. Schow's fiction is, by the standards of some of his colleagues, as pure as the driven snow.

From **Kevin M. Lemke** of Columbia, Missouri, we have this:

I know this is an odd statement, but I am afraid that you may have made a great mistake by publishing issue #296. It's just too good! From now on this issue will serve as the yardstick I will measure you by and I fear that it will be no easy task to achieve such heights again.

While I have enjoyed Weird Tales® *since it was revived, each issue had a few low points for me. But not this one. Absolutely everything was top notch! I would especially like to thank you for the David J. Schow stories. They showcased his great talent and versatility beyond the simple "splatterpunk" that is usually attached to his name.*

Without a doubt, my favorite story in this issue was Schow's "Monster Movies." I can't recall when I last read a short story that mesmerized me so. While this story is a radical departure from such work as "Jerry's Kids Meet Wormboy," it is no less intense, although perhaps the intensity occurs on a more emotional than visceral level. I saw brilliance reflected in this story (and in the interview) and think that this man is the writer to watch *in the '90s, regard-less of what field he publishes in.*

Second place goes to Rutherford's "Knight of Darkness, Knight of Light." His line, "The desire for death bound his thoughts like a crown of black ice," will remain in my mind for many years. I certainly hope Rutherford has plans to expand his novella to novel length.

Janet Aulisio's work is the finest you've published yet. (I'm sure this will work a few J.K. Potter fans into a frenzy.) Her dark, spare style beautifully complemented the contents of the magazine.

Another of our Eyrie Regulars, **Peni R. Griffin**, writes:

Ranking the stories was a tough call this time. "Soft" was the best, but "Monster Movies" was my favorite. Mr. Schow does not understand religion, but each one of us can only tell the truth we know as well as we can, and it behooves us to be gentle with one another's blind spots, insofar as they are not willful. He got all the important stuff right.

I didn't like "Knight of Darkness, Knight of Light" when I started, but it grew on me. A sincere pumpkin patch story.

THE MOST POPULAR STORY

Readers never agree on favorite stories, and even the most popular story can get a couple of last-place votes, but for *Weird Tales®* 296 we've got a hands-down winner: "Knight of Darkness, Knight of Light" by Michael Rutherford beat any competition almost two-to-one. Second place went to "The Shaft" by David Schow, and third to "Soft" by Darrell Schweitzer.

Thanks again to all readers who voted or wrote letters. Remember that The Eyrie is precisely as lively and interesting as *you* make it. Ω

THE DEN

by John Gregory Betancourt

Two months ago I accepted a job with Byron Preiss Visual Publications, Inc., as their science-fiction editor. (No, I'm not leaving *Weird Tales*® . . . just cutting down a bit.) BPVP is a book packager, which means simply this: we come up with the concept (either by ourselves or with an author) for a book or series, sell the idea to a publisher, and then create the whole package (cover art, illustrations, text, graphic design, etc.) We don't do the manufacturing or distribution, just the creative stuff.

If you browse bookstores, you've probably seen a number of series BPVP has done, including *Isaac Asimov's Robot City* and his *Robots and Aliens, Bill the Galactic Hero,* and various hardcover anthologies such as *The Planets* and *The Universe.*

It's been interesting so far. I'm seeing an entirely different side of the publishing industry (I'm used to viewing it solely as an author).

However, I've come to realize book packagers are getting an unjustly bad reputation in the science-fiction field of late. Norman Spinrad and various others have been lambasting them as unnecessary evils for months. Even my co-editor, Darrell Schweitzer, has been criticizing them in his book review

column in *Aboriginal Science Fiction.*

Frankly, I think these critics are wrong, and not because I've "sold out" and joined a packager. I thought long and hard about packaging before I decided to take the job with BPVP.

Let's look at the points the various opponents of packaging bring up, and see if we can dispel some myths:

1). Packaged books take rack space away from "real" books.

Wrong. Packaged books *are* real books. Those who say otherwise haven't been paying attention to what packagers are doing in our field. Byron Preiss Visual Publications (I use them as my example solely because I know them best — and also because they're the largest packager in science fiction) does dozens of books each year. You *can't tell* which books BPVP did unless you look on the back cover and see the credit line, "A Byron Preiss Visual Publications Book."

The most noticeable part of what BPVP does is the "shared-universe" series, which is often (but not always) tied in with a famous author. Hence *Isaac Asimov's Robot City, Philip Jose Farmer's The Dungeon,* or *Roger Zelazny's Alien Speedway.* But shared-universe books are just a drop in the

bucket. Packagers do single-author trilogies like Tom De Haven's *Walker of Worlds* — which just got a rave review in *Locus*. Packagers do anthologies: *The Universe, The Planets,* and *The Microverse* are all major hardcover coffee-table-sized books, half science fiction and half essay. (Connie Willis's story from *The Microverse* just won a Nebula Award, in fact.) Packagers do collections by major authors — Frank Herbert, Fritz Leiber, Philip Jose Farmer Isaac Asimov, and Arthur C. Clarke, to name a few. Packagers do original novels — like the ten novels BPVP packaged for Walker's Millennium imprint a few years ago, or the eight we're doing for Atheneum now. Authors like Robert Silverberg, Charles de Lint, Tanith Lee, Esther Friesner, David Gerrold, Richard A. Lupoff, Barry Longyear, Katherine Kurtz, Roger Zelazny, and Poul Anderson did original novels for this series.

Is a new novel by Roger Zelazny "taking rack space away from a real book"? Or a collection of Asimov's Robot stories? I think not.

The critics meant the shared-universe books, though, not novels by major writers. From most of their comments, I don't believe they've actually condescended to sit down and *read* any of the series they're criticizing. That would ruin their objectivity, right? Whatever, they've missed one key *advantage* of the shared-universe books. Simply, they keep children reading who would otherwise move on to comics or television or other less challenging pursuits.

Most of the shared-universe series that BPVP does are aimed at a young-adult audience. Children are more likely to stick to reading if they have a series they're following (such as *Robot City*), which now has over half a million copies in print. By keeping young people reading science fiction, these books are doing the field a favor . . . because someday these children are going to be buying and reading adult novels in the field,

too.

2). Publishers take money away from "real books" to do shared-universe series.

Publishers are in the business of making money. If they can make money by developing a new writer to best-sellerdom, they will. If they can make money with a shared-universe series, they will. It's not an either/or situation. You can't paint the world in black and white to strengthen weak arguments. (Well, you can; but someone's going to call you on it.) The truth is that publishers put out as many books each month as their sales reps can sell effectively. Having a couple of strong-selling series (and most shared-universe series sell a lot of copies) actually *strengthens* a publisher's line — it gives the sales reps more bargaining power with booksellers.

3). Doing hack-work for packagers takes away from a writer's "real" work.

This assumes that everything done for a packager is by its nature hackwork. Not so. There are a number of writers out there who are more prolific than their normal publishers want them to be. For a long time it's been the general wisdom that too many books out too fast will lessen a new writer's sales. Several of my friends are on a one-book-every-nine-months (and *no more!*) schedule from their publishers. What should a new writer do when he finishes a book in 5 or 6 months? Take up golf? Knitting? Write short stories (which have no guarantee of selling)? Or accept a contract to write a novel for a packager? Not all packagers issue "work-for-hire" contracts (where for a flat fee the packager owns all rights to a book). Byron Preiss Visual Publications doesn't; we offer an advance against royalties. Packagers provide a way for a professional writer to make a living *as* a writer.

Moreover, it doesn't have to be — and

15

shouldn't be — hack-work. A writer with imagination can operate within the limits created by a shared-universe series and come up with interesting, valid fiction. (I suspect that's why the *Star Trek* novels do so well — they're written largely by fans these days . . . people who *care* about doing a good job.) It's a matter of mindset. You shouldn't take a job if you don't intend to do it to the best of your abilities. It's the writers who go into a packager's project cynically intending to do the least amount of work for the most money who are doing the field a disservice.

When I wrote a novel in the *Dr. Bones* series for BPVP a couple of years ago, I certainly tried to be as original, ambitious, and creative as I would have been in a novel I wrote from scratch. Now that I'm an editor there, I expect that same commitment to quality and originality from everyone I work with, regardless of the series.

Let's admit it — we all read packaged books as children and enjoyed them. Who here didn't read *Tom Swift*? The *Hardy Boys*? *Nancy Drew*? Or any of the other quality series?

There's no reason those same high standards can't apply to series books packaged in the science-fiction field.

Lost Angels, by David J. Schow
Onyx, 252 pp., $3.95 (pb)

Dave Schow (as any regular reader of *Weird Tales*® knows, since he was Featured Author just two issues ago) is one of that rare breed of writer, the master of short fiction. You can tell just by picking up one of his collections (this is the second), opening it up at random, and beginning to read.

One example: "The inside of Darkmoon Occult Supplies' front door was festooned with tiny brass bells. Grant's eyes quickly dealt with the chaotic junkyard of merchandise and decorations and zeroed in on the store's only occupant." (pp. 72-73)

It's the clean, clear prose of an experienced hand, no doubt about it. You feel *compelled* to continue, because it's that gripping.

There are five novellas collected here, including "Monster Movies," which appeared in *Weird Tales*® a couple of issues back. The other four are all thematically linked (involving love lost), and three of the four belong in anyone's Best Of The Decade list.

"Red Light" is the story of a fashion model whose image is starting to wear out. Gripping, taut, and very tragic. "Brass," involving deals-with-dark-forces and the mystical properties of a brass bed. Deftly carried off, when it could have degenerated into parody. "Pamela's Get," about a girl whose friends don't realize how much they owe her — until she's gone. "Monster Movies," about the nature of fantasy, is delightful nostalgia that works because the protagonist is a little bit of everyone. Lastly, "The Falling Man," a hodgepodge about tarot that completely lost me. It's Schow working on his own weird level. Perhaps someone with more of an interest in tarot cards would have enjoyed it more; I was too confused.

All in all, four real gems make this a collection that should be on everyone's "must-keep" shelf. If you missed it, go out and hunt *now*.

The Night Man, by K.W. Jeter
Onyx, 283 pp., $3.95 (pb)

Jeter's latest is an uneasy horror in the worst sense. Not because the horror makes you uneasy, but because you're left not quite knowing if it worked. After a lot of thought, I've decided it doesn't.

The plot is simple: In a town where football jocks can get away with anything short of murder (including child abuse, wild parties, vandalism, harassment, mutilating small animals, etc.), Steven is the child they abuse. Steven's drunkard mother insists on sending Steven along everywhere his sister goes

(she's a cheerleader, dating one of the jocks), so they see him often and get plenty of opportunity for physical and emotional torment.

Poor little Steven just withdraws into a fantasy world where he's alone and they don't exist. And he dreams The Night Man into existence.

The Night Man rides around in a sleek black car and kills jocks, usually in imaginative and very gory ways. The book ultimately devolves into a series of murders, one right after another, which only the most jaded horror fans will enjoy. It's not so much the bad guys getting their just deserts after a long build-up, it's more a series of scenes from a slaughterhouse, as X follows Y follows Z to the grave.

Of all the characters here, I liked The Night Man the best. There is a long list of villains taking over center-stage to become sort of anti-heroes. The most recent example I can think of is Freddy Krueger from the *A Nightmare on Elm Street* movies, who holds whole audiences fascinated. However, The Night Man's appeal stems not from his charms (he has few), but from the human characters, who have none whatsoever. Someone needs to explain to Jeter that horror is about emotions, especially the reader's emotional response to horrible things happening to characters he likes. Unlike science fiction, which can fall back on strange settings or brilliant new ideas (and often does), horror is primarily about *people*. No one here is sympathetic. Young Steven is a pathetic wimp; Steven's family is disgusting; the jocks are wholly unsavory. Taylor, the well-meaning worker at the juvenile hall, is the closest stab at a sympathetic character — but he's more pathetic and ineffective than anything else.

There should be more to a horror novel than just a kind of neat villain. I expect more from someone as talented as Jeter. I read recently that he intends to give up science fiction and pursue horror writing. If his next book isn't better, I plan to write him off as one of those flash-in-the-pans who showed great promise, but threw it all away to join the slice-&-dice school of hack-hack-hack horror.

Kane, by Douglas Borton
Onyx, 350 pp, $4.50 (pb)
DreamHouse, by Douglas Borton
Onyx, 285 pp., $3.95 (pb)

Borton's two most recent novels have a lot in common. In fact, they're both variations on the same plot with different characters and explanations tacked on.

Dreamhouse is a typical haunting-ghosts-get-nasty story, in which a house captures the spirits of a murdered tribe of Indians. The Indians' spirits go a little crazy and lash out at the residents of nearby Otterton, California. A slay-fest ensues, with characters (some nasty, some nice) getting murdered in brutal but imaginative ways. The three little pigs who murder the police officer were particularly amusing.

Kane is a much more somber and less overtly fantastic version of the same story. Only this time it's a man named Kane (as in the Biblical Cain) who wanders into Tuskett, California. Since he's cursed to wander the Earth forever, he's sort of pissed off at humanity. So a slay-fest ensues, as he sets about killing off characters (some nasty, some nice) in brutal but imaginative ways.

In both *Dreamhouse* and *Kane* the biggest problems — outside of a plot that's far too predictable, and seems deliberately geared to appeal to the *Friday the 13th* movie audience — are the books' resolutions. In both, the endings come too fast and too easily. The reader is left completely unsatisfied, feeling faintly cheated. (If it's that easy, the characters should have done it sooner.)

As always with Borton, the writing is smooth and the characters believable. I

just expect more from someone with his obvious talents. Perhaps next time he'll try to stretch himself a bit more, rather than settle into a predictable niche.

Quick Chills: The Year's Best Horror Stories from the Small Press, Volume One, edited by Peter Enfantino
Deadline Publications, 172 pp., $14.95 (hc)

This new "best of the year" horror anthology concentrates on stories from the small press. Selected are 14 stories from 13 authors (the repeat is Bentley Little), from eight different magazines: *Pulphouse, The Horror Show, 2AM, Midnight Graffiti, The Scream Factory, DeathRealm, Grue,* and *Eldritch Tales*. You can't argue with a line-up like that; if I had to pick the best small-press horror magazines, I'd chose every one on the list. The only worthy omissions I can think of are W. Paul Ganley's magazine *Weirdbook* and Nina Kiriki Hoffman, whose strong little horror stories are always gems.

The authors here are a good selection, though: Edward Bryant, Jeff Radt, Bentley Little, Richard Lee Byers, Don Hornbotsel, Tracey Albert Knight, Wayne Allen Sallee, Buzz Dixon, Brian Hodge, Rickey Shanklin, J.E. Dressler, Ken Wisman, and Joe Lansdale.

While I don't always agree with the editor's choice (a few stories are a bit rough), it's an interesting selection. If you're not reading all the source magazines, you should consider picking up *Quick Chills* for a taste of contemporary horror where it brews best — in the underground.

Note: like the magazines it mines for stories, this anthology is a small-press endeavor, from binding (odd, but sturdy) to typesetting (home computer) to print run (600 copies). Order from: The Scream Factory, 4884 Pepperwood Way, San Jose, CA 95124. Make checks payable to Joe Lopez.

Deadspeak, by Brian Lumley
Tor, 487 pp., $4.95

Lumley's fourth installment in what Tor has been billing "The Necrosocpe Trilogy" is merely labeled "Necroscope IV" now. Interesting.

Of course it's much like the last three, which is good, because it's a formula that Lumley clearly makes work. This time Harry Keogh has been stripped of all his necroscopic powers by his son, a vampire now resident in a parallel universe, so he's no longer the superman he used to be. A good plot twist: Harry had become too powerful to be an effective protagonist.

So when a new vampire appears, Harry must not only face him, but also find a way to defeat him, getting his own powers back in the process.

There were only two elements I disliked in *Deadspeak*: First, the introduction of magic. (Though the series has the trappings of horror, the "supernatural" abilities demonstrated — right down to the vampires themselves — have all been explained in a thoroughly pseudoscientific way thus far. The existence of working magic undercuts the rationalism behind the earlier books' basic premise.) Second, the invocation to Yog-Sothoth in one of the spells, and the new implication that the Cthulhu Mythos is involved. Give me a break. . . .

Though not quite up to the level of the earlier books, it's close. Four instead of five stars. Fans of the series won't want to miss it.

Of note . . . :
I have here a one-volume encyclopedia. No, wait — it's merely that big! It's . . . Stephen King's 1153-page new edition of *The Stand*, now uncut, somewhat revised, and somewhat expanded. I haven't had a month to read it yet, but die-hard King fans should be aware of its existence.

According to the promo literature sent along, over 500 pages (150,000

words) have been reinstated by King. The setting of the book has been changed from 1980 to 1990. A new beginning has been added; the book starts earlier in the story than the 1978 edition. And there's a new ending — the story continues beyond the 1978 edition's ending. As King explains in his new preface to this edition, "I am republishing *The Stand* as it was originally written not to serve myself or any individual reader, but to serve a body of readers who have asked to have it. I would not offer it if I myself didn't think those portions which were dropped from the original manuscript made the story a richer one, and I'd be a liar if I didn't admit I am curious as to what its reception will be."

As part of its special marketing strategy, Doubleday has arranged a "*Stand* Hotline" (1–800–44 S T A N D) which started January 2nd. The toll free number provides callers with a 75-second recorded message. As of May 5, 1990, it was still operating.

Another book of note is Ursula K. Le Guin's *Tehanu: The Last Book of Earthsea* [Atheneum, 226 pp., $15.95, (hc)], which concludes the Earthsea trilogy — oops, series. I've begun *Tehanu*, and it's quite good — exactly what I'd expect from Le Guin. If you enjoyed her three previous Earthsea books, this is one you probably won't want to miss. A longer review next time.

A reminder to publishers

Review copies of new books, magazines, and related items should be sent to me at: 37 Fillmore St., Newark, NJ 07105. Many thanks.   Ω

PIERS ANTHONY
HARD SELL

MARS LTD.
WELCOME

FOR SALE

SEPTEMBER HARDCOVER

TAFFORD

MEET FISK CENTERS, TYPICAL 21st CENTURY MAN-

Yanked out of his comfortable retirement by the promise of mega profits in Martian land, Fisk is thrust from one preposterous predicament to another.

He saves an orphan girl from a deep space pilot with evil intent, hawks high rise cemetery plots, and barely escapes embalmment alive by an over eager robot mortician.

Then the fun really begins...

AT YOUR FAVORITE FANTASY AND SCIENCE FICTION SPECIALTY STORE OR, ORDER DIRECT FOR $18.95 PLUS $1.50 PER ORDER FROM:
　　TAFFORD PUBLISHING
　　P.O. BOX 271804
　　HOUSTON, TX 77277

JABBIE WELSH

by Chet Williamson

art by Janet Aulisio

Martin Faraday and Linda Beaumont had not heard any of the stories about Jabbie Welsh when they moved into the old farmhouse on Washburn Road, but even if they had they still would have bought it. Having lived in a succession of small New York City apartments for over a decade, and having lived in one of those apartments together for two years, they were ready to share a house, anxious to live in the city no longer. They both longed for privacy, and Linda welcomed the feeling of permanence a house would bring to their relationship.

They had first met backstage at the Beaumont. He was a set designer with a number of successful off-Broadway shows to his credit, and she designed costumes, so they hit it off quickly, and in a few months were living together in her loft on Christopher Street. The next two years were good ones, and when the opportunity came along to buy an old house upstate, they jumped at it.

A realtor in Albany had been scouting for them a few months, and called them immediately when the Welsh place became available. When they saw it standing alone across the field like a castle in a desert, they looked at each other and nodded in agreement. A walk through the old building confirmed their impression that it was right. It smelled damp, but was otherwise in good shape, and would need little restoration. After only a short round of haggling, they agreed on a price.

During the closing, Linda thought to ask about the house's history, and the realtor told them that it had been built in the 1850s by a wealthy farmer named Josiah Welsh for his wife Rachel. When the Civil War came, Josiah marched off as captain of a New York regiment, leaving his wife and a young daughter behind. He died two years later at Gettysburg. The daughter married, and the old woman lived there until her death, when the daughter and her husband took possession. Their family, the Washburns, had lived there ever since, until the last of the Washburn line, a widower who died childless, left the property to a friend who had put the house up for sale.

Martin and Linda moved in in September. The month coincided with the busiest preparations for the New York theatre season, so they found themselves commuting on an irregular basis. Martin drove down for a few days of concept, then returned to do his blueprints in an arboretum they had turned into a makeshift studio. While he worked, Linda drove down for fittings or to choose fabrics. To their dismay, they found that they only spent two or three days together each week, but somehow the house made it worth the trouble, and they made the most of the time they were able to share together.

They were just sitting down to a late dinner one evening at the beginning of October, when Linda mentioned the old woman. "I had a funny one today. A visitor. It was the weirdest thing. I was upstairs, sitting in the rocker in the front window, doing some sketches for *Volpone*. I looked down at my pad for a few seconds, and when I looked back up, there was a woman walking down the drive. But the drive's so long I don't know why I didn't see her before. It was

like she dropped out of the sky or something."

"Maybe she was behind the trees."

Linda shook her head. "I don't think so. Oh, she could've been, but I don't think she was. No one would come that way."

"What'd she want?"

"I . . . don't know."

"Didn't she come to the door?"

"Yes, yes. And she knocked. But I didn't answer."

"Why not? Was she selling something?"

"Well, she wasn't carrying anything. I thought at first she might be a religious nut — a Jehovah's Witness or a Mormon or something — so I didn't think I'd open the door. But then I figured since she walked all the way out here — I didn't see a car — I could at least see what she wanted. So when she knocked I went down to the front door with every intention of letting her in.

"But then I saw her shape through the sheers over the glass door, and . . . I just *couldn't* — I couldn't open the door. She seemed like a dark shadow, a bringer of bad news or something, so I went to one of the front windows for a closer look at her.

"She was in her late fifties maybe, and her clothes . . . well, they would have been perfect for *Mourning Becomes Electra*. I swear, Martin, it was a perfect post-Civil War ensemble, maybe 1870, 1880 at the latest. A fantastic recreation — buttons, hooks, everything looked authentic. I couldn't see her face too well at first — she wore a hat that covered it at the side. But then she turned, really slow, till she was looking at the window I was peeking out of. I don't know how, but I'm *sure* she knew I was watching her. It was like she could see right through the curtain, like she was playing a game with me. She was the cat and I was the mouse. I ran upstairs as quietly as I could, and when I went down later she was gone."

"But you saw her face?"

Linda nodded. "Grim. Like an old battle axe. Sort of a beaky nose, and a real pale complexion. And her eyes . . ."

"What about them?"

She shook her head in frustration. "I don't know. There was something weird about them, but I can't . . . not like she was blind, but they were different somehow."

"You mean different colors?"

The frustrated look vanished. "That's it. One was dark, brown or hazel, and the other was a really pale blue."

Martin sat back, his dinner forgotten. "Sounds like a gem. Sorry I missed her." He tried to make his tone light, but he was worried. He had lived in a small town until his late teens, and knew that not only cities bred crazies. "Wonder if she'll come back."

"God, I hope not."

"You were really scared of her, weren't you?"

She laughed uncomfortably. "Yeah. I was."

He rose from the table, went over, and put his arms around her. "Don't worry, babe. She was probably just a harmless old coot out to convert you to her particular denomination. If she comes back, don't answer the door."

"She was just so damn *weird* looking."

"That's great. Somebody who's lived in the village ten years calling an up-stater weird."

She laughed, and they started to talk of other things.

But a week later, Martin found out just how weird the woman really was. Linda was in the city for fittings, leaving Martin with some plans for an O'Neill revival at Circle-in-the-Square. He had just tossed down his drawings in disgust, and stepped out on the porch with the intention of stalking through the maple grove fifty yards away and beating the bushes with a dead stick until they gave him some inspiration, when he saw a

strange woman at the bottom of the porch steps.

Her clothes were those of another century, and somehow her face was too. It looked as though it would have been right at home on any of the faded tintypes Martin had considered for set dressing on the O'Neill. Linda had been right. *Grim* was the operative word. And if he needed more proof that this was the same unwelcome visitor Linda had seen, he had only to look at the eyes, one a dark brown, the other a blue so pale that it looked like a white marble with a small black blot upon it.

He stood for a moment, looking down at what seemed an apparition from a long buried past, then said (rather stupidly, he thought later), "Hello. Can I help you?"

Her jaw tightened. "You can," she said in a hard and grating voice.

That was all. He shrugged, and gave a little laugh. "Okay, uh, how?"

"This is my house. You're in my house." Her head moved in quick, peckish motions as she spoke, reminding Martin of the way a crow's head darts and jabs as it feeds on roadkill.

"Your house? I think you're mistaken. I own this house."

The woman ripped out an oath that Martin had heard and said thousands of times, but this was the first time he had ever been shocked by it. It seemed so obscenely incongruous coming from this staid old spectre of lost gentility, that he suspected she was truly a madwoman. "*Your* house," she snarled in her gravel voice. "This is a *Welsh* house. Are you a Welsh?"

"No, I'm not."

"God damn you, at least you speak true there."

"Look, who are you, anyway?" Martin spoke roughly, in response to the woman's remarkable rudeness, and to unwind the cold wire of fear that was twisting around his chest.

"A Welsh. Jabbie Welsh. And this is my house and has always been."

"Listen, this house belongs to me, and I don't care if you're a Welsh or a Corleone. I bought it from a Mr. Bryant, who it was left to by a Mr. Washburn . . ." Her eyes flared at the mentioned of Washburn's name. ". . . and it's mine, mine and Miss Beaumont's, and if you want to see the deed, have your lawyer contact mine."

"There are things older and stronger than deeds, you young bastard! As for Bryant, I never heard of him. And a Washburn shall *never* bide here! Now will you be gone from this house or not?"

Her eyes burned into his with a force that nearly staggered him, and he felt light-headed, as if in a dream. "No," he said weakly. "I said this is my house, and I have no intention of leaving."

"On your head then," she said coldly, and from somewhere in her voluminous dress she took two long and tapered needles that shone blindingly in the midday sun. She held one in each bony hand, and slowly started up the porch steps.

Martin realized later that there was not a single, sudden moment when he knew what she meant to do with those sharp devices. Instead the knowledge came upon him like a murky image that sharpened with each step the woman took, until he finally saw her clearly, plunging the long needles into his face over and over until his blood blinded him. By the time he realized her intentions, she was nearly on him.

He barely had time to throw himself backwards into the house and slam the door behind him with an outstretched foot before he toppled onto the entrance hall carpet. From the other side of the door came a sound like fingernails on a blackboard, and he knew it was the needles sliding against the glass pane. A duller sound followed as they scraped across the wood underneath, then silence.

He lay there for a moment, heart

leaping like a rabbit trapped in a pit. Then he sprang to the door to make sure the lock was snapped, that the insane old woman would not, in another second, burst through, needles raised above her head like the thunderbolts of Zeus. He thought of the gun in the den, and ran to get it. It was a .22 revolver, a present from his father when he had first moved to the city, that had lain untouched for years. Now he was glad for the comfortable feel of its cold metal in his palm, and the reassuring and businesslike click the chamber made as it snapped shut on half a dozen verdigris-coated cartridges.

When he returned to the front door, he pushed the curtains aside with an umbrella, then stepped around for a look.

There was nothing there, not a sign of a black-garbed bulk of female lunatic with knitting needles poised. He ran to the back door, gun held out in front of him like a crucifix warding off a vampire. The door squeaked slightly as he opened it, but there was no other sound, and he slipped out and circled the house, ready to fire at the slightest hint of motion. He moved more cautiously as he came around the front of the house, but there was no sign of the old woman. As he looked around, he realized that the grove was the only cover she could have taken. But the nearer he came to the densely packed trees and bushes, the less he relished the thought of entering their labyrinth. Dead leaves lay in thick piles underneath, and their crackling would announce his presence to anything standing in wait behind an overgrown bole.

Instead he turned back to the house, pulling out the key to open the front door he had locked from the inside. As he slipped it into the lock, he became aware that something was wrong, something was missing. Then he remembered the rasping scrape of the needles on glass and wood that should have made a scratch inches long in the dry and flaking white paint.

But there was nothing — no line of whiteness on the glass, no snakelike scratch in the wood of the door. Nothing. He stayed inside the locked house until Linda drove in late that evening. When he told her what had happened, she started to shake as if all the windows were open to the October chill.

"I knew it," she said. "I just knew there was something horrible about that woman."

"You know," said Martin, "the thing that frightens me the most — in retrospect, that is — is that I was actually ready to kill her. I found myself hoping that she'd try to resist being held, that I'd be forced to fire. And goddammit, Linda, I wouldn't have tried to wound her. I think I would've aimed right at her chest."

Linda put an arm around him. Now only her hands were trembling. "I know. I think I know how you felt."

"I felt *violated*, dammit. Jesus, all those years in New York and never robbed, never burglarized. We move up here and a nut tries to stab me with needles! It doesn't make any sense."

"There's another thing that's weird. Those needles. They must have marked the door. So why aren't there any scratches?"

He shook his head. "I don't know. Now I think maybe I didn't hear the needles hit at all. Maybe I just *expected* to hear them, so I did."

"What do we do now?"

"Go to the police. I'll tell them what happened. Who knows, there may be an escaped maniac running around here. With our information they may find her a little sooner."

But there was no escaped maniac, as Martin learned from the police the next day. The chief said he would send a man out to look the place over that afternoon, and told Martin he had received no other complaints concerning a woman

named Jabbie Welsh, or anyone of her description. As far as he knew, no one named Welsh had lived in or near the town for a long time.

The deputy came out at three o'clock. Martin told him the story and walked him around the property, but they found nothing. The thick carpet of dead leaves in the grove was undisturbed, and the woman had left no footprints in the soft dust of the driveway. The deputy, a gaunt, older man named Joe Kready, looked at Martin oddly when Martin finished his story.

"Jabbie Welsh, Mr. Faraday?" he asked. "You're sure she said Jabbie Welsh?"

Martin nodded. "Positive."

"Now that's a queer one." Kready rubbed the two-day stubble on his chin.

"Why?"

"Name's familiar. My daughter June, she went to Cornell and majored in history. Teaches at the NYU branch now, but anyway her thesis or whatever was a criminal history of the county, and she came across a court case — this was a few years back, mind, so I don't recall too much — but this case concerned someone named Jabbie, and I think it was Welsh. I remember it 'cause it's such a queer name, you see? Not her Christian name, but what other people called her."

"A nickname."

"Sort of. Anyway, this woman was widowed, and when her son, or it might have been a daughter, left her, she went crazy. People stayed away from her, but when a visitor came one time — it might have been a tax collector or such, *damn,* I wish I could remember — she killed him. Stabbed him with needles."

"Jesus."

"So it seems to me, Mr. Faraday, that somebody's playing you a pretty sick joke."

"You mean that someone might have dressed up like this Jabbie Welsh?"

Kready shrugged. "Don't know what else it would be."

Martin laughed in disbelief. "But why? Why would someone do that?"

"Christ, I don't know. But there's all kinds. You listen now. If that woman comes back again, just stay inside and give us a call. You got a gun?" Martin hesitated, then nodded. "That's good. You use it if you have to."

"Mr. Kready, do you . . . or does your daughter still have the notes from that case?"

Kready licked his dry lips. "June might have something. I'll call her. If I find out anything else, I'll get back to you."

They talked a few minutes more until Linda came down from where she had been working in the studio. Kready seemed a bit put off when Martin introduced her as Linda Beaumont rather than Faraday, but didn't let his moral discomfort show for too long, and became positively ebullient when Linda asked him if he knew of a good carpenter in the area.

"Oh, yes, ma'am. My cousin Fred Pritchett. He's a great one for carpentry. Makes rocking chairs and other furniture and sells them to shops in Albany. What do you need done?"

Linda led him up to the master bedroom, where she showed him a built-in mahogany wardrobe that hung open like an idiot's mouth. "It's a beautiful piece," she said, "but it needs refinishing and could stand a new door. The only thing is it can't be removed."

"You think your cousin would be interested?" asked Martin.

"Oh sure. I'll have him give you a call about it."

Fred Pritchett called the next day. He sounded cheerful over the phone, and said he could get to it that week. Linda told him they would both be tied up in New York City most of the time, but promised to drop off the house key so that he could come out and work on it at

his leisure.

"Do you think that's wise?" Martin asked when she told him about it. "Letting a stranger in here after what's been happening with this crazy lady around?"

"He's not a stranger. He's the deputy's cousin."

"I meant what if this Jabbie person would come when he's alone? She might hurt him."

When they dropped off the key, Linda told Pritchett that they had had a little trouble with a stranger, and not to let anyone in while he was there.

"I know, Miss Beaumont. My cousin Joe told me about it. Don't worry, I'll be careful. Besides, my boy'll be with me. Thanks for the key, and you have yourself a good time in the city. We'll lock up good after we're done."

Martin and Linda did have a good time. It was the first they had been in Manhattan together for almost two months, and in the evenings they ate at the old restaurants, visited friends, and caught some new shows.

"I'd forgotten," said Martin one night as they were walking down Fifth Avenue, "what this city's like when you're with someone you love." Linda said nothing, only snuggled closer to him as if to banish the chill. They walked without speaking, turning at 44th Street toward the softly glowing marquee of the Algonquin a block away.

Linda had just started to recall to Martin a particularly clever line in the play they had just seen, when suddenly a squat, dark shape seemed to *roll* from a doorway onto the sidewalk in front of them. Linda gasped, clinging to Martin's arm with a strength that made him wince.

It was an old woman, wrapped in so many layers of nondescript clothing that she looked like a ball of gray rags with a wizened face. One arm protruded tumor-like from the mass, thin, ungloved hands clutching a worn shopping bag filled with her life's debris. The other arm extended outward toward Martin while her voice rasped, "A dollar, mister? You got a dollar?"

He stared at her for a few loud heartbeats, then fumbled for his wallet, from which he drew a bill. When the withered hand took it, he barely heard the mutter of thanks that followed him as he steered himself and Linda around the hag and toward the safety of the hotel. He looked back once, but the woman was gone.

They went to the Blue Bar as they had planned, and ordered their drinks. Martin drained his scotch in under a minute, and laughed hollowly. "Christ, I've been panhandled a thousand times since I've lived in this town, and that is the *first* time I've ever felt *scared.*"

Linda kept nodding. "I know. There was just something about her. She reminded me so much of . . ."

"Yeah. Jabbie Welsh." He quickly signaled for another drink.

"It wasn't that she *looked* like her," Linda said. "It's just that . . . I thought she was going to attack us or something. God, that seems so crazy."

Martin lit a cigarette. He had quit smoking when they moved upstate, but had bought a pack at dinner that night, to Linda's disappointment. "We don't have to go back," he said softly. "We could live in the city again."

"Are you kidding? I love that house, Martin." She took a long pull from her glass. "They'll catch this woman. She'll do something else crazy sooner or later."

"We just better make damn sure that she doesn't do it to *us.*"

They drove back the next day, arriving just after noon. An impending storm had turned the sky to the color of dusk as they had traveled north, and light rain had just begun when they reached the end of their drive. A red mini-van was parked near the house, and a few lights glowed thinly through the sheer

curtains, giving them a cloudy view of the house's interior.

"Must be Pritchett and his son," said Linda, as Martin turned off the engine.

"Hope they haven't ruined the piece," said Martin. "They sure took their time getting to it."

Linda started to walk toward the front door. "I'm going to see how they're doing. Can you handle the bags?"

As she pushed open the door and stepped into the entrance hall, Linda immediately became aware of the smell. At first she thought she had left the milk on the counter to ripen for three days. But it wasn't that. It was deeper, richer than sour milk.

Then she listened, expecting to hear hammering upstairs, but the house was as silent as the empty theatres in which she had passed so much of her life.

"Mr. Pritchett?" she called. There was no answer. She had just started up the stairs when Martin clattered through the door, a flight bag in each hand, an artist's case wedged under one arm.

"What's up? They're not here?"

"No one answers." She called louder. "Mr. Pritchett?"

They waited for a few seconds. Then Martin set down his bundles. "Come on. Let's see."

The way his voice shook alarmed Linda, but she followed him as he nearly ran up the stairs, and as they padded down the hall she was surprised to find the smell growing stronger.

It was at its height in the master bedroom, where Fred Pritchett and his son lay on the floor, their heads pillowed by velvet pools of blood, their eyes and faces pierced by innumerable puncture wounds that made them look as though they had been stricken by a disfiguring plague. Except for the riddled faces, the bodies were untouched.

Linda screamed and bit a knuckle to keep from gagging, while Martin turned away and vomited helplessly on the worn hall runner. When there was noth-

ing left but dry, ragged gasps, he straightened up. "The phone. We've got to call the police."

Linda looked around in desperation. "The gun. Let's get the gun first. She may still be . . ."

Martin's voice cut at her. "No, she's gone! They've been dead at least a day. Christ, can't you smell it?" And he lurched out of the room toward the phone in the studio. She followed, filled with the age-old terror of being alone with the dead.

Chief Montgomery and Joe Kready arrived in twenty minutes, an ambulance behind them. A state police car pulled in ten minutes later, and while the medical examiner and police photographers did their work upstairs, the two local officers talked with Linda and Martin. Kready had gone white when he saw the bodies, and the color had not returned to his face. He asked no questions, simply sat on a settee staring down at the old, patterned carpet. When the chief finished and left the room, Kready stood up and walked over to where Linda and Martin were sitting, as if he had a secret to share.

"I talked to my girl," he said in a near-whisper, "told her about the trouble you were havin' and asked if she knew any more about the Welsh place . . ." He paused, and they could tell that the horrible picture upstairs was being played back in Kready's mind. "Goddam," he muttered. "Sixteen years old. That boy was only sixteen. Who'd do that? Who'd want to do that? Oh, Fred . . . oh Jesus H. Christ . . ."

"Mr. Kready," Linda said gently, "I'm so sorry. Please, please sit down."

Kready shook his head and blinked away tears. "No. No thank you, miss, I'm all right . . . Anyways, June sounded real funny when I told her about this. She said to me to tell you to be careful, that there were other peculiar stories hooked up to your house. Well, I knew you were gonna be away for a few days,

but I forgot about . . . about Fred and Terry comin' out. I just forgot." His voice started to bubble again, but he cleared his throat and went on. "She's comin' up to town tonight, June is. She said she wanted to meet you two, talk to you about all this. Could you come over?"

Martin nodded. "I don't think we'll want to stay in the house anymore. Not while that maniac is loose. What time?"

They left the house and the corpses to the mercies of the police, packed their bags, and checked into the Holiday Inn south of town. After a quick shower and a scarcely touched dinner, they drove to Kready's house and arrived at eight.

June Kready was a solemn, dark-haired girl, too buxom to be stylish. She wore the frank, unassuming expression of one who cares more for the company of books than of people. She came straight to the point.

"Your house has a bad history, Mr. Faraday." Linda lifted her head, wanting the girl to address her as well, but June's gaze remained on Martin. "You might have heard a little about it, but not all, I imagine."

Martin told her what he and Linda had learned from the realtor, as well as what Kready, seated uncomfortably in a fully erect lounger, had told them of Jabbie Welsh.

June nodded throughout the narrative. "There's more to it," she said, "and a few mistakes as well. When her husband didn't come back from the war, Rachel Welsh slowly went mad. Paranoid, I suppose. She believed people were trying to take her house away, seduce her daughter, who knows what else. She knitted constantly, and was never without a skein of gray yarn and her needles. Her neighbors gave her the nickname Jabbie, in part because of her chattering conversation, but mostly because of the way she used her knitting needles to make a point, or to ward off her imaginary persecutors.

"One of those 'persecutors' went a little too far and paid for it. He was a tax collector, name of Crane. The daughter, Eleanor, handled most of her mother's business affairs, but it got to the point where she couldn't bear to live with the old woman anymore, and didn't have the guts to have her committed. She left her mother and married a young man named Washburn who'd been trying to court her, much to her mother's displeasure. This supposed desertion sent her over the edge, and when this Crane came out to the house to inquire after the delinquent taxes, Jabbie Welsh killed him, stabbed him with those knitting needles."

"In the eye?" Martin asked. Linda thought he looked horrified, yet fascinated.

June Kready shook her head. "The accounts don't say. They were pretty circumspect about such details back then. At any rate, Crane's wife reported him missing, and knew that he had been planning to go to the Welsh home, so the law came out to investigate. They found Crane dead on the front porch, and Jabbie Welsh inside the house, sitting and knitting by a cold fireside. When the sheriff and his men tried to take her, she attacked them, and one of them struck her in self-defense. She fell against the fireplace, her head hit the bricks, and she shattered her skull. Died instantly. A few weeks later Washburn and the daughter moved back in, and the house stayed in the Washburn family right up until you bought it."

Martin nodded. "Except for Jabbie Welsh's death, that pretty well jibes with what we've heard."

"There's more," said June, and her puritanically solemn face grew even more rigid. "Supposedly, Jabbie Welsh appeared again. In 1895 one of a pair of tramps the household had turned away was found dead in a nearby grove of trees, his eyes and face pierced by some sharp object. His friend said they were

going to sleep there that night when an old woman stepped from behind a tree and started to stab his companion with long needles. *He* was found guilty of the crime and hanged.

"Then in 1919, when the family returned from a short vacation, they found a traveling drummer dead on the lawn. He had been stabbed, the wounds centering on the head. The murder was unsolved.

"The most recent occurrence . . . " She looked sadly at her father. ". . . not including what happened today, was in 1937. A young couple was parking in the driveway of the house, again at a time the family was away. The girl said that someone came up to the car and began stabbing her boyfriend through the open window. She didn't say whether she thought it was a man or a woman, since what happened affected her reason. She died a few years later in the state asylum. And that," she concluded, "has been the unpleasant history of the Welsh house."

All four of them were quiet for a minute. Then Linda's high laugh broke the silence. "You don't mean to tell me, Miss Kready, that a ghost has been responsible for what happened today?"

June looked at her with strangely cold eyes. "Can you come up with a better explanation, Miss Beaumont?"

"But the *physical* aspects," Martin said, "the fact that people were actually killed, not by fright, but by stabbing — doesn't that rule out anything supernatural?"

June shrugged. "Does it? If psychic research has any validity at all, there are some ghosts that transcend the merely ethereal. Poltergeists, for instance."

"But that's broken crockery," Linda said angrily. "Pranks. We're talking about *murder*."

"What's the difference?" said June. "If a ghost can throw a dish, why not a knife or a spear? If it can turn a

doorknob, why couldn't it pull a trigger?"

Martin cleared his throat. "There's something else we're forgetting. Jabbie Welsh was mad. A lunatic. So wouldn't her . . . her ghost tend toward the same random violence?"

"It might," June agreed, "but I don't think those killings were random. The victims might have been seen by a paranoid mind as interlopers, threats to the family or the house."

"All right!" Linda said. "Assuming all this *bullshit* to be true, what do we do about it? Call the *National Enquirer* and try to get their cover?" She felt furious at both the bizarre turn the talk had taken, and the way in which June Kready had studiously ignored her.

"You can do two things," said June, her calm irritating Linda all the more. "You can leave the house, try and sell it, maybe burn it down, or —"

"Destroy her."

They all turned, surprised to hear Joe Kready's deep voice. He had not spoken since they had arrived, and Martin had almost forgotten he was there. But now he rose from the lounger, his tall form looking like some spirit-possessed evangelist in the dim light.

"Destroy her," he repeated. "It should have been done years ago. I should have known what she was when you first told me about her, Mr. Faraday." His eyes were hollow, and his expression begged forgiveness for whatever misplaced guilt he felt. "I should've figured it out. If I had, Fred and Terry'd still be alive."

June put her arm around Kready's shoulders. "Daddy, there was no way to know." She shook her head. "We don't even know now for sure. It all sounds so crazy."

"No," said Martin quietly. "On the contrary, it all makes sense."

"Martin, are you —"

"Just a minute, Linda. June's right. There's no other explanation. We're dealing with a ghost here. A physical

ghost, who's strong enough and solid enough . . . and mad enough to kill. Only we've got to finish her first before she kills again."

"Oh, that's *great*, Martin," Linda said. "That's just fucking *great!* There's some wacko around here killing people *in our house,* and all you can do is leap on the lunatic fringe bandwagon. Well, not me, ace! You can take your crucifixes and wooden stakes and shove 'em! I'm going back to the city." She snatched up her coat from the sofa and stormed to the door.

"Linda, I —"

"Miss Kready, will you give my . . . *friend* a ride back to the motel?" June nodded.

"Yeah, I'll just bet you will. I'll leave the key at the front desk, Martin. I'll be at Charlotte's if you . . ."

She didn't finish, merely opened the door and slammed it behind her. There was dead silence in the room.

"I'm . . . sorry. I apologize for her. She's been under a strain with everything, and —"

"Forget it, Mr. Faraday," June said. "Even with all the facts it sounds crazy to me too."

"It's crazy, but it's real," said Joe Kready. "And it's gotta be stopped. So what do you say, Mr. Faraday? It's your property, but that thing killed *my* cousin and his boy."

Martin automatically dug into his pocket, only to realize he had smoked his last cigarette on the drive up from the city. June offered him a Winston and he took it. "All right, Mr. Kready. I'm willing on one condition. That's that before we try to destroy this . . . this *ghost,* we make sure, dead certain that it *is* what we think it is, and not just some crackbrained old woman. I don't want the police coming after us with a murder charge."

Kready smiled grimly. "I *am* the police. But all right. What you say makes sense."

Martin looked at June. "What about you, Miss Kready? Are you coming with us?" He hoped she was. She seemed oddly confident, and made the lunacy sound real, the solution practical.

June Kready smiled for the first time and nodded. "I'll be there. Folklore's a lot more interesting close-up."

"Anyone else?"

"I got a brother Bob," Kready said, "and Fred had two, Cyrus and Frank. They'll help us out, along with Fred's older boy, Wyatt. That's seven of us."

"Seven," June said. "Lucky number."

"Yesterday I'd have laughed at that as a superstition," Martin said. "Today I'm not so sure. But are they going to go along with this ghost stuff?"

"They'll believe me," nodded Kready, "and if not me, June. They know she's no fool."

"So . . . when do we do it?"

June shrugged. "I don't think it matters. Jabbie Welsh has appeared both day and night. Why not tomorrow afternoon? That'll give us time to get ahold of the others."

"All right. What shall I bring? I've got a gun out at the house."

"I know," said Kready. "That'll be good. I'll bring a pistol for June and a shotgun for myself."

"And something made of iron," June said. "A sword, an axe maybe."

Martin felt a lump come into his throat. An axe. Jesus.

"Well, we'd better get you back to your motel, Mr. Faraday. We've got a strange day ahead of us."

On the way to the Holiday Inn, June and Martin's conversation was more relaxed. It seemed to him that the battle plans had been made, and now the soldiers could talk about themselves and each other for a while. The first time she called him Mr. Faraday, he told him to make it Martin, but her reaction was not what he'd hoped for. Instead of further loosening her up, the remark made her more distant, and she called him noth-

ing at all.

It was not until he heard the sound of her car driving away that he realized he had been wanting to sleep with her, partly to get rid of the tension that was knotting his gut, and partly to strike back at Linda. He thought about calling her at Charlotte's, but remembered that she would still be on the road, so he had a drink in the bar, and went to sleep watching Arsenio Hall.

June called him at ten the next morning and asked him if one o'clock was all right to start out. He agreed and tried to work the rest of the morning on some roughs, but found it useless, and ended up watching game shows. When June picked him up at one, Joe Kready was with her, along with a heavy-set, red-faced man of about fifty who Joe introduced as Bob, his brother. The others, Joe said, would meet them at the house.

The sky threatened snow. It was cold enough for it, and Martin wished he had worn something heavier than his windbreaker. The Kready men both had on red wool hunting jackets, and the contrast made Martin feel all the colder in the poorly heated car.

The three Pritchetts were there when they arrived, huddled together in an old green pickup truck. Cyrus and Frank, Fred's brothers, seemed bluffly hearty, as if they were about to start on a deer hunt. But Fred's son Wyatt was as grim as death, and merely nodded when Joe introduced Martin. The seven of them looked, Martin thought, like a small army. Most of the men had a rifle or a shotgun, as well as a holstered pistol on their belts. Cyrus and Bob had hatchets dangling from loops in their poplin trousers.

"What kinda gun you got, Mr. Faraday?" Frank asked.

"A .22 revolver. Only it's in the house."

"Ah, screw that. Wait a minute." He reached into the back of the pickup and withdrew a red canvas case. He unzipped it and took out a rifle. "Here ya go. Thirty aught six. This'll stop whoever we find a helluva lot better than your popgun. She's already loaded, so be careful."

"How we gonna do this?" asked Wyatt sullenly. "Junie, what do we do?"

She answered while she stuck a clip into her pistol and chambered the first round. "I hate to say this, but I think we ought to split up. Not alone, though. Pairs. I don't think she'll appear if there are so many of us together. She could be scared off."

Cyrus laughed bitterly. "If what you say's true, Junie, that one ain't scared of the devil."

"What do we do if she shows?" asked Bob.

"Don't shoot first," said June. "Ask her to give herself up. She won't. She'll most likely come at you with the needles, so be ready. Do whatever you can. If you can kill her, do it."

They were all silent for a moment. Then Frank said shyly, "Should we say a few words first? A prayer?"

Joe Kready nodded and bowed his head. They all followed suit, and Martin looked down at the ground. "Lord," Joe intoned, "help us to do your will. We don't understand what's been happening here, but if there's evil, help us search it out and destroy it. Watch over us, and over the souls of Fred and Terry. We pray in Jesus' name, Amen." He straightened up and looked at the others with a firm resolve. "All right. June, you and Mr. Faraday come with me, Bob with Wyatt, Cyrus with Frank. We'll take the house. Bob, just roam around outside. Cyrus, Frank, look to the grove. Stay together. You see anything funny, give a holler."

They all moved cautiously away, as if expecting to kick a rabbit from the dry brush. Joe, June, and Martin walked up the porch steps and into the house. The smell still remained, and June wrinkled

her nose at it. They went single file through the first floor, Joe leading, then June, with Martin securing the rear.

The second floor was next. Martin looked out the window of the large front room and saw Bob and Wyatt moving behind the woodshed. He could see the grove, but Cyrus and Frank were hidden by the thickly grown trees.

Suddenly he heard a gasp from June. He swung around and saw her standing in the hall, just outside the door. "There!" she cried, and pointed toward the stairs. In a second Martin and Joe were by her side. Her hand dropped, and both men looked toward the head of the stairs. There was nothing.

"She was there," said June, panic edging her voice. "An old woman dressed in black, standing at the top of the stairs. Then she . . . she blanked out — just disappeared."

A gun crashed outside, then another. A man's scream cut the air, and Kready dashed to the window. "Cyrus!" he yelled.

Martin and June were beside him instantly. Through the window they saw Cyrus Pritchett running emptyhanded from the grove of trees. Even at that distance they could see the terror on his face.

Then there burst from the thick trees a woman in black who Martin knew was Jabbie Welsh. Her speed belied her thick skirts, and she caught up with Frank before he even reached the doorway. As the man turned his head to look back in horror, she struck with the needle she wielded in her right hand.

Martin saw the sharp metal flash dully, piercing Cyrus's cheek as easily as if it had been dry parchment. He thought he saw the red point protrude from the underside of the man's chin, but couldn't be sure.

As he watched Cyrus fall, watched the old woman straddle his body and plunge her needles again and again into his upturned, screaming face which grew redder and wetter every moment, Martin felt that he watched in a dream and was powerless to move, be it to flee or to help the man who lay dying outside his house.

Joe Kready muttered a strangled curse and ran from the room, his voice growing louder as he careened down the stairs, until he was screaming in hate and rage. Then Martin heard June's voice soft beside him.

"But she was *here*. She was up *here*." The girl seemed, like Martin, drugged by the sight of the drama below. As they watched, they saw Bob and Wyatt beat Joe Kready to the woman. Wyatt was in the lead, and when he was less than five yards from the woman, he pointed his .12 gauge at her and let fly with both barrels.

The shots caught her high in the chest, shoving her back and away from Cyrus, who had finally stopped moving. Martin saw the lead hit, saw the black satin and lace tear apart, saw skin and muscle and blood laid bare by that tremendous wad of shot.

And he saw too the woman quickly get to her hands and knees, stand, and run toward an unbelieving Wyatt Pritchett like a nightmare sprinter, leaving a stream of blood in her wake.

She dug the thin spikes into the boy's head, driving him to the ground, while Bob Kready pumped round after round into her from his rifle. Her body jerked as each slug hit, and she seemed disoriented for a moment after one bullet pierced the left side of her forehead, scattering pieces of her into the air like obscene confetti. But she merely shook herself and fell to with the needles once again.

"How? My God, how?" Martin heard June's voice through an aural fog that thickened each word.

Now Bob was swinging his rifle at Jabbie Welsh, slamming it against the sodden mass of flesh that his slug had exposed. But still she kept stabbing the

slick, red face of Wyatt Pritchett.

"How can she do that? How can she be that strong?"

Joe Kready came into view, springing across the driveway with his hatchet raised like a crazed Indian in a western movie. Screaming, he buried it deep in the woman's back and fell upon her, bearing her to the ground. She twisted beneath him, and shot one of her needles out and up, catching Kready directly in the soft round cavity just above the breastbone. He gave a quick, bubbling gasp through the newly-made hole, and folded into death.

"How?" June Kready whispered, gazing at the still body of her father on the ground below, not moving, both she and Martin trapped like a pair of deer in a headlight's beams. "I don't believe it . . ."

Then it came to Martin, a needle of crystal driven into his own eyes, stabbing the wisdom deep into his brain. "Belief," he said, and then louder, "*belief.*"

Jabbie Welsh was after Bob now. He had thrown down his rifle when Joe had died, and stood helpless for a pair of heartbeats. Then he turned and ran toward the pickup truck. His weight made him slow, and with uncanny ease she caught him and bore him down, out of Martin and June's sight, on the other side of the truck. He screamed three times, while ribbons of blood coursed into the air like gay, red streamers, spattering the truck top.

"She's strong because we believe," said Martin, and it suddenly seemed so simple, so elemental, that he knew he was right. When he turned to June, his face was alive again, his eyes glowing with the certainty of his knowledge. "Stop!" he cried. "Don't think of her, don't look at her —"

"She killed my father!"

"Forget it! She's not *there*, she's *not!*"

"She doesn't —"

"She's real! She's there now! She

killed them all!"

Martin shook her so roughly that her teeth snapped shut on her tongue, and she gasped with the pain. "You're wrong! Look out there . . . look out, but *don't see her!*"

He turned back to the window and looked down. Bodies littered the yard, and Martin thought he saw, just for an instant, an old woman, pale and ethereal, whose name he made himself forget. Then she was gone: the image winked out like a candle, and disbelief poured its cooling waters on his mind.

"She's *there!*" June screamed. "Oh my God, *look!* She's there!"

Martin looked, saw nothing. His fingernails bit into the heel of his hand as he struggled to maintain his self-imposed ignorance.

"She — " June stopped, then turned toward the door to the hall. Martin saw her eyes go wide, and she threw up her hand in front of her to ward off something only she saw.

Her right eye collapsed into a red ruin, and she shed tears of blood and fluid. Then her arms dropped, and she stood like a lamb accepting the slaughter.

Nothing there. . . .

An indentation appeared in her cheek, deepened, and the flesh parted as if of its own accord. Her mouth fell open, the muscle holding it closed torn by . . .

Torn by fancy, torn by imagination . . .

She fell to her knees, and Martin watched as the red marks appeared, one after another, in open mouth, running eyes, fragile cheek, nose, forehead, chin, neck . . .

Nothing! Only her belief, her BELIEF!

And Martin Faraday closed his eyes to banish the crazy vision, the thing that could not be. He threw himself to the floor, blotting out his thoughts, pulling blackness into his brain to deaden his mind, to eclipse the belief that could bring him death. . . .

. . . to destroy himself before he could be destroyed.

That was how the chief and two state policemen found him that evening, after Cyrus Pritchett's wife Mary called him and said that Cyrus and Frank had gone out to Martin Faraday's house and hadn't come back.

Cyrus, Wyatt, Bob, and Joe were all dead, scattered among the leaves on the lawn and driveway. They found Fred Pritchett in the grove of trees. June Kready's mutilated body lay less than a yard from where Martin Faraday cowered, drawn into a fetal position, open eyes seeing nothing. He did not respond even when the chief slapped him sharply in the face.

Three weeks later Linda Beaumont handed Charlotte Peters a cup of instant coffee and sat down beside her on the sofa in the living room of what had been the Welsh house. Charlotte, a hard-faced woman in her late thirties, was helping Linda, who did not want to be alone in the house, to pack. It was late afternoon, and they were nearly finished. They wanted to be away from the house before nightfall.

"Never?" asked Charlotte.

Linda shook her head. "They don't think so. It's as if his mind just . . . just blacked out completely, like all his thought processes were switched off."

Charlotte sipped her coffee. "What's the hospital like?"

"Horrible." Linda shivered. "But it doesn't matter. He has no idea where he is. He probably never *will* know. And they'll never find out the truth."

"The truth," said Charlotte. "Honey, we already know the truth."

"I'm . . . not sure. . . ."

Charlotte sighed. "Don't get on this Jabbie Welsh thing again — it'll drive you crazy too."

"I've been trying to tell myself they're right," Linda said. "That after I told Martin about the old woman, he *imagined* Jabbie Welsh and the needles, and that's why there weren't any scratches on the door. Maybe it *was* a drifter who

killed the two workmen. And then maybe the stories and the killings influenced Martin to . . ." Linda broke off. "No. No. I can't believe it."

She took another sip of coffee, and suddenly tears burst from her eyes. "Oh God, Charlotte, Martin loved this place so . . . and he was so kind, so gentle, he couldn't have done it. . . ."

The older woman put her arms around Linda. "Okay, baby, shh, it's okay."

"How could he?"

"I don't know . . . I don't. But he did."

Linda's eyes grew large as she blinked away tears. "No, I *saw* her. I saw her that first time." She looked up into her friend's face. "The old woman."

Charlotte shook her head. "You saw an old woman, nothing more. She never came back, but when you told Martin about her, it triggered something in him, and —"

"No, Charlotte!" Linda's eyes were huge now, and alive with purpose. "Martin didn't kill them!"

"Who did?" Charlotte demanded. "Who did, Linda? Who else could have? Jabbie Welsh? A ghost?"

"Yes!"

The word hissed through the room, and Charlotte pushed herself back from Linda, frightened by the force and the secret meaning of the word.

"Yes," Linda repeated, in a voice so soft that Charlotte had to strain to hear. "I believe it now. I honestly —"

But the sharp knock on the door interrupted her.

Ω

ANI-YUNWIGA

This is our land! Each snow-crowned mountain peak,
Each saw-toothed range, each swamp and level plain!
Alien, we challenge you who come and seek
A foothold in our country once again!
The lightning strikes when we hold up one hand
and thunder rolls and crashes when we speak!
Older than Earth itself, we silent stand
Against all comers — ! Hear them moan and shriek
And plead for mercy that they do not give,
For justice that is sham and mockery —
The broken treaties, and the "choice" to live
Or die where soldiers "drive" us . . . *who are free!*

Dare you encroach upon our hunting ground?
Dare you to laugh and prate of "Squatter's Right"?
Ah, if you only knew how Time turns round
And Space contracts and Day becomes Dark Night
For the True People — we who know no fear,
Since Yesterday is Now . . . and There is Here!

— Mary Elizabeth Counselman

THE GLASS FLOOR

by Stephen King

art by Bob Walters

INTRODUCTION

In the novel *Deliverance,* by James Dickey, there is a scene where a country fellow who lives way up in the back of beyond whangs his hand with a tool while repairing a car. One of the city men who are looking for a couple of guys to drive their cars downriver asks this fellow, Griner by name, if he's hurt himself. Griner looks at his bloody hand, then mutters: "Naw — it ain't as bad's I thought."

That's the way I felt after re-reading "The Glass Floor," the first story for which I was ever paid, after all these years. Darrell Schweitzer, the editor of *Weird Tales*®, invited me to make changes if I wanted to, but I decided that would probably be a bad idea. Except for two or three word-changes and the addition of a paragraph break (which was probably a typographical error in the first place), I've left the tale just as it was. If I really *did* start making changes, the result would be an entirely new story.

"The Glass Floor" was written, to the best of my recollection, in the summer of 1967, when I was about two months shy of my twentieth birthday. I had been trying for about two years to sell a story to Robert A.W. Lowndes, who edited two horror/fantasy magazines for Health Knowledge (*The Magazine of Horror* and *Startling Mystery Stories*) as well as a vastly more popular digest called *Sexology*. He had rejected several submissions kindly (one of them, marginally better than "The Glass Floor," was finally published in *The Magazine of Fantasy and Science Fiction* under the title "Night of the Tiger"), then accepted this one when I finally got around to submitting it. That first check was for thirty-five dollars. I've cashed many bigger ones since then, but none gave me more satisfaction; someone had finally paid me some real money for something I had found in my head!

The first few pages of the story are clumsy and badly written — clearly the product of an unformed story-teller's mind — but the last bit pays off better than I remembered; there is a genuine *frisson* in what Mr. Wharton finds waiting for him in the East Room. I suppose that's at least part of the reason I agreed to allow this mostly unremarkable work to be reprinted after all these years. And there is at least a token effort to create characters which are more than paper-doll cutouts; Wharton and Reynard are antagonists, but neither is "the good guy" or "the bad guy." The *real* villain is behind that plastered-over door. And I also see an odd echo of "The Glass Floor" in a very recent work called "The Library Policeman." That work, a short novel, will be published as part of a collection of short novels called *Four Past Midnight* this fall, and if you read it, I think you'll see what I mean. It was fascinating to see the same image coming around again after all this time.

Mostly I'm allowing the story to be republished to send a message to young writers who are out there right now, trying to be published, and collecting rejection slips from such magazines as *F&SF, Midnight Graffiti*, and, of course, *Weird Tales*®, which is the granddaddy of them all. The message is simple: you *can* learn, you *can* get better, and you *can* get published.

Copyright © 1967 by Health Knowledge, Inc. Copyright © 1990 by Stephen King.

If that little spark is there, someone will probably see it sooner or later, gleaming faintly in the dark. And, if you tend the spark nestled in the kindling, it really can grow into a large, blazing fire. It happened to me, and it started here.

I remember getting the idea for the story, and it just came as the ideas come now — casually, with no flourish of trumpets. I was walking down a dirt road to see a friend, and for no reason at all I began to wonder what it would be like to stand in a room whose floor was a mirror. The image was so intriguing that writing the story became a necessity. It wasn't written for money; it was written so I could *see better.* Of course I did not see it as well as I had hoped; there is still that shortfall between what I hope I will accomplish and what I actually manage. Still, I came away from it with two valuable things: a salable story after five years of rejection slips, and a bit of experience. So here it is, and as that fellow Griner says in Dickey's novel, it ain't really as bad's I thought.

— Stephen King

———— - ————

Wharton moved slowly up the wide steps, hat in hand, craning his neck to get a better look at the Victorian monstrosity that his sister had died in. It wasn't a house at all, he reflected, but a mausoleum — a huge, sprawling mausoleum. It seemed to grow out of the top of the hill like an outsized, perverted toadstool, all gambrels and gables and jutting, blank-windowed cupolas. A brass weather-vane surmounted the eighty-degree slant of shake-shingled roof, the tarnished effigy of a leering little boy with one hand shading eyes Wharton was just as glad he could not see.

Then he was on the porch, and the house as a whole was cut off from him. He twisted the old-fashioned bell, and listened to it echo hollowly through the dim recesses within. There was a rose-tinted fanlight over the door, and Wharton could barely make out the date **1770** chiseled into the glass.

Tomb is right, he thought.

The door suddenly swung open. "Yes, sir?" The housekeeper stared out at him. She was old, hideously old. Her face hung like limp dough on her skull, and the hand on the door above the chain was grotesquely twisted by arthritis.

"I've come to see Anthony Reynard," Wharton said. He fancied he could even smell the sweetish odor of decay emanating from the rumpled silk of the shapeless black dress she wore.

"Mr. Reynard isn't seein' anyone. He's mournin'."

"He'll see me," Wharton said. "I'm Charles Wharton. Janine's brother."

"Oh." Her eyes widened a little, and the loose bow of her mouth worked around the empty ridges of her gums. "Just a minute." She disappeared, leaving the door ajar.

Wharton stared into the dim mahogany shadows, making out high-backed easy chairs, horse-hair upholstered divans, tall narrow-shelved bookcases, curlicued, floridly carven wainscoting.

Janine, he thought. Janine, Janine, Janine. How could you live here? How in hell could you stand it?

A tall figure materialized suddenly out of the gloom, slope-shouldered, head thrust forward, eyes deeply sunken and downcast.

Anthony Reynard reached out and unhooked the door-chain. "Come in, Mr. Wharton," he said heavily.

Wharton stepped into the vague dimness of the house, looking up curiously at the man who had married his sister. There were rings beneath the hollows of his eyes, blue and bruised-looking. The suit he wore was wrinkled and hung

limp on him, as if he had lost a great deal of weight. He looks tired, Wharton thought. Tired and old.

"My sister has already been buried?" Wharton asked.

"Yes." He shut the door slowly, imprisoning Wharton in the decaying gloom of the house. "My deepest sorrow, Mr. Wharton. I loved your sister dearly." He made a vague gesture. "I'm sorry."

He seemed about to add more, then shut his mouth with an abrupt snap. When he spoke again, it was obvious he had bypassed whatever had been on his lips. "Would you care to sit down? I'm sure you have questions."

"I do." Somehow it came out more curtly than he had intended.

Reynard sighed and nodded slowly. He led the way deeper into the living room and gestured at a chair. Wharton sank deeply into it, and it seemed to gobble him up rather than give beneath him. Reynard sat next to the fireplace and dug for cigarettes. He offered them wordlessly to Wharton, and he shook his head.

He waited until Reynard lit his cigarette, then asked, "Just how did she die? Your letter didn't say much."

Reynard blew out the match and threw it into the fireplace. It landed on one of the ebony iron fire-dogs, a carven gargoyle that stared at Wharton with toad's eyes.

"She fell," he said. "She was dusting in one of the other rooms, up along the eaves. We were planning to paint, and she said it would have to be well-dusted before we could begin. She had the ladder. It slipped. Her neck was broken." There was a clicking sound in his throat as he swallowed.

"She died — instantly?"

"Yes." He lowered his head and placed a hand against his brow. "I was heart-broken."

The gargoyle leered at him, squat torso and flattened, sooty head. Its mouth was twisted upward in a weird, gleeful grin, and its eyes seemed turned inward at some private joke. Wharton looked away from it with an effort. "I want to see where it happened."

Reynard stubbed out his cigarette half-smoked. "You can't."

"I'm afraid I must," Wharton said coldly. "After all, she was my . . ."

"It's not that," Reynard said. "The room has been partitioned off. That should have been done a long time ago."

"If it's just a matter of prising a few boards off a door . . ."

"You don't understand. The room has been plastered off completely. There's nothing but a wall there."

Wharton felt his gaze being pulled inexorably back to the fire-dog. Damn the thing, what did it have to grin about?

"I can't help it. I want to see the room."

Reynard stood suddenly, towering over him. "Impossible."

Wharton also stood. "I'm beginning to wonder if you don't have something to hide in there," he said quietly.

"Just what are you implying?"

Wharton shook his head a little dazedly. What was he implying? That perhaps Anthony Reynard had murdered his sister in this Revolutionary-War-vintage crypt? That there might be something more sinister here than shadowy corners and hideous iron fire-dogs?

"I don't know what I'm implying," he said slowly, "except that Janine was shoveled under in a hell of a hurry, and that you're acting damn strange now."

For a moment the anger blazed brighter, and then it died away, leaving only hopelessness and dumb sorrow. "Leave me alone," he mumbled. "Please leave me alone, Mr. Wharton."

"I can't. I've got to know . . ."

The aged housekeeper appeared, her face thrusting from the shadowy cavern of the hall. "Supper's ready, Mr. Rey-

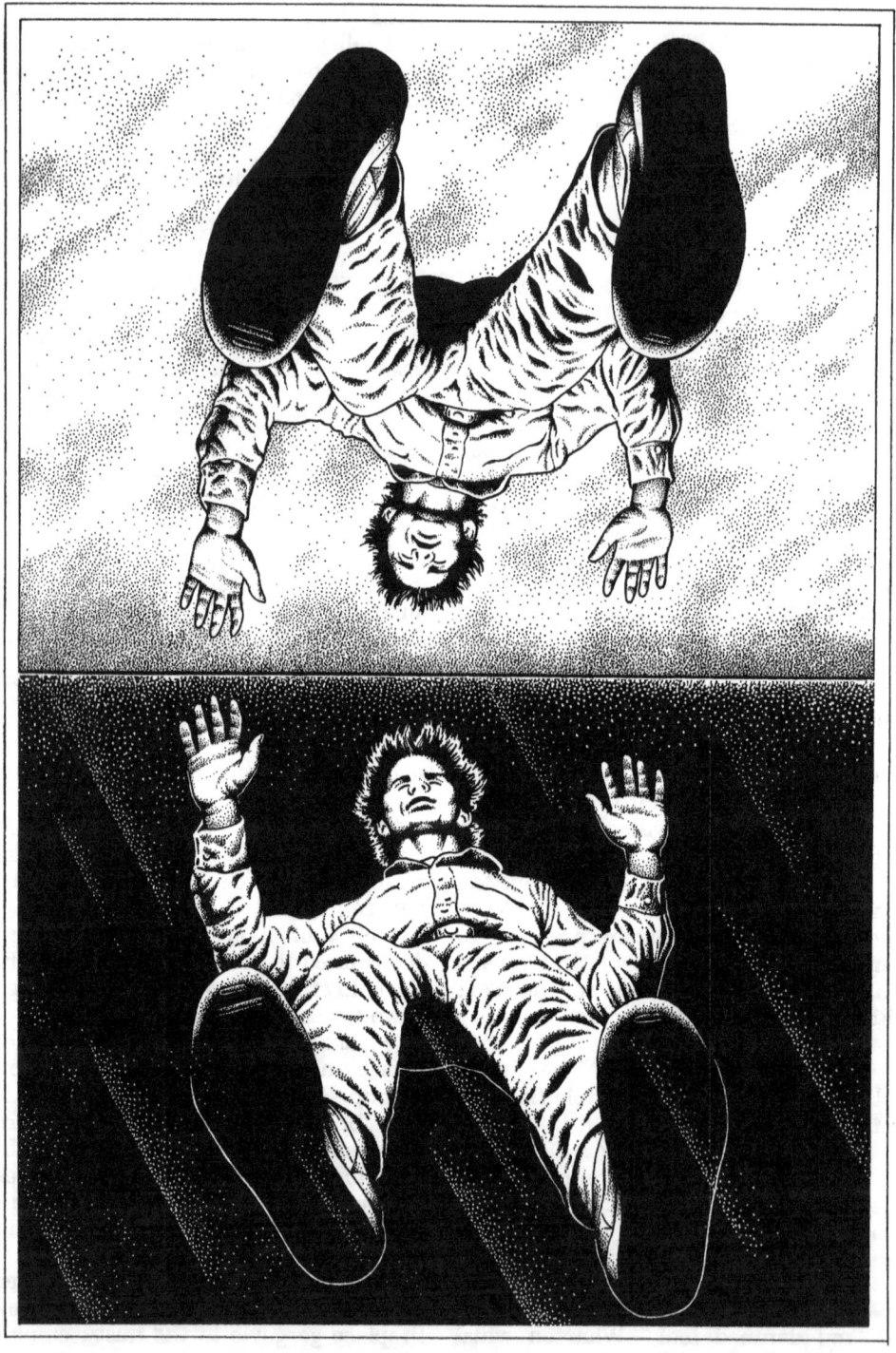

©'90 Walters

nard."

"Thank you, Louise, but I'm not hungry. Perhaps Mr. Wharton . . . ?"

Wharton shook his head.

"Very well, then. Perhaps we'll have a bite later."

"As you say, sir." She turned to go.

"Louise?"

"Yes, sir?"

"Come here a moment."

Louise shuffled slowly back into the room, her loose tongue slopping wetly over her lips for a moment and then disappearing. "Sir?"

"Mr. Wharton seems to have some questions about his sister's death. Would you tell him all you know about it?"

"Yes, sir." Her eyes glittered with alacrity. "She was dustin', she was. Dustin' the East Room. Hot on paintin' it, she was. Mr. Reynard here, I guess he wasn't much interested, because . . ."

"Just get to the point, Louise," Reynard said impatiently.

"No," Wharton said. "Why wasn't he much interested?"

Louise looked doubtfully from one to the other.

"Go ahead," Reynard said tiredly. "He'll find out in the village if he doesn't up here."

"Yes, sir." Again he saw the glitter, caught the greedy purse of the loose flesh of her mouth as she prepared to impart the precious story. "Mr. Reynard didn't like no one goin' in the East Room. Said it was dangerous."

"Dangerous?"

"The floor," she said. "The floor's glass. It's a mirror. The whole floor's a mirror."

Wharton turned to Reynard, feeling dark blood suffuse his face. "You mean to tell me you let her go up on a ladder in a room with a glass floor?"

"The ladder had rubber grips," Reynard began. "That wasn't why . . ."

"You damned fool," Wharton whispered. "You damned, bloody fool."

"I tell you that wasn't the reason!" Reynard shouted suddenly. "I loved your sister! No one is sorrier than I that she is dead! But I warned her! God knows I warned her about that floor!"

Wharton was dimly aware of Louise staring greedily at them, storing up gossip like a squirrel stores up nuts. "Get her out of here," he said thickly.

"Yes," Reynard said. "Go see to supper."

"Yes, sir." Louise moved reluctantly toward the hall, and the shadows swallowed her.

"Now," Wharton said quietly. "It seems to me that you have some explaining to do, Reynard. This whole thing sounds funny to me. Wasn't there even an inquest?"

"No," Reynard said. He slumped back into his chair suddenly, and he looked blindly into the darkness of the vaulted overhead ceiling. "They know around here about the — East Room."

"And just what is there to know?" Wharton asked tightly.

"The East Room is bad luck," Reynard said. "Some people might even say it's cursed."

"Now listen," Wharton said, his ill temper and unlaid grief building up like steam in a teakettle, "I'm not going to be put off, Reynard. Every word that comes out of your mouth makes me more determined to see that room. Now are you going to agree to it or do I have to go down to that village and . . . ?"

"Please." Something in the quiet hopelessness of the word made Wharton look up. Reynard looked directly into his eyes for the first time and they were haunted, haggard eyes. "Please, Mr. Wharton. Take my word that your sister died naturally and go away. I don't want to see you die!" His voice rose to a wail. "I didn't want to see anybody die!"

Wharton felt a quiet chill steal over him. His gaze skipped from the grinning fireplace gargoyle to the dusty, empty-

eyed bust of Cicero in the corner to the strange wainscoting carvings. And a voice came from within him: Go away from here. A thousand living yet insentient eyes seemed to stare at him from the darkness, and again the voice spoke . . .

"Go away from here."

Only this time it was Reynard.

"Go away from here," he repeated. "Your sister is beyond caring and beyond revenge. I give you my word . . ."

"Damn your word!" Wharton said harshly. "I'm going down to the sheriff, Reynard. And if the sheriff won't help me, I'll go to the county commissioner. And if the county commissioner won't help me . . ."

"Very well." The words were like the faraway tolling of a churchyard bell. "Come."

Reynard led the way into the hall, down past the kitchen, the empty dining room with the chandelier catching and reflecting the last light of day, past the pantry, toward the blind plaster of the corridor's end.

This is it, he thought, and suddenly there was a strange crawling in the pit of his stomach.

"I . . ." he began involuntarily.

"What?" Reynard asked, hope glittering in his eyes.

"Nothing."

They stopped at the end of the hall, stopped in the twilight gloom. There seemed to be no electric light. On the floor Wharton could see the still-damp plasterer's trowel Reynard had used to wall up the doorway, and a straggling remnant of Poe's "Black Cat" clanged through his mind:

"I had walled the monster up within the tomb . . ."

Reynard handed the trowel to him blindly. "Do whatever you have to do, Wharton. I won't be party to it. I wash my hands of it."

Wharton watched him move off down the hall with misgivings, his hand opening and closing on the handle of the trowel. The faces of the little-boy weathervane, the fire-dog gargoyle, the wizened housemaid all seemed to mix and mingle before him, all grinning at something he could not understand.

Go away from here . . .

With a sudden bitter curse he attacked the wall, hacking into the soft, new plaster until the trowel scraped across the door of the East Room. He dug away plaster until he could reach the doorknob. He twisted, then yanked on it until the veins stood out in his temples.

The plaster cracked, schismed, and finally split. The door swung ponderously open, shedding plaster like a dead skin.

Wharton stared into the shimmering quicksilver pool.

It seemed to glow with a light of its own in the darkness, ethereal and fairy-like. Wharton stepped in, half-expecting to sink into warm, pliant fluid.

But the floor was solid.

His own reflection hung suspended below him, attached only by the feet, seeming to stand on its head in thin air. It made him dizzy just to look at it.

Slowly his gaze shifted around the room. The ladder was still there, stretching up into the glimmering depths of the mirror. The room was high, he saw. High enough for a fall to — he winced — to kill.

It was ringed with empty bookcases, all seeming to lean over him on the very threshold of imbalance. They added to the room's strange, distorting effect.

He went over to the ladder and stared down at the feet. They were rubber-shod, as Reynard had said, and seemed solid enough. But if the ladder had not slid, how had Janine fallen?

Somehow he found himself staring through the floor again. No, he corrected himself. Not through the floor. At

the *mirror*, into the *mirror* . . .

He wasn't standing on the floor at all, he fancied. He was poised in thin air halfway between the identical ceiling and floor, held up only by the stupid idea that he was on the floor. That was silly, as anyone could see, for there was the floor, way down there. . . .

Snap out of it!, he yelled at himself suddenly. He was on the floor, and that was nothing but a harmless reflection of the ceiling. It would only be the floor if I was standing on my head, and I'm not; the other me is the one standing on his head. . . .

He began to feel vertigo, and a sudden lump of nausea rose in his throat. He tried to look away from the glittering quicksilver depths of the mirror, but he couldn't.

The door . . . where was the door? He suddenly wanted out very badly.

Wharton turned around clumsily, but there were only crazily-tilted bookcases and the jutting ladder and the horrible chasm beneath his feet.

"Reynard!" He screamed. "I'm falling!"

——— - ———

Reynard came running, the sickness already a gray lesion on his heart. It was done; it had happened again.

He stopped at the door's threshold, staring in at the Siamese twins staring at each other in the middle of the two-roofed, no-floored room.

"Louise," he croaked around the dry ball of sickness in his throat. "Bring the pole."

Louise came shuffling out of the darkness and handed the hook-ended pole to Reynard. He slid it out across the shining quicksilver pond and caught the body sprawled on the glass. He dragged it slowly toward the door, and when he could reach it, he pulled it out. He stared down into the contorted face and gently shut the staring eyes.

"I'll want the plaster," he said quietly.

"Yes, sir."

She turned to go, and Reynard stared somberly into the room. Not for the first time he wondered if there was really a mirror there at all. In the room, a small pool of blood showed on the floor and ceiling, seeming to meet in the center, blood which hung there quietly and one could wait forever for it to drip.   Ω

ALONE

By night I view the City of the Dead
But not alone, depending on the point
Of view. With chilling rain to anoint
My lowered brow, I pass the small green bed
Where lies the infant shade that died unfed;
And there a murdered matron by her stone
Weeps silently, hears not her neighbor's moan,
Remembering his suicide with dread.

I view them all, the Dead, but they are blind
To me, to one another, to the pain
All around them, save only for their own.
Am I alive? I wonder. And my mind
Balks at contemplating how swift the rain
Chills more than my sad being to the bone.

— Jessica Amanda Salmonson

THE MURCHESON BOY

by Patricia Anthony

art by Stephen E. Fabian

In the tarry blood on the chicken wire white, delicate feathers were stuck. They trembled in the wind that soughed through the pines. On the sandy floor of the coop were whole hens, looking somehow deflated in the first stages of death. Around the bodies were pieces of chickens, which looked worse.

It was near ten of a hot May morning, but the coop had trapped a shaded twilight. The air was claustrophobic; rancid with the rusted-iron stench of blood and the ammonia-reek of chickens.

"So whatcha gonna do, DeWitt?" Hody Knight asked as he turned his pale moon face towards the sheriff. He stood, his prissy bow mouth slightly ajar, his doughy hands stuck into the ragged pockets of his overalls.

DeWitt looked away from him and kicked at the severed, beady-eyed head of a leghorn. The head was easier to look at than the man. Hody had been a snot-nosed kid who had grown up into a snot-nosed adult. There was always something green and moist lying on Hody's upper lip. In the quiet of the hen house the sheriff could hear the man's heavy liquid breathing. "Shit, Hody. What do you want me to do? We ain't got no proof it was them Murcheson dogs."

Hody hawked pensively into a stained handkerchief. "Seen 'em run off that way."

The sheriff bent and fingered the hole in the wire where something had burst, not torn, through. "You told me it was dark night, Hody. Don't see as how you could spot a thing."

"Might find some chicken blood on them dogs still, if you wasn't too afraid to run over there."

Straightening, DeWitt felt the beginnings of a kink in his back. The humid air in the hen house had given him the queasy start of a headache. "Let's go look outside," he said.

Swiveling, he strode through the coop door and out into the yard. A fat laying hen, one of the few survivors, made a warm thock-thock sound in her throat and hurried away like a wind-up toy.

"What was your dogs doing?" The sheriff glanced up fast in time to see Hody's consternation. The big man looked marshmallowy, as if he contained more air than meat; and his two blank blue eyes sat in a balloon face that was empty of expression. Hody was a child's drawing of a man.

"They was barking."

"Uh huh." DeWitt stopped to inspect broken twigs. Something big, strong and determined had crashed its way through the brush.

"But they didn't go out. Don't blame 'em any. Them Murcheson dogs is pit bulls."

"Don't have to be dogs, Hody. Could've been a bobcat."

Hody hawked and spat, perilously near DeWitt's shined boots. The sheriff moved out of range.

"Ain't seen a bobcat round here since 'sixty-eight. Seen a lot of them Murcheson pit bulls, though."

"Uh huh." Hands on his thick belt, DeWitt ambled over to his squad car. Out of the relative cool of the shade, the late morning sun made DeWitt squint and his latent headache blossom into full-grown pain. The metal of the car latch was hot to the touch.

"You gonna arrest her?" Hody asked with a wide, idiot's grin.

"Yeah, Hody. I'm gonna arrest her. Accessory to chicken murder. Vet'll have to give her a lethal injection."

"No need to make fun, DeWitt," Hody said as the sheriff gunned his engine and put the squad car into reverse. "Weren't your chickens."

"Right," DeWitt called back. The wind tore his reply away as he negotiated a fast three-point turn in Hody's yard, splattering gravel.

DeWitt drove down the farm-to-market road a mile, turning in at the next mailbox. Above the clay road to the Murcheson house red oaks and pecans had interlaced their branches into an evening-quiet tangle of green. The ruts in the weed-choked path jarred DeWitt's teeth together, punctuating his headache.

When he drove up he saw Miss Murcheson already standing on her porch, her hands to either side of her wide hips. She'd apparently heard the car coming.

"Sheriff," she said simply.

DeWitt waited a few cautious minutes before unfolding himself from the front seat. Leaving the door open, he touched the brim of his hat and glanced around the yard for signs of her dogs. His right hand never strayed far from the reassuring weight of his service revolver. "Been some trouble up to Hody Knight's place," he began.

"Come on up in the shade, DeWittless. No sense you and me yelling across the yard at each other."

"Yes'm." His suspicious eyes took in the empty yard. A rusting chair led from a pine to a naked scar in the grass that was as perfectly circular as if made by a compass. The studded leather collar was still fastened at the end, but her male dog was gone. "Dogs run off?" he asked. He stopped in the shade of the stairs' overhang and propped one foot on a riser.

When Miss Murcheson didn't answer, DeWitt dared a glance in her direction. With her granite-grey hair and dry-leaf skin, she seemed like the wrong end of an Earth Mother. Her print house-dress was faded into a non-color, the exact hue of bones.

"I said, them dogs run off?"

"Who wants to know?"

"I do. I want to know bad. Could be them dogs is off running in a pack. Most of the feral dogs round here is farm mutts; but if we got a pack of pit bulls, could be real dangerous. Once they has a taste of blood, cain't never train 'em not to kill."

Talking to Miss Murcheson was like talking to a mountain. The words sort of settled around her oblivious shoulders and soaked in for a while until she percolated up an answer. "My dogs is dead."

"All of 'em?"

"All of 'em."

"Uh huh. How they die?"

"I shot 'em."

DeWitt squinted up at her. She looked uncompromisingly solid, as empty of moisture as a dead tree. "Why?"

"Got tired of feeding 'em."

He didn't like the answer, but it made some sense. He could see Miss Murcheson killing dogs for that. He could picture her killing a person for a lot less. "Uh huh."

Some movement out of the corner of his eye caused DeWitt to swivel. He crouched. His fingers fumbled for the snap on his holster.

"Just the boy," Miss Murcheson said.

There was a child standing hunched in the dust of the yard. Two deep-set eyes were punched into the brown clay of his face as if they had been put there by a careless, inattentive workman. His clothes were torn and streaked. At the end of his long arms hung huge hands: a man's hands.

DeWitt's own hand trembled on the diamond-patterned gun butt.

"Just the boy," Miss Murcheson said again.

There was something wrong with that boy.

She whistled and the boy lifted his head, staring at her from under the deep shadow of his brow. When she whistled again the boy came to her in a shuffling, crab-like walk. He climbed the stairs using his hands and feet both, as naturally as a monkey.

DeWitt backed away and stood in the sun, staring at them. The boy wrapped his long arms around Miss Murcheson's thighs and returned the sheriff's gaze. Something about the boy's eyes made DeWitt's stomach contract with cold, even in the East Texas noon heat.

"Your boy?" DeWitt had to swallow before he spoke.

"My boy now."

There was, the sheriff decided, some family resemblance, but it had more to do with expressions than the shape of the boy's lumpy face. Together the two looked like an American Gothic gone wrong.

"You . . ." DeWitt hesitated, wondering how to phrase the next question. He wanted to phrase it right because fear had made his sweat freeze down his spine and across his palms, so chilly he expected his skin to be brittle.

He was as afraid of the two people-shaped things on the porch as he was of himself. He was afraid he'd draw his gun and shoot them dead, not because they were doing anything particularly wrong or particularly illegal; but he'd shoot them out of disgust, like he might kill a rattler.

The look on Miss Murcheson's face went beyond an Indian's stoicism. Her patience was more like the patience of a rock. The boy's knotted, greasy hair fell down over his low forehead and hung in an unspeakable waterfall of black over the caves of his eyes.

"Where'd you get him?"

"From my sister's people."

DeWitt had heard enough lies to recognize one. "So if I was to go back to the station and enquire about a missing kid, I wouldn't find him on the list."

Miss Murcheson did an eerie thing: She laughed. He'd never heard her laugh before and didn't want to hear it again.

The laugh ended as suddenly as if she had been strangled. "That chicken killing. Was probably Hody's own dogs, like as not. Or maybe Tanner's dogs to the other side."

"The Tanner's got chihuahuas, Miz Murcheson. Don't seem likely."

"You tell Hody Knight for me. You tell him there's one way to teach his dogs, if he's got the balls to do it. Tell him to take baling wire and tie a chicken carcass round that dog's neck. That dog's gonna paw it off and bury it, but tell Hody just to dig that carcass up and tie it on again. Tell him to tie it real good, 'cause that carcass's gotta stay on two weeks till that chicken's real ripe. Dog won't eat nor sleep. It'll drive him crazy. But when that two weeks is up, he won't go killing chickens no more."

DeWitt backed up until his hip hit the fender of his squad car. He felt his way around the fender until he was at the door.

"You tell Hody Knight that for me," she said. "See if he's got the stomach for it."

It was the height of August when the first of the sheep were killed. DeWitt stood next to Scharina Wallace and looked down at the carcass at his feet. The sheep's eyes were gone, plucked out after death by either a turtle or a blackbird, and its empty blind gaze was riveted towards a far line of trees. Its mouth was open, and the overall expression on the face was that of ovine amazement.

"Be dogs," Scharina said.

"Wouldn't be surprised." Not as surprised as the sheep, DeWitt thought as he glanced down. The wound to the throat had killed, but it was the soft parts, the anus, the guts, that had been

eaten. The pelt had been ripped from its ribs. The flesh stretched across them was dry and hung like gruesome papier mâché to the barrel-stave bones.

"A.J. be out in the pasture tonight," Scharina told him. Her mahogany cheeks glistened with sweat. Her tight black curls wore a sprinkling of moist diamonds. "Got him a shotgun. Gonna kill me some dogs."

"Yeah. You tell A.J. to be careful. As DeWitt walked away he thought about the Murchesons' pit bulls. Then he thought about that Murcheson boy. DeWitt remembered the way the child had knuckle-walked up the stairs. He remembered the size of his hands and the flat look in the sunken eyes.

"Was a real messy kill," Scharina said as she walked beside him. Her head was down. "Messier than coyotes."

"Yeah," the sheriff said. He didn't like the look of the kill. He didn't like the look of that Murcheson boy, either. It was less like the boy had been born deformed than it was as if he hadn't quite made it to human.

DeWitt swiveled to look into Scharina's dark eyes. "You tell A.J. be careful, hear? You tell A.J. don't take no chances."

"Say he hide in a tree."

"Yeah," DeWitt said doubtfully as he cast his gaze up to the sky where vultures were already circling for a landing. "Yeah. Tell him not to take no chances."

From August to early October, the Sheriff's Department was quiet. Then, within a week, all Hell broke loose. Three of the Tylers' heifers were torn apart and the Andersons lost five sheep. DeWitt gathered some volunteers from the town to hunt predators; and while the men were out sipping beer, cheap heroism on their minds and their .30-.06's on their shoulders, Forgey Dentwilder's wife left him. Forgey came back, found her gone, got drunk, and shot out the Main Street signal light.

At three-thirty in the morning when he would have been better off asleep, DeWitt stood in jail and listened to Forgey cry. "She left all her stuff, too. All the stuff I give her, like it wasn't worth nothing. Shit!" Forgey shouted suddenly and slammed his hand against the unlocked bars of the cell. As quickly as his rage had come on, it disappeared. He was weeping again.

In the harsh overhead light Forgey looked bad. His eyes were swollen and puffy. His shoulder-length hair fell in greasy ribbons down his neck.

"Went off with that tractor salesman she was eyeing."

"Yeah. Like as not," DeWitt said, feeling badly that the wife had left while Forgey was out with the volunteers.

Because he felt guilty, DeWitt released Forgey the next day on his own recognizance. After that atonement, he began to worry about the dead livestock and forgot about the missing woman.

Then a week later A.J. Wallace disappeared.

By the time DeWitt made it out to Scharina's place, her family had already started arriving. That, more than anything, was a sign they'd given up on A.J. Black families gathered when someone was dead.

The men on the porch eyed the sheriff with sullen suspicion. He ran the gauntlet of their stares into the house.

The women were in the front room with Scharina. A side table was already piled high with food. When Scharina saw DeWitt her mouth opened in an O of anguish. She bent double at the waist and wailed.

"Get me Robert," DeWitt told a woman he didn't recognize. "Go get me Robert so he can tell me what's going on."

The younger boy came out of a back room and stood in a doorway. The sheriff put a hand to Robert's shoulder and

walked him out to the squad car. At his back he could feel the sharp resentment from the men.

"A.J. was out in a tree in the east pasture," Robert told him.

"Yeah. Any sheep dead?"

"Three."

DeWitt sighed and stared at his boot. "Let's go out there."

They found the three dead sheep. They found the tree, shotgun pellets embedded in the trunk. DeWitt followed a trail of blood and broken branches about four miles to where it ended in a thicket. He told Robert to stay back and then went in himself. A.J. was there. His throat had been torn out. The soft parts of his belly had been eaten.

DeWitt walked Robert back to the house.

"Sheriff?" Robert asked in a small voice. DeWitt had always felt the boy was either awed of or scared by his badge.

"Yeah?"

"Does dogs climb trees?"

DeWitt looked away quickly from the narrowed, dark eyes. "Mebbe it was a wildcat. Mebbe a puma."

"But I seen those sheep, sheriff. Weren't a claw mark on 'em."

The sheriff wrapped one arm about the boy's thin shoulders. "Shhhh," he whispered in what might have been construed as solace; what might have been interpreted as the safekeeping of secrets. "Shhhh."

When Robert started to cry, DeWitt hugged him tight. Back to the house, the sheriff told Scharina the news himself and called for the coroner. Then he went to his trunk and exchanged his .38 for a .45 automatic. He filled two extra clips and stuck them into his pocket. He checked the barrel of the automatic for stray grease and slid the nine-round clip in. His hands were shaking.

Miss Murcheson was waiting for him, an over-and-under shotgun cradled in her arms like a baby. When he got out of the car, he drew his .45, but left it dangling at his side.

"You want to put that shotgun away, now," he told her.

She didn't put it down; but she didn't point it at him, either. She just stood there.

"You didn't kill them dogs, did you," DeWitt said, watching her carefully. DeWitt was so scared he knew if she moved, if she even shifted her weight, he was going to shoot her.

She must have read something in his face, because she didn't even blink.

"They was purebreds. You wouldn't of killed them dogs. You would of sold 'em. If they was in any shape to be sold."

The sun slanted down across the porch, cutting the woman into half bright and half shadow.

"What kind of creature can kill a pit bull, Miz Murcheson?"

Her eyes darted to the right.

DeWitt froze where he stood, wondering if she was trying to draw his attention away. Then he wondered if there was something even worse than Miss Murcheson standing at his side.

"Go on, now," Miss Murcheson spat.

The wind shifted a little, bringing the greenish stench of rot into the sheriff's nostrils. Raising the .45 hip-high, not aiming, really, but prepared, DeWitt turned his head.

The boy stood in the yard, his thick neck strung with baling wire. The lump that had been Mrs. Dentwilder nestled its swollen, blue lips into the hollow of the boy's neck. Her platinum hair, in tangled disarray, spread down the flayed ruins of her shoulders. The corpse had been chewed apart from the waist down.

"Go on, now, honey," Miss Murcheson cajoled. Her voice was soft with a sort of maudlin, despairing love. "You go on round back."

Looking right at DeWitt, the boy licked his lips.

"Only way to break 'em," Miss

Murcheson was saying. "He tore her off and buried her three times already. Another week should do him. He'll be all right, then. Won't do it no more."

DeWitt's right arm twitched, bringing the .45 up into position. Out of the corner of his eye DeWitt saw a quick metallic glint as she wrestled the heavy shotgun to her shoulder.

The sharp clap of the .45 was as sudden and bewildering as thunder from a clear sky. It was so unexpected that for a moment DeWitt was sure it was her that had done the shooting, not him. He would have stopped and checked himself for pellet holes if the kick from the automatic hadn't jerked his arm over his shoulder. Across the blue-white fog of cordite, he saw Miss Murcheson fly backwards. Droplets of blood spray-painted the weathered wall behind her.

"Jesus wept!" he shouted in terror.

He'd never shot anyone before, but he had seen the effects of bullets. DeWitt felt amazement and then a weak-kneed sort of relief when Miss Murcheson pulled herself up from the porch.

"Don't you hurt him, DeWitt," she was saying. Her left arm was waving frantically for his attention. Her right hung heavily at her bloodied side.

Across the yard the boy was sniffing the air, his nostrils wide and quivering. His pale eyes were alert and steady the way a dog's are before the kill. He was staring right at Miss Murcheson's bleeding shoulder.

"Don't you hurt him, now," she was still saying when the boy leapt.

Miss Murcheson saw the boy coming and uttered a short cry of anguish. Still screaming, she sprinted towards the trees. The boy bounded after her with his long, leaping strides. It would have been smarter for her to have picked up the shotgun. It was the running away that killed her. Shouldn't ever run from a wild animal. Miss Murcheson knew that.

But the sheriff also knew that there were some people you couldn't bring yourself to shoot. Not ever. No matter what they had done. There were some people you'd just rather die than kill.

DeWitt's first bullet took a chunk out of the porch railing. His next hit the platinum head of the rotting corpse, sending bits of flesh up in a pink and grey explosion.

It took DeWitt fifteen minutes to track them through the pines. By the time he found them, Miss Murcheson was pretty well dead. Her eyes were still moving and her hands still twitched, but the boy had already started feeding.

DeWitt took slow aim, holding the gun with both hands, and pumped six quick rounds into them. Some bullets hit the boy's knotted face; some hit the woman under him. DeWitt would later excuse himself by thinking he couldn't have helped that.

But he could have helped the next thing he did. When the automatic was empty, he put another clip in. He fired until that one was gone. He pumped every bullet he had into both bodies, partly out of his own fear; and partly out of his own disgust.

Then he buried them. All three of them. He didn't know quite why he did that, either, except he really didn't want to know what that boy was or where he had come from. He was tired and really didn't feel like telling Scharina or anybody else the story. His job was to protect people, after all.

He went back to the house, cleaned up the blood, wiped the shotgun free of prints and put it into its place above Miss Murcheson's mantle. She had a pot of beans going, and he turned the gas off under them. When he left he locked the door.

He drove back to town and got another group of volunteers together. Under DeWitt's direction, they shot every coyote and feral dog in the county. They celebrated when the predation stopped.

Ω

HERA'S MADNESS

by Kij Johnson

art by George Barr

A man is an unusual thing in the Amazon court during the rainy season. Most envoys travel in the summer when the roads are firmer and the bandits not so desperately hungry. Whatever the season, no one arrives alone and unheralded.

My women were inside the great hall when the stranger was brought to me. They lounged on the long tables pushed against white walls hung with weapons, cleaning their blades or shouting criticisms to the women in mock combat in the center of the hall.

My consort Antiope was fighting a younger woman with spears and weighted nets, shouting instructions for the use of the strange combination to her opponent. Intent on picking Antiope's voice from the surrounding noise, the girl forgot her feet and stumbled over a boarhound that suddenly burst across the space. For a moment it seemed she would regain her balance; then she fell in a tangle of net, spear and hound. The spectators laughed and beat their weapons together in appreciation. The noise drew the rest of the dogs from their bones by the fire into the hall's center to bark in loud high voices at their howling companion. Antiope knelt in the soft rushes to free her opponent from the mess: I couldn't hear her laughter over the din, but her shoulders were shaking.

The man in the doorway cut a swath of silence across the room. He was bigger than any man I had seen, and at first he seemed half-lion, for his head was hooded by a huge lion's mane, and great golden paws crossed his chest to tie over his heart, fastening an entire skin. He bent his head to pass under the entry lintel, though not even Antiope, who is the tallest of us all, can reach that lintel. The guardswoman who brought him in barely reached his chest. He was unarmed, but his hands were as big as clubs and looked equally capable of driving stakes into summer-hard ground.

I walked from my seat by the fire across the ringing silence to the giant. Antiope ran to stand protectively at my shoulder, the spear and net ready in her hands.

"Welcome, stranger. Know that you are in the court of the Amazons. I am their queen, Hippolyte." Up close, he seemed even larger: my eyes were just even with the claws of the lion's front feet. "Share our fire. I will have food and wine brought." I gestured to Antiope. She eyed the man warily, then made some private decision and ran off to perform the task. But she took the weapons out of his reach, I noted with amusement.

"Thank you, Queen. I am grateful for your openhandedness. It's a hard wet walk from your port to your halls this time of year. But I have to tell you now, before I eat your meat and drink your wine, that I come with a shameful request." His voice was low and harsh. It rumbled far below the lightness of sound usual to my court — women's and dogs' high voices, and the brilliant hiss and clang of weapon against weapon. The cold had turned his skin pallid green, but warming in the hall he flushed olive, a Greek complexion. Water slid from his wet black ringlets to lay clammy tracks across his flat features and drop into his

close dark beard.

I was getting a crick in my neck from craning up at him. I rolled my head, listening to the crackle behind my ears. "Eee, you're tall. Let's sit down before my neck breaks. We'll talk after I've served my duty as host."

He followed me to the backed benches beside the greater hearth, lifting his big feet over the hounds and wineskins and pottery that lay near the fire. He gestured toward the mess, his voice warm with what might have been amusement. "You keep an informal court, Queen."

"In the winter, yes. In summer, I hold as high a court as any, but I personally don't care for these things. When it's so cold and rainy out, this is the best place for the women to gather and practice." I kicked at the thick rushes that lay over the packed-earth floor. "The padding makes for a softer fall." His eyes met mine and I saw his understanding.

"My lord." Antiope knelt formally on the ground offering a tray to the giant, as she would for an official envoy. On it sat meat and redware vessels and a chased silver cup. Not waiting for her to mix the wine and water, the man lifted the cup.

"I have never seen work like this," he said curiously, turning the silver in his great hands so that it ran with firelight. The little finger of his right hand ended in a jagged stump, as if it had been bitten off.

Antiope stood, forgetting her role. "It was the gift of a Persian prince to Hippolyte." She caught his wrist to hold the cup still as she filled it. "The pattern is pounded into the metal from the back. See, it's a hunt. Here's the hart."

"It must be a treasure of your court." His head bent close to the tiny figures, as if he were a child poring over some new thing.

Antiope laid down the tray and made obeisance again, but with her face turned so that I could see the laughter there. Then she left us alone.

One-handed, the man hauled the huge lionskin off and dropped it before the fire to dry, where it gave off a sharp smell as it heated. Even without it, he looked like a lion — burly of build, with shoulders broad enough to lift an ox. I have seen statues of the Greeks' Zeus, and they looked like this man, with his shoulders and his flat face. Still, he seemed mortal enough in spite of his size. Dark bruises and pale scars mottled his chest and arms. Four recent parallel scars scraped across his collarbone, I guessed the marks of the beast whose skin lay drying on the hearth. I recognized the pattern: I killed a leopard in my sixteenth summer, and I still bear the tracks over the pucker of my breast-scar.

The stranger did not seem inclined to talk as he curled over the tray eating and drinking in silence. After a time, I left him alone and walked to where Antiope lay in the rushes, teasing White-Ear with a piece of venison on a stick. She looked up with the sudden warm smile that always fills my heart, and in that brief moment of greeting, the boarhound snatched the meat, stick and all, from Antiope's slackened grasp and bolted for the disused court hearth. My consort twisted to catch her but missed, and only wallowed in the sweet rushes.

"My dinner," Antiope said ruefully, and glared at White-Ear, who grinned back at us from around the slab of meat. With a neat movement, my consort turned and hopped to a crouch beside me. "What are you laughing at, O Queen?"

"Not you, ever strong and brave one." Her cheek was warm and firm as she laid it against my knee. "What do you think of our visitor?"

She rolled her eyes. "A very lion of a man."

"You saw it, too? What do you think he comes for?"

"It is a strange time of year for guests. The animals in the hills —"

"He came by sea, but he doesn't look like they would frighten him much."

She looked amused. "No doubt *he* eats *them.*"

We were silent for a time, with the quiet of women who have loved and fought together, watching the big man. He hunched as if absorbed in his own sorrows, but sometimes the long-legged hounds and the children sparring with their short spears eased him for a moment, and he laughed as if he were a child himself. As the light dimmed to purple in the high windows that circled my white hall, my women ate and roughhoused the dogs that bickered for scraps. Most sat on the rushes ringing an open place near the fire where two women wrestled, naked bodies knotted with exertion, musky sweat mixing with the bite of the pervasive smoke. I saw my guest stood watching, the silver cup in his hand, and moved to his side to explain.

"It is a way of the Amazons." I had to speak loudly to be heard over the shouts. "Oreithyia, the younger one, has sued Lysippe for her love, and they are deciding her worth in this fashion."

"She is so young."

"Not so young. Her right breast is to be removed this winter so that she can draw the great bow and fight as one of my warriors."

"Do you always pick your — partners in this way?"

"In the summer, we have footraces, or we ride our horses to the sea and back to prove ourselves."

He rumbled a laugh. "But is it always a competition?"

I smiled, remembering my gentle wooing of Antiope. "No, not always. But often." We fell silent to watch. Antiope's heart is mine and I no longer enter these contests, but I still love to watch the slide of muscles beneath proud scars and the fierce beauty of faces pulled taut in the rictus of combat.

The contest was a short one. The girl fought hard and with an earnestness that charmed us all, but Lysippe is my warmaster and has reached her twentieth year. Oreithyia fell holding her shoulder, her jaw clenched against a cry. But it was Lysippe who helped her rise and held her as the dislocated shoulder was set. And when Oreithyia passed out, Lysippe allowed no one to help her, but carried the girl from the hall herself, her dark head bent close over the small pale face.

I watched them leave. "Perhaps the little one won, after all."

The stranger looked down at me from his great height. "She was valiant. I would be proud of a son who fought so well."

"They're all my daughters. Come, it's time we talk. Let's do this right." I led him to the court hearth, where one of the youngest warriors had laid a fire. I seated myself in my golden chair and he dropped onto the ivory and blackwood seat before me. Seeing us move, my women settled close to hear him, the first new voice since the rains began.

"You are welcome, stranger, to the Amazon court of Hippolyte. We have shared our fire and meat, and you have tasted our wine. Now, please share your story with us, that we may rejoice in your victories and marvel at your accomplishments." I finished the formal words and waited expectantly, but he said nothing, his head bent so that I could not see his face. I sighed. "Tell me your name and story, and what drives you over the wet and dangerous hills and across the yet wetter and riskier sea." He raised his head, and I saw it was rage and not fear that had bent it before.

"I am called Alkaeus by some, and by others Herakles —" A murmur like the summer wind passed through the listening warriors. His was a familiar name in the tales that came in summer.

He looked over the faces turned to him, the heads leaning close to whisper.

"You know my name, but I tell you, for all the wondrous tales you have heard, I was born under a cursed star. It seems a glorious thing to be a god's son, but the gods in their plans leave me nothing for myself."

"Explain this. To be chosen by the gods doesn't seem so bad to me. Our god chooses no one and nothing."

"Your god allows you to choose for yourself. My father bred me for his own reasons, and Hera tortures me for spite against her husband."

I hesitated. "Hera — is your goddess, the queen of your gods?"

He nodded, his four-fingered fist clenched around the stem of his cup.

"Aren't you concerned that she might hear your anger and strike you dead?"

"She cannot. What can she do worse to me than she already has?" His question ended with a wordless roar, an anguished sound that silenced even the scuffling dogs. He leaned forward and spoke into the stillness. "Here is my story, Hippolyte — such as it is.

"I am the son of Zeus himself, who bred me on Alkmene of Mykenae to be strong enough to aid the gods if they ever need it. Hera never forgave my mother for Zeus' passion, and she hated me. She tried to kill me when I was a child.

"When I was young, I married and sired sons and fought wars and killed men. What every man does. Except I angered Hera in one of those wars, and she drove me mad, so that with these hands" — and he spread them out, so that I could see their size, the palms like basins — "I killed my sons."

The women gathered around us spoke softly among themselves. I leaned towards him. "We mourn with you. Children, even boy children, are not so common here that we view their death with tranquillity." He continued as if he hadn't heard.

"With the madness she forms in me, she strips from me everyone I love. Her

hatred led to this, to my killing my children. And as absolution for what her hate did, I am bound for twelve years to Eurystheus, a coward and no ruler of men."

He straightened in his chair, and wordlessly Antiope went to fill his cup with wine. "He sets me tasks, a man I wouldn't ask a slave to bow to. I have killed wild animals for him. When I fought a boar in Erimanthus, I killed my friend Kiron —"

"The horse-man?" I broke in. He lifted his head slowly, as if only just remembering the presence of my women in the silent hall.

"Kiron taught me to hunt game and to play the harp. I loved him, and he died because of one of Hera's vicious tasks. My last arrow, the one that killed the boar, glanced off bone and struck Kiron on the knee. It destroyed the joint. He died in agony. Folus tried to wrench it free and stabbed himself. So I lost two friends. Folus and I used to run in the woods and wrestle after music lessons with Kiron. He was my host when he died by my arrow. Hera's madness kills them all." He raised his hands to me again. Red firelight played along their blunt lines, across the ragged stub of the missing finger.

"But Hera wasn't there," I said gently. "Yours were the hands."

"She has set my destiny, and now it rules my actions. She bound me to Eurystheus, who hides in a vase rather than look at the skins of the beasts I kill for him, or the living beasts I trap for him. Once I ran down a gold-horned hind and took her alive when she could run no longer. She was beautiful and strong, and holy to Artemis, and it bit like gall to take her away from her country for a man too cowardly to face even that gentle beast."

"Why don't you leave him, if he's such a coward?"

"I am bound to him. But I did for a while, to travel with Jason. I hoped I

could outsail even Hera's hate on the *Argo*. And for a time, I did. We danced and wrestled and had contests of strength, and I saw another country of women like yours. But she caught up. We came to a barren island, and she stole Hylas, who is my nephew and my shield-bearer. I waited for him until my companions on the *Argo* sailed without me, and even after that, until I was summoned back to the king. So he is gone as well. Because of Hera."

He tilted his face to the dark roof timbers. Pale lines crossed his cheeks where the clenching of his jaw had slowed the blood. Light from the court hearth gleamed in unshed tears.

"I lost my sons and my friends because of Hera's madness, but I have lost worse things even than that. Fighting the beasts had the credit of honest battle, muscle against muscle. But Eurystheus swapped me like a slave-boy to haul the shit of someone else's cattle, to kill my pride." His great fists knotted. "And now —

"This is his latest task, Hippolyte." His eyes glowed like bronze on the anvil as they met mine. "This is the request I bear from Eurystheus, my master."

I held up my hand to still the harshness of his voice, to silence the pain. "No. Tomorrow night, Alkaeus."

"But —"

"You're the only guest we've had this season. And yours is no tale full of liar's courage and an easy ending. Let us digest it, a little at a time."

Without a word he stood and walked away from the hearth. My chatelaine ran to meet his long strides. From my golden seat, I saw her catch up with him, touch his great elbow and lead him towards the long guest hall, empty this time of year except for him. The rest of my women drifted back to the winter hearth, which is, after all, much warmer. Their voices were solemn with the tale he told.

I stared into the flames of the court hearth. "Hippolyte," a voice said beside me. I turned and Antiope lay in full obeisance on the rushes.

"What is it, strong one? Get up and stop being foolish."

She sat up and brushed straw from her chest. "I have a request. I was going to wait until spring to breed a daughter, but I think I must do it now."

"With the stranger, Alkaeus?"

"He bears a god's blood, but I thought I'd use one of the dogs instead." She smiled up at me, her face beautiful in the dropping fire.

I took her hand, and traced a scar along its palm. "He's brave and strong, and you would bear a Queen for the Court. But be careful. You've heard him. It's dangerous to come too close to one involved with his hasty and intemperate gods, even if only for the time needed to take his seed. His goddess — Hera, it was — might take a life for the one he starts. Are you sure?"

She raised her head and met my eyes. "I am sure."

"Then I am happy for you," I said, and I kissed her. She jumped to her feet and looked down at me.

"I love you, Hippolyte."

"And I you. Go quickly and come to me afterwards, and I will ease the pain."

—— - ——

I sang with the women of my court for Antiope, and danced and shot my bronze bow at a mark on the wall (though I am thirty, I am still the strongest shot of my people, and only my warmaster is more accurate), but I was back at the court hearth, absently sharpening a spear, when Antiope ran into the hall. The women who had not yet gone to the dormitories laughed and cheered her, but she passed them and fell into my waiting arms. There were tears on her face and blood on her thighs, but she smiled at me nonetheless.

"How was it, heart's desire?" I whispered to her.

She made a face. "Like shitting a rock,

55

only backwards." Then she laughed. "But I will bear a daughter from it, I know I will."

I took her to the Queen's chamber, and with warm oil I rubbed her muscles free of pain. And then we loved with the knowledge of the warrior that would grow inside her. After a time, she fell asleep in my arms, and I laid her down in the furs and walked softly to the door of my chamber. I watched her sleep in the red light of the brazier, then turned and left.

Perhaps reluctant to share space with the few women still drinking by the greater hearth, Alkaeus sat in the blackwood and ivory chair by the court hearth, warmed only by the embers of the fire set earlier. He wore his lionskin over his head, and the steady orange light filled the eyeholes with false life. I collected a cup and wineskin, and walked to him. White-Ear slept in my golden chair, an awkward pile of limbs and ears. She growled half-heartedly when I pushed her down, then dropped at my feet, eyes gleaming between half-closed lids.

"You see how my subjects mock me in the winter. Why aren't you sleeping? Is your bed uncomfortable?"

"I never can sleep, after —" He gestured with a four-fingered hand.

"Thank you for your gift, Alkaeus. The daughter you've bred will be strong and proud of her sire. Where's your cup?"

"And if she's a son?" he rumbled, his voice muffled from leaning over to pick up the silver-chased cup beside the leg of his seat.

"Why should she be? It's my consort that bears her."

He allowed me to fill his cup, drank, and turned it absently in his hands. "I know you'd like to wait until tomorrow, but I must return as soon as possible to Eurystheus."

"By your own account, he's no true king. Stay for the winter with us in the Amazon court. I have hunting I could show you, and there's a place in the sea where the fish are so big even you'd have to dive in and wrestle them into the boat."

He smiled, his dark skin creasing under the rough lion's head; but he shook his head. "It's not him. It is Hera. There's no rest from her."

"And if you didn't go back? What else could she possibly take from you if you didn't return?"

"My honor."

I looked at him for a long time, as I tugged White-Ear's velvety namesake. She rumbled softly in response. "Then you must go. When will you leave?"

"With the tide tomorrow."

"At least I can ride with you to the docks. Amazon horses are good and will get us there quickly."

"I will gladly accept your company, Hippolyte."

"Done, then. And your mission. You've given my consort what she most desires. Ask what you will, and it's yours."

His face hardened with the anger I had seen earlier, and he turned his face to the dim hearth. "You don't know what it is, yet. I wouldn't ask this from a slave-girl, but I must ask you, knowing you will refuse and that I will add the death of another friend to my dishonor." He swallowed heavily, then burst out, "I'd return without asking you and brave the coward's anger, but Hera sets my fate. And she destroys those I love when I deny her."

His anger startled the boarhound under my hand. She scrambled up and retreated to the other fire. I snapped my fingers for her, but she did not return.

"What is this request?"

His nine fingers twisted across the cup's chasing. "I am to bring the girdle of the Amazon Queen to the king's daughter Admete, that she might share in Hippolyte's beauty."

I had to laugh. "My belt?" I fingered

its plain length. My belt is no flimsy gaud to hold a maiden's gown modestly. It's hard and worn and holds my axe. "She wouldn't want this ugly strap, nor the beauty of bright spears and brave death, which are all I have. Ask for something else."

He did not look up, seemingly lost in the feel of the little hunt running beneath his great fingers. When he spoke his voice was almost gentle.

"You are a warrior, one I would be proud to fight beside. But I can't choose my battles or my comrades. If you can't give me the belt, then I must fight you."

"Over a belt? If it is so important to you, it's yours."

"No!" From the corner of my eye, I saw that his roar brought up the heads of the women at the other hearth. When neither of us moved, they ignored us again. "It's more than a belt to him. It's that I dishonor an honorable warrior, and hate myself more for this." Alkaeus tapped his own belt, as serviceable as mine. "In my country, this is a symbol of a woman's virtue. If I take yours back, he — everyone — will believe that the symbol is the deed."

"What deed is that?" I asked softly.

"Rape. That I've had the queen of the Amazons, who beds no man." The silver cup made a sudden small noise and collapsed in his clenched fist. He looked across the bright air at me. "I'm sorry, Hippolyte."

I stood and the brush of my sandals against the rushes seemed very loud. I touched him, and the contorted metal shape fell from his cold hand.

"You'd fight me for a piece of leather that says you've had sex with me against my will." I looked down from where I stood into his haunted eyes. "I'm old, Alkaeus, and perhaps you would win. Or perhaps you would die and my dogs would chew on your forgotten bones. But I won't fight to fulfill your fate — not for a goddess's hate, not because your king thinks I will, not for false

honor. There are more ways to gain something than to force it." I unwrapped the belt and dropped it to lie beside the broken cup. "It is yours."

When I, Antiope, woke in the grey of early morning, Hippolyte was gone. My bones ached and the brazier was cold, so I pulled a fur around myself and went to the great hall, to stand before the fire that always burned in the winter months. A woman sat there alone, finishing the dregs of the evening's wine.

"Where is the Queen?" I asked her.

She raised her head and looked at me. "She left in the first greyness with the hero, Alkaeus. They were riding to the port, to his ship."

Something gleamed on the tiles of the court hearth, beside the gold chair of the Queen. I walked to it and picked up a mangled silver shape that broke into pieces in my hands. The metal was cold and dusted with the ashes of the dead fire.

The woman at the greater hearth spoke across the hall. "It was the Persian cup. He crushed it in his hands, and then they left."

From the woman's words, I somehow knew Hippolyte was being taken from us. His shameless request was her company back to his king's court, and without her permission (for surely she would have told me if she had agreed, surely I would have been allowed to accompany her) he stole her.

I yelled the battle cry and snatched up my sword and her bronze bow and clashed them together. In moments, my sisters ran from their sleeping halls. Their bodies were strong and hard, and the weapons they tore from the wall shone sharp in the pale light that seeped in the high windows. Lysippe the warmaster ran to my side looking for Hippolyte.

"Amazons," I shouted. "Our Queen has been taken by the stranger Alkaeus, who is no hero but a traitor. We must follow."

The women shouted and the walls rang with the clashings of their anger. I ran to the stables, Lysippe at my side, mounted my horse bare-backed, weapons in my hands. We rode all the several leagues after them in the spears of winter rain, and only our sweat kept us from the chill of nakedness.

I was the first over the breast of the salt-bleached hill by the water. This is what I saw: my Queen and the man whose seed I had taken standing on the pale wood of the single wharf, her axe and knife hung securely from her dress belt, men setting the red sails of the docked Greek ship, the unworried faces of the dockwomen close by, Hippolyte and Alkaeus grasping each other's forearm in the mark of sisterhood — I saw all these things and halted my horse, who rose under me, even as my warriors poured over the hill, their battle cry ululating in the cold heavy air.

I suddenly remembered the woman in the hall whose words had led me here, and I could not remember her face, whether it was Amazon or stranger. In despair, I watched Hippolyte and Alkaeus turn towards the warriors, her proud face only surprised, but his dark with her imagined betrayal. He pulled my Queen to him by the arms they still clasped, and tearing her axe free, he struck her on the side. Even through the war cries, I heard the axe cleave her flesh. He flung her to the ground as blood fell from her mouth, and ran to the Greek ship, its crimson sails already belled out and pulling it free of the dock.

Only then, when it could do no good for any of us, could I move. I pulled back the great bow of Hippolyte, and shot a black-fletched arrow across the grey air between me and the man whose seed I had taken. The wind with a sudden snap tore the arrow sideways, so that it drove into the mast beside him.

Six months have passed since I lost my love at the hands of Herakles. I am

Antiope, now Queen of the Amazons. Hippolyte warned me about his intemperate gods, that the destiny his goddess thrust upon him was a danger. And no woman (or man, either) can deny her destiny. But my Queen was stripped of hers. She died at his hands to be but a line of his many-booked tale.

And I am left to sit in the golden chair at the court hearth, and I am left to smile at the sweaty summer envoys bearing their jewels and cups. No woman stands behind me, but the men who fill the guest hall do not know what this means; instead they stare at my swelling belly and wonder what manner of daughter I will bear. As do I.

I cannot forget that day. While my arrow still quivered in the mast beside his head, he met my eyes, and even across that distance and through the rain and spears that fell between us, I saw the grief there; and, on his face, the tears that fell unbidden.   Ω

THE LEGEND OF THE MAN-MOUNTAIN

After the *Quinbus Flestrin* had gone away,
And Lilliputians who had known him —
Roped him,
Walked beneath the archway of his ragged breeches,
Driven coaches round his table —
Were getting scarce,
He became a legend.

Grandparents told the youngsters
Tales of the Man-Mountain
Who had saved them from the Blefuscudian armada
(And urged a peace on them
They weren't quite sure they wanted,
Granting too much to Blefuscu,
Some would add,
But then the conversation had a tendency
To turn to politics
And acrimony).
Gossip still found scandal
In the favor that the Treasurer's lady showed him.

The youngsters knew it wasn't so,
And couldn't be.
A Man-Mountain couldn't live.
He'd collapse of his own weight.
No, they said, someone tall,
Even ten *glumguffs* tall,
A war-hero grown sadly unpatriotic,
That was the truth
Age and exaggeration had forgotten.

— Ruth Berman

THE HEART'S DESIRE

by Chet Williamson

art by Frank Kelly Freas

"What's yours?"

"It's foolish, Peter. I have none."

"No. *That's* foolish. Everyone has one."

"Not me."

Michael Lindstrom, without a heart's desire, smiled at his friend and sipped from a glass of white wine.

"Come on, Michael," Peter said. "A moment somewhere? Somewhere along the way you lost, but still remember, bright as your youth. If I had one, you had one."

"What *was* yours?"

Peter Riley's face drifted for an instant."It'll sound . . . stupid. Undoubtedly. But it is *the* time. The *best* time. I was eleven."

"Oh Jesus."

"Hear me out. I was eleven. And I was on a baseball team."

"Little League."

"Nothing so grand. A park league. Summer at the town park. I was not a good player, but I liked it. I wanted to be good. And I practiced every evening, made my dad throw me balls and I'd hit them. Or try to. In those afternoon games I'd stand out in right field, nervous as Hell when I was about to bat. Oh, I got hits. Maybe one out of five or six. Always a single, and usually because somebody bobbled a ball or made a bad throw. But one day — *the* day — I was at bat with a guy on first, one run behind, and two outs. It was the bottom of the seventh — we only played seven — and my whole team was muttering under their breaths, and some out loud. But that first pitch, the very first pitch — well, I belted it. I absolutely ripped that mother. That goddamn ball went back over the left fielder's head, hit, and bounced, and went right into the creek. And by the time the kid fished it out, I was long home, and everyone was yelling and cheering and clapping and pounding my ass off they were so damn happy. It wasn't a championship game or anything like that, but *I* won it. Me. That was the day. And there's never been another to touch it for sweetness."

"Not even when you lost your virginity?"

"I'm not even sure when that was. Technically."

"And you've relived that home run."

"Yeah. Several times."

"Doesn't it lose its novelty?"

"No. Each time there's something new."

"Come on. You can't mean you actually experience it. I can't believe that."

"But I have. It's time travel, Michael, honest to God."

"I also can't believe you're calling it that."

"Me and a hundred other people. And why not? You can't go back physically. That's science fiction. Mentally is the only conceivable way. Your own memory, your subconscious has it all in there. Every tiny detail. And Wagner knows how to make you remember."

"And how much have you paid Wagner all told for that privilege?"

"It's not inexpensive."

"No. That type of thing never is. 'Sell all you have and follow me.' "

"Don't make it sound like a religion."

"I wanted to make it sound like an obsession. Or an addiction."

"It's harmless. Helpful if anything."

"Does Jennifer think it's harmless?"

60

"Jennifer's been very supportive of it. Of me."

"Financially as well?"

"I can *handle* the cost, Michael."

"Doesn't she get a bit jealous? Of your running away from her back to the town park?"

Peter paused a moment too long. "No. I'm . . . refreshed when I come back from the experience. Renewed. I'm a better husband for it."

"And how long before all that freshness and renewal wear off and things get shabby again?"

Peter laughed. "Michael," he said quickly, "I just can't describe it. It's something you have to experience. I mean, everything is there, the smell of kids, the feel of the sun on your t-shirt, the infield dirt under your Keds — *Keds,* for Christ's sake — the old, taped bat in your hands — *everything*. The sensation is *total*."

"You sound like you did when you tried to talk me into doing acid in college. Then, if you'll recall the precious sensations, I had to hold you all night while you cried and told me to watch out for the blue willies. What the Hell *were* the blue willies anyway?"

"I don't remember."

"Well, I'm sure Dr. Wagner could remind you."

Michael's wife came up to them. "All right, what are you two up to?" She put an arm around each one, kissing them both soundly.

"Michael is giving me Hell again, Maggie," Peter said.

"Oh, your treatment . . ."

"It's not a treatment," Peter protested.

"Sure it is," said Michael. "Fight reality with a checkup and a check. A big

one."

"Michael, it *is* reality."

"No, Peter. *This* is reality. Here and now. That *was* reality."

Peter turned to Maggie.

"Don't get me in this argument," she said.

Peter nodded. "I never *could* talk him into anything, could I? Where's Jennifer?"

"Upstairs," said Maggie. "I think she was going to be sick."

Peter tried to smile. "We all have our ways of escaping from reality, huh? But what's yours, Michael?" Peter turned and disappeared into the crowd.

"You shouldn't be so hard on him," Maggie said, taking her arm from Michael's shoulder.

"I can't approve of what he's doing."

"He seems to be getting something out of it."

"Oh yes. An alcoholic wife."

"Michael . . ."

"They're lies. He's lying to himself, Maggie. He's found one moment of triumph that's become the core of his life, filled with seeds, and he goes back time after time to get one more."

"It's his choice. What can you do?"

"I could expose it."

"Why?"

"It would sell, for one thing. And the other thing is that it makes me angry to see my friend throwing away his money and his life to dreams."

There was that and more, enough to make Michael Lindstrom decide to do an exposé on temporal revisualization, to make him call Dr. Paul Wagner's Park Avenue office for an appointment, to make him lie when he met the doctor, expressing admiration for his work and acknowledging Wagner's compliments toward Michael's own writing with a grace and a gratitude he could not feel. He told Wagner that he wished to do a first-person article on the procedure, and asked for Wagner's cooperation.

Wagner gave a smile of practiced sincerity. "There's no pledge of secrecy, Mr. Lindstrom. I'll be happy to have you as a patient, and you can tell as much or as little as you like. Do you . . . have a certain time in mind that you wish to revisit?"

Michael chuckled. "You make it sound so simple. 'Step into my time machine and let's go.' "

"Hardly that. But it is quite simple, really. When you know how."

"How?"

"Drugs — harmless, government-approved drugs — and hypnosis. It's in your mind, Mr. Lindstrom. It's really all in there."

"This sounds awfully sixtyish — Timothy Leary stuff."

Wagner shrugged. "Styles change. The mind doesn't."

"It's just very hard to believe," said Michael with a penitent's smile, "that it's all still there . . . in as much detail as I've heard about."

"It's there," Wagner said plainly. "Things you didn't even know you'd seen. You'll scarcely believe it. But you'll be there. And so will everything else. Just as it was."

"I assume it's very expensive."

"And I assume your publisher will pay for it, so that needn't worry you."

Michael smiled wryly, thinking it best not to appear too innocent, too trusting. "You doctors."

"Or doctors' *wives*," Wagner said, his smile showing his teeth for the first time. They looked white, and bright, and young, like the rest of him. "Now. Suppose you tell me."

Michael pursed his lips, looked at Wagner, looked down at his hands in his lap, and back up again. "A woman," he lied. "A woman I once knew."

"A lover?"

"Must you know that?"

"I should."

"No. Not a lover. Though I loved her. And I think she loved me. I was young, in college. It was before I met my wife. It

was our second, maybe third date, I can't remember. But we were walking on the beach. With no one else around. We must have walked for miles without seeing a soul. And we didn't say a word. Not all the way. Then, when the beach ended . . ."

"Ended?"

"Isn't that strange," said Michael, "but that's how I remember it. It just ended. A cliff, a sea-wall, I don't know."

"You will," Wagner said quietly. "What happened next?"

"I held her. I kissed her. Nothing more. And we walked back. And that day I felt happier, more at peace with myself, than I've been before or since."

"What happened? Between the two of you."

"She died. Three weeks later. Swimming alone on that same beach. Drowned. A young boy saw her go down. They never found her body."

Wagner nodded slowly. "What was her name?"

"Anne." *Beautiful Annabel Lee. In her tomb by the side of the sea.* Michael laughed inside at the lie, the false Anne, the seaside and walk he had never known. "And that," he said aloud, "is the moment I want to reclaim."

"One thing, Mr. Lindstrom," said Wagner with a frown. "What brought you here? Your desire to see and be with this girl again? Or your desire for a story."

"Both. Combined business and pleasure trip."

Wagner looked at him for so long that Michael grew uncomfortable. Finally he spoke. "Ready then?"

"Now?"

"It doesn't take long. A matter of minutes."

"That's not much for the money."

"It will seem far longer, I promise. But first I'll have to ask you to sign this," and he handed Michael a piece of paper and a pen from a desk drawer. "It simply releases me from any legal actions stemming from a psychological complaint. I remain liable, however, for any adverse physical reaction." Michael read it and signed.

Wagner stood and walked to a metal cabinet that contrasted starkly with the tasteful opulence of the room's other furnishings. He returned to Michael's side bearing a tray on which lay an unmarked vial, a syringe, an alcohol swab, and a Band-Aid. "Do you mind needles?" Michael shook his head, shrugged off his jacket, and rolled up his right sleeve. Wagner inserted the syringe in the vial and drew out a cc of thick, milky fluid.

"What is that?" Michael asked.

"Ah. My secret," Wagner replied, wiping the skin over Michael's biceps with the swab. "Safer than aspirin as far as side effects. This'll sting a bit."

The needle slid into Michael's arm, and he looked away. "There," said Wagner. "All there is to it. You'll begin to feel drowsy in a minute or so."

"Do I lie down?" asked Michael, looking in vain for a couch.

"No. Sitting is fine. You won't be aware of your body. Now just relax."

Within seconds, Michael felt a lethargy steal over him, as when he would fall asleep on trains. He closed his eyes. He didn't hear Wagner speaking, could not remember later if Wagner had said anything at all.

The beach appeared slowly, but with such a sense of reality that he felt as if he were awakening from a dream. It was real, it was true, and the wet sand was cool where his bare feet pressed it down. Wind, blowing from a gray sky, ruffled the sleeves of his jacket and played with his hair. The smell of the sea was fresh and strong, and the hand he was holding was warm.

He turned — not his dream-self, he thought, but *he* — and looked at her, and knew that he had never seen her before, but knew that she was here, was real, and that no one would ever be able to

take her place. She gazed back at him with deep, thoughtful eyes that had owned him always, then turned her face out to the sea so that the breeze took her hair and made it shimmer like a curtain of obsidian rain.

Had he wanted to speak, he could not have. His knowledge would have choked him. But his voice and thoughts, those of fifty-year-old Michael Lindstrom, were imprisoned within the young body, with whose flesh he saw, and touched, and heard. His consciousness rode above, like a hawk over a storm, observed all, felt, but could not express the feeling. They walked on through the cool day, over the wet sand, and from time to time he would look at her, kiss her cheek or her lips, and when he looked ahead, or down at the sand, he prayed to himself to turn his head, to look at her again, to never look away, never leave her alone, because then she would not vanish, not leave him, not be claimed by the sea.

It was a cliff at the end of the beach. That which he had not remembered, which had never existed, was there now, tall and gray, its lower flanks gleaming with salt spray. He and Anne (*Anne*) watched the waves caress the rock, moved to where beach and sea and cliff all met, then sat in the sand and held each other. Michael shivered as the chill crept over his buttocks and touched the base of his spine. He hugged Anne tighter, thinking, *tighter still never let go never,* and he wanted to crush her to him, make them inseparable for always, but his young arms would not obey old desires.

After too short a time they rose and walked back, back the way they had come. It seemed to Michael that they ran where he would have crawled. He could feel Anne's arm around him, could feel the wind cool his flesh, could feel Anne's hair, black as the sea's depth, brush his cheek, whisper at his ear, and then another reality impinged —

— a reality of a three-piece suit, a leather chair beneath him, his hands resting on its arms, and Dr. Wagner beside him, gazing into his face with a loving concern.

"Welcome back," Wagner said softly.

Michael could not speak. He felt as though he had been wrenched in time and place, experienced sudden confusion that approached panic before he remembered what he had done, why he was there. He looked at his right hand, and was surprised when he found Anne's hand missing. He spread his fingers apart, examined them, looked down at his shod feet. He could still feel the sand. "It was all a lie," he said huskily. "None of it was true."

"You saw it," said Wagner. "You were there. Weren't you?"

"There was no *there* to be!" Michael said with an anger that startled and unmanned him. He knew that he should have felt smug, triumphant. He felt neither.

"You were lying then," the doctor said. "I suspected you were."

"Did you?"

"Annabel Lee, wasn't that it?" Wagner smiled gently. "A fairly simple allusion."

"If you knew it was a lie, why did you do it? Let me take it?"

"Mr. Lindstrom, half of what my patients want to relive are lies. They never happened. At least not as grandly as most of them remember. But if that's what they want, that's what they can have. At last."

"But that's . . . a fraud . . ."

"Not really. The rooms are inside. I just provide the key."

"For such simple things? My friend, and his home run?"

"Maybe it was, maybe it wasn't. Maybe it was only a single, maybe even only a walk. That doesn't matter. *Now* it's a home run. Not many of us have had those perfect moments. Not even one. Life can be very sad when one has to pretend to remember happiness."

"You sell dreams," Michael said.

"No." Wagner's face was expressionless, his tone flat. "I sell the heart's desire. Sometimes what was, but more often what should have been."

Michael held up an admonishing finger, then saw it tremble, and lowered it guiltily. "I'm going to . . . to tell about this," he said, his lower lip quivering. "This cannot, should not happen."

"If you feel you must, you may," Wagner said calmly. "I'm not sure what exactly you've found that you consider worthy of exposing, but you're welcome to whatever it is. Just one thing — think about it for a day or two. Before you start writing. And ask yourself if your knowledge will make any difference to those who come to me. Ask yourself if they don't already know what you know.

"And ask yourself too, if the truth be known, whether people will stop coming to see me, or whether more will start to come."

Michael tried to stop shaking. "Why do you do this?"

"Because I can. Because it helps to ease the pain."

"What if I don't *want* my pain eased?" Michael flared. "Or what if I *have* no pain?"

"Then you shouldn't have come here. I am, after all, a doctor. My purpose is healing."

Michael made no reply.

"If you have no more questions, there are other patients I must see."

Michael stood up. "This is not . . . the last of this," he said, before he moved to the door.

"No," Dr. Wagner said. "I don't suppose it is."

Maggie was in the kitchen when Michael Lindstrom arrived home. When he embraced her, her bare arms felt rough and leathery, her hair was the texture of straw against his cheek. Her smile was stiff and unfriendly, a stranger's smile, and her voice, as she tried to draw out his secrets over dinner, was cawing, strident. He stayed up late that night, and drank more than was customary for him.

The following day, when Dr. Wagner was told by his receptionist that Michael Lindstrom had made a second appointment, he was not surprised. The doctor prided himself on his ability to recognize deep pain, pain that would be long in healing, healing that would leave scars as deep as the pain that had made them necessary.

Ω

MOVING?

Don't leave *Weird Tales*® behind!

Just let us have your old address
(and ZIP code)
and your NEW! IMPROVED! address
(and ZIP code),
so we can do our very best to keep up
with you.

WEIRD TALES TALKS
WITH CHET WILLIAMSON

by Darrell Schweitzer

Weird Tales: I seem to remember you from Lovecraft fandom in the middle '70s. You weren't writing modern horror fiction then, or at least I didn't know about any. So, what *were* you writing at the outset of your career?

Williamson: I was always a *real* big fan of Lovecraft's. I was in the Esoteric Order of Dagon, which is an amateur press association dedicated to Lovecraft and weird fiction. I belonged from about 1973 to 1983. I didn't really start to write fiction seriously until around 1979 or 1980, when I started writing short stories. My first sale was to *Twilight Zone* in 1981. That's what started it. I began my first novel in 1982. That was the start.

WT: What novel was that?

Williamson: *Soulstorm.*

WT: You seem to have started writing much later in life than a lot of people do, presumably your mid-twenties at least. So, what did you plan to do with your life before you knew you were going to be a writer?

Williamson: I started out wanting to be an actor. I *was* one for many years, I was a member of Actors' Equity. I did a lot of summer stock and regional shows and industrial shows, and through doing the industrial shows I began to *write*. I was doing comedies — parodies, even a *sci fi* one — about people in business, to be performed at business conventions. And when I began to realize that I was constructing plots and characters, I thought, well, why not do this in real fiction? So I did, and it took me a while to get to the point where I was producing

stuff day after day, but eventually I did and it got to the point where I enjoyed being a creator more than I enjoyed being an interpreter.

WT: When you started writing fiction for yourself, did you know from the start that you were going to be a horror writer, or did you try other things first?

Williamson: No, I didn't try other things. I've loved horror since I was a kid. The stock-boy in my grandfather's grocery store terrified me with Edgar Allan Poe stories in the basement. I discovered very quickly the Ballantine horror anthologies that were out in the early '60s. Lovecraft was being reprinted then. So with my love of horror and my interest in Lovecraft, it was only natural with my interest in Lovecraft that when I started to write, I would write horror. It just seemed to be the thing that appealed most to me.

WT: I can't help but wonder: did the stock-boy read you the stories or enact them?

Williamson: He *told* them. He was a very good storyteller, and the cellar itself was a really scary place because it went back to lower levels and got darker and darker as it went. As I got older I explored more, back into the deeper cellars. It was a great place to hear Poe.

WT: Since you got into all this by way of Lovecraft fandom, it surprises me that you didn't turn out large numbers of Cthulhu Mythos stories narrated in the First Person Delirious by scholarly Rhode Island recluses who get eaten by Things at the end. Why not?

Williamson: When I think of influ-

ences, I have to say that Lovecraft really wasn't an influence in my writings. I think it's because I didn't start writing fiction until later in life. This is just my theory, but I think that when you're younger you tend to copy the kind of fiction you enjoy. I started relatively late, so I had already formed an outlook — I wouldn't call it a world-view — and I was also influenced by contemporary fiction as well. I had read a lot of horror, not just Lovecraft. It's funny, though. I was reading Peter Cannon's new book on Lovecraft, the Twayne Authors Series volume, and I came to the discussion of "The Picture in the House." Now, I hadn't read this story for years and years, and of course the climax concerns the blood dripping through the ceiling. And I remembered that, and I thought, Gee, in *Dreamthorp* I have a scene in which blood is dripping through the ceiling onto a velvet hat, and I wondered if that image might have been an influence. But *then* I remembered, *Wait a minute. I dreamed that.* I had a dream, and had written it down, thinking that someday I might use it in a book. But, one step backwards: Was the dream inspired by my memory of Lovecraft? So I got a copy of *Dreamthorp* and a copy of "The Picture in the House." "The Picture in the House" describes it as *a large, irregular patch that slowly dripped crimson* and in my book it was *a large, irregular spot from which the blood dripped.* So, phrases and images just lodge in your mind and they might pop up years later, because I'm sure that when I was a kid and read that story for the first time, it made a tremendous impression on me. I must be influenced more than I know. . . .

WT: But you still didn't write about large tentacular seafood and add new books to the Mythos library of eldritch tomes.

Williamson: No. I saw that as a dead end. I had read so much of that kind of material, and after a while there's a real

sameness about it. It wasn't the kind of *believable* horror that I wanted to write. Also, it's understood only by a very small group of readers. From the beginning I wanted to get a wider readership than people who are only into the Cthulhu Mythos, the Yog-Sothoth Cycle of Myth.

WT: I think the limitation of that sort of stuff is that no one other than Lovecraft ever actually wrote a scary one. The artistic development of the Mythos ended in 1937.

Williamson: I think you're right. Most of them aren't very frightening. The worst wind up being silly in-jokes, and the best are literary exercises that are very well done, but fun for only a few readers.

WT: This gets back to something Les Daniels suggested, that no one becomes a horror writer simply because it's an expedient way to make money, or for any conscious, deliberate reason. We do it because we're *warped.* We're that way from the beginning . . . Obviously your fascination with the dark cellar and Poe when you were a kid meant you were one of us.

Williamson: Unfortunately I had a very happy childhood . . . [laughs] but I was always fascinated by the dark side, and as soon as I could go to the movies alone I saw all the American International matinee Poe films. I bought the early issues of *Famous Monsters of Filmland.* I built the Aurora models. I fell in love with all that kind of stuff. Yeah, I was warped. My parents, God love 'em, took me to *Psycho* when I was eleven and it scared the *Hell* out of me. I don't think they knew how scary it was going to be. It was great. And there was *Thriller,* which was on TV when I was fourteen. I ate that stuff up like crazy.

WT: You were fortunate in that your parents allowed you to be exposed to that sort of thing. I was very strictly *not* allowed, but turned out this way *anyway.* . . . You may well be better adjusted in your warped nature.

Williamson: [Laughs.] That may be. My parents were pretty permissive in what they let me read. But at that time you could feel pretty safe that if you bought a horror novel you were not going to find explicit sex and violence in it. It was more suggestive. I remember that when Monarch Books came out with their series of *Gorgo* and *Reptilicus* novelizations, there was *sex* in those. My mother always did keep a watch on what I read, and she went through *Reptilicus* and when she came upon the *roseate nipples* . . . that was the last of *Reptilicus*. She let me keep the cover . . . That was around 1961, so they were spicy by the standards of the era. But today it's a little harder. Kids are so inundated with graphic horror — you've got eleven- and twelve-year-old kids who've seen all the *Friday the Thirteenth* and *Nightmare on Elm Street* movies, and the suggestive horror, which I really find more frightening, just doesn't affect them. Hopefully with a little age and maturity it might, but the explicit stuff seems to have a desensitizing effect on a lot of kids.

WT: I suppose what sums up the current state of the movie field for me was one of those instant-remainder coffee-table books that I saw in a store, about horror films with lots of photos and the like — the image on the cover (to instantly define to the browser what the book was about) wasn't a werewolf or the Frankenstein monster; it was a *knife* descending. So the public's whole idea of what horror is no longer has anything to do with the supernatural as much as it does with spurting arteries.

Williamson: Yes. You're right. The stuff that gives me the chills, the *frisson*, is the supernatural and the suggestion of the supernatural. Did you see *The Lady in White* a couple years ago? It was wonderful, a pure supernatural film. There was a physical element of menace in it, but there was an awful lot of the supernatural in it. I hadn't seen that

kind of movie in ten, twenty years. And it was *genuinely chilling*. To me, M.R. James is still able to produce the shivers. There are some stories I can read — and the climax is just the realization that you were talking with a dead person, with a ghost — but it's so skillfully done and so realistic that it really does produce a shiver. That's a subtlety that I'm afraid is lost in a lot of stuff today, in films primarily, but also in the literature. It's a shame.

WT: At least a high-quality, subtle horror novel is still commercial, in the way that a similar film probably isn't.

Williamson: Absolutely. I think there is room in the field for both kinds of work. I think you can have the most explicit, graphic horror and still have a fine book. You can also have very subtle, sophisticated suggestion and have it be just as good. It all depends on the writer and the way he or she approaches the material. I think the movies are skewing our view of it a little bit. They seem to be the primary vehicle for horror just now, rather than books.

WT: Yet for the first time we have a horror category in publishing, and multi-millionaire horror writers.

Williamson: There aren't that many of them, really. You can count the multi-millionaires on probably three fingers. Of course Stephen King is the one who is always pointed to, but King is so absolutely unique in the way his career has gone and the magic he has cast on readers. It's a thing that hardly ever happens. He's the best-selling author of our time. But if you look at the best-seller list at any one time, you only find a few names associated with horror novels. The lists are loaded with techno-thrillers and romances, and the Danielle Steeles and Sidney Sheldons and James Micheners. So horror is making some inroads, certainly. If people are becoming aware of horror, and the horror bestsellers are leading people to seek out other such books, great, but I'm not all

that convinced that's happening. I think you'll find people who read everything Stephen King writes, but won't necessarily go out and look for more horror novels. It's the same sort of person who reads everything Tom Clancy writes, but doesn't go out and search for other good techno-thrillers.

WT: Still, the big change has been that for the first time writers are making *careers* as horror writers, whereas even someone like Algernon Blackwood, who wrote lots of horror, also wrote children's books and other things completely out of the field. But now there are writers who are expected by their publishers to turn out a new horror novel every eighteen months or so, one right after another. I can't help but wonder how long any writer can keep it up.

Williamson: I don't know. I can only answer for myself. I write on spec. So I don't *have* to turn out something every so often. I see myself continuing to deal with the darker side of humanity, but whether I'll continue to write what you could classify as pure horror novels, I don't know. I think as you continue to write, you have to continue to grow and learn. Once you stop — and start, in essence, to write the same book over and over again — some of the best part of life has stopped.

WT: Horror is basically a single mood or note, and I wonder if anyone can make a career over, say, twenty years, striking the same note. *The Haunting of Hill House* seems to have just *happened* in the middle of Shirley Jackson's career. She could not have written twenty-five of them.

Williamson: No, of course not. I don't see on the other hand how someone can write twenty-five or thirty mysteries. If I had the kind of career Agatha Christie had, I'm sure I would have gotten really bored writing puzzle mysteries all my life.

WT: I have a theory, which may apply more to someone like John Creasey, who wrote many hundreds of mysteries, and that is that such a writer has only one trick. That's all he can do, and he doesn't feel the emotional textures of the story, and is really not a *storyteller* at all, but a puzzle-constructor. But the horror writer is very much exploring emotional experiences and textures which can't necessarily come on cue, let alone several hundred times.

Williamson: That's one of the reasons I like horror more than other genres. It seems that in other genres you're limited in some way. In a mystery you're limited to solving a problem. Whether you're writing hard-boiled or tea-cozy, there's a crime that has to be solved. In a western you're limited to a certain historical place and time. In science fiction, although the borders of that are a lot less strict than other genres, generally you're working in terms of the future. But horror is a literature of emotion, and emotions can take place anywhere at any time. You can have a horror western, horror science fiction. You could have a horror romance, of all things. It's a very wide-ranging genre. What you tend to *find* mostly is contemporary horror. The worst of it is indeed contemporary, one-note, the kind of books that are written over and over again. But that's a very narrow part of what horror can be. For that reason I don't mind being called a horror writer, because horror is just an emotion.

WT: For marketing purposes, it would seem that if you set a horror novel in, say, Minoan Crete, it wouldn't be published as a horror novel. It might be published as fantasy, or as a historical. This would determine what sort of cover it would get, where and how prominently it would be displayed in the publisher's catalogue, and even how big an advance you got for it. Or whether or not the publisher would accept it at all.

Williamson: You may be right. I'm

dealing rather ideally in my definition of it, but still I think that I can go anywhere I want with it. Hopefully if you try to take a change in direction, readers will follow you. There are a lot of readers who want just a straight horror novel, though. So if someone who normally writes in a certain way does something very different, those readers are disappointed. They might not read the next book. But that's a chance you have to take.

WT: There's a theoretical point I've always wondered about, which is what would have happened if, well into his career, Stephen King wrote the equivalent of *The Sound of Music*. How would his enormous readership, brought together out of an interest in his horror novels, suddenly take a light, romantic comedy from him? Would he be able to sell it? What would his editors do? They'd be tearing their hair out.

Williamson: King took a change of direction with the *Gunslinger* series. That is not the typical contemporary horror that he's been doing, but the books are selling well and readers are following him. Admittedly it's not as radical a change as writing a light, romantic comedy, but I think if he did write a comedy, an awful lot of his readers would go along with him. I value that, because they've found an author who has a voice that they like. Like them, I tend to read *writers*. I don't read genres. If there's a writer whose work I like, I'll read whatever he's written, no matter what genre it's in, because I like his voice. I like the way he tells a story.

WT: Well, you've written in other genres. You even had a story in *The New Yorker*.

Williamson: Yeah. Humor. Al Sarrantonio just picked that up to reprint in *The Fireside Treasury of New Humor*. And I've written one suspense novel. I may do another; I may not. I've also written some science fiction, but my heart is really in the horror field. That's

what I enjoy doing the most, what I feel the most comfortable with. As long as I have a passion for it, I'll continue to write it.

WT: Could you give our readers a quick run-down of each of your novels?

Williamson: Sure. *Soulstorm* was the first one. I had to work on a relatively small scale with that book, because I didn't want to get lost in a large cast of characters and many locations. So I thought the classic haunted-house story would be a good place to start. There are a lot of influences which I think can be seen in that book, more so than in my later ones. It's a real head-bashing horror kind of thing, not too subtle, but I think a lot of fun. My second novel, *Ash Wednesday*, was a more thoughtful book. What I wanted to do was a passive horror story, in which there are no monsters, no things that come after you. The situation is that one day a small town wakes up to discover that all its dead have returned as semi-transparent, naked wraiths. They don't move. They don't speak. The entire action of the book is dependent on the reactions of the people in the town to these intimations of mortality. The third book was *McKain's Dilemma*, a suspense novel set in Lancaster County where I live. That was an attempt to create a very realistic private eye. The fourth was *Lowland Rider*, which was a descent-into-Hell story, in this case Hell being the New York subway system, which I certainly look on as pretty hellish. Then there's *Dreamthorp*, which is a lot more graphic and explicit than anything I've done to date. It had to be, because I was dealing with a sociopathic killer. In that one, also, the protagonist turned out to be a woman. I hadn't intended that, but she took over the book, and I was very glad. The story is ultimately her triumph. That's where we are now.

WT: There sure are a lot of novels about sociopathic killers of late. It seems

to be a trend: *Koko* and *The Kill Riff* and most especially Rex Miller's *Slob*, and *Slob II: The Revenge of Slob* or whatever it was, and so on. I assume that you wrote yours without any deliberate intent of copying any of these. It must be something in the air.

Williamson: Yeah. It is something in the air. Fiction reflects society, and this is so much in the news today. The book, I must emphasize, is not solely a sociopathic-killer book, although he does feature in it. It's a book mainly about people who are searching for a home, a haven, and the kind of love that one finds there, including the killer. Sociopathic killers need love too. . . . But, yes, it's so much around us today that I suppose it was inevitable that one of these fellows would eventually creep into one of my books. I don't expect to write another one. But you have to do it once.

WT: Surely no writer can allow himself to follow trends. You have to either make trends or stand alone, and the rest is sheer luck.

Williamson: I think you're right. I try very hard not to be imitative. Originality is a very valuable commodity to me and to readers. I would like a reader to finish a book and not merely close it and go on to the next one, but to think about it a little because he or she hasn't read anything quite like that before. They say that there are no new plots, and it's true in a way, but there are and always will be good new ways of retelling the old ones.

WT: How does the technique of the horror novel differ from that of other types?

Williamson: A lot of people have said that they write horror primarily to scare the reader. I don't. That's one of the furthest things from my mind. If the reader wants to be scared and my books keep him awake at night, that's fine, because it shows that I've touched inside them. But primarily what I want to do is

write a novel, and I don't especially care if it's a horror novel or not. But because of the way I think, that's what it's probably going to be. What I'm mainly concerned with are my characters, and their problems, and the way they solve them. Primarily I want to tell a good story with characters that are going to interest the reader from the beginning and make him or her stay with me till the end.

WT: Are there any more arbitrary techniques or requirements? I am thinking of the case of Raymond Chandler's *Playback* which was making his publisher really frustrated because it was supposed to be a mystery and there wasn't even a corpse until half-way through. So, are there any things you have to do in that sense of pacing — at what point do you introduce a menace, and so on?

Williamson: If I can, I like to introduce a menace as early as possible, and then go back and fill in the pieces. There should be some sort of menace or hint of it — in a genre horror novel — on the first or second page. But also on the first or second page — and what is more important to me — there has to be a real person doing something which the reader becomes interested in. It is not totally necessary to have the menace on the first page. If you can just interest the reader enough to keep going, tell an interesting story, then the menace will come. Depending on the way it's packaged, they *know* that a menace is going to come, so, in a way, holding it off longer and longer may make it all the more frightening and powerful when it finally comes, because of the slow, gradual buildup. But it all depends. You can have a murder take place on the first page and go terribly explicit and have it work just as well. I don't think you should be limited by any particular framework.

WT: You're limited by the mere fact that this is a horror novel. In real life, if

something strange starts happening, we do not immediately assume that vampires or Nameless Things are responsible, but in the horror novel, since the reader knows this *is* a horror novel — I mean, it's got one of those black, embossed covers and it says "horror" quite clearly on the spine — the reader is going to come to that conclusion quite quickly, perhaps well before the characters plausibly can. Therefore, if you don't follow up that conclusion fairly quickly, your characters are going to seem awfully dense. So the *pacing* of reader expectations may be a function of category.

Williamson: I see what you mean. But if the character jumps to the conclusion too quickly, the character looks like a New Age Shirley MacLaine-following bozo. You have to anchor it securely in the real world. In the real world most sane, rational people are not willing to accept the fact of a vampire or a werewolf — neither of which I've used. You'd be willing to accept *anything* before that. You'd accept the most bizarre psychological explanation, the weirdest conspiracy theory, before you would admit to the existence of the supernatural. So there has to come a point in the book where there is no other solution. It's like what Sherlock Holmes said about when all other explanations have been ruled out, whatever remains, however improbable, has to be the answer. So there has to be that moment, and hopefully with the pacing that moment will come before the reader finally tosses the book down and says "Boy, what a thick-skulled dimwit." So, yeah, there is some skill and craft involved in getting to that point.

WT: This is actually the classical Lovecraftian theory of horror, that the real horror isn't so much the big, menacing thing with claws, but the implications of what that thing's mere existence means to our view of reality.

Williamson: That's right, and in the

books where I use supernatural menaces of any sort, I try to make the most shattering moments come at the realization of *My God. This is real. This exists.* It's just as hard for the reader to believe that — you do suspend your disbelief when you read a horror novel, to some extent — but to *really* make the reader suspend that disbelief, the writer must make the characters convincing and well-developed and have them in the same position as the reader would be in, in the same state of disbelief, to make it effective. When that moment comes, your whole view of life is completely turned around.

WT: Which would preclude the possibility of a New Age horror novel. Skepticism on the part of the writer and the reader seems to be required, or else both will take the supernatural elements completely for granted, and there won't be any build-up or suspense or shock.

Williamson: Sure. If all these things exist and we believe in spirits and entities under every bush, where does the interest arise? What's so wonderful, so awesome about an intrusion from the supernatural world?

WT: What would happen, then, if more and more of your readers start to actually believe in this stuff — if Shirley MacLaine wins?

Williamson: I like to think she won't . . . [Laughs.] But whether you are a New Age believer or a rational human being, you can still enjoy a good novel in any genre. So I don't see that as much of a problem. I'd be happy to have New Agers read my books and take them for what they're worth — to them.

WT: Yet it would seem that horror fiction itself is the product of a culture which does not believe in the supernatural. Back when everybody did, there was no horror fiction, as in, say, medieval Europe. Fritz Leiber has a thesis that John Webster was the first horror writer. He was writing in the 1620s. There was then just enough skepticism

that people could begin to play games with the supernatural, and use it to symbolize psychological states, and so on, although most people still believed in the Devil. Yet disbelief had crept in just enough. This may also explain why no one is writing horror fiction in, say, India or central Africa today — for all they are writing novels — because everyone still believes in the supernatural.

Williamson: I never really had thought of that. Reading horror requires some skepticism, because horror is about shaking people up and questioning their established beliefs, and the suggestions that there are more things in Heaven and Earth, Horatio. So of course in a world where everyone believed explicitly in ghosts and demons and witches, there would be no need for horror, because there would already be that cleansing that I think horror does to people's everyday lives.

WT: Ultimately what the rational people are afraid of more than anything else is the possibility that Shirley MacLaine is right.

Williamson: [Laughs.] I see what you mean. But my books are all essentially about the fear of death, the fear of separation from someone you love, the fear of being ill or disfigured. Very realistic fears. It's not the fear of ghosts, but the fear of what the thought of ghosts represents. In a way ghosts are nice, because they insure life after death. But the vampires, the werewolves, the demons all represent death and destruction. *That* is the harsh reality, no matter what society we're in. I think we use horror as a kind of palette from which to paint those very real feelings. If you were to tell someone "This is a novel about how we deal with the inevitability of death," I think they would put that sucker down and go find the next Garfield book. But if you can couch it in a horror novel or in a story supposedly about the supernatural, they'll find it much more accessible and easier to swallow, but what you're saying will still come through.

WT: What are you writing just now?

Williamson: I just finished a novel dealing with professional theater, which I was involved with for a number of years. It is a horror story, although it tends to verge more into the mainstream. The next novel, which I am planning now, you may not even call a horror novel. It has elements of horror in it, but it also has a touch of fantasy, a touch of thriller. Hopefully the scope is a bit larger than some of the things I've done before. I think it might have an appeal to a wider audience. I hope.

WT: Thank you, Chet Williamson.

Ω

UNLIKELY SUICIDES: NUMBER 29

At the end of our block lives McBatt,
A witch with an untidy hat.
  I went to her house
  And got changed to a mouse,
But no one would lend me a cat.

— **Dan Crawford**

IN HER SHOES

by Ian Watson

art by Vincent Di Fate

When David Latimer left school before going to art college, he took a job in the real world for a few weeks. His parents had not thought this such a good idea, yet David craved independence, which a job seemed to promise. He would be earning a wage: meagre enough, though much to a schoolboy. After years as an only child who was quite protected, he wished to be his own person. Here was proof of his rebellious, artistic streak which he had nurtured quietly.

The year was 1960, the wage for such as David was four pounds a week. The job was accounts clerk in a shipping company. Squabbling kittiwakes nested on the stone window ledges, streaking the riverside office block white with their droppings. Cargo vessels moaned and hooted on the foggy river. Sometimes the sun shone, heating the office like an oven.

At lunchtime he walked through the city in company with other junior clerks, who seemed enrolled for life, to a cheap clean restaurant for a businessman's lunch: cream of tomato soup, roast beef, jam pudding and custard. Senior accountants in the office talked endlessly about a pub they would pop into at night, The Balloon, and its luscious landlady.

The job was a form of imprisonment; and besides, David botched it. He couldn't understand the filing system. He was asked to tot up a portage account, to tally the thousands of pounds which a ship spends in foreign ports, and found five different answers. Unfortunately he had already inked in the first, and second, and third. His

supervisor's only comment was a quiet, "Shit." After a month David quit, promising himself never to do an ordinary job again.

Nor did he; not that he avoided hard work in his lifetime. At art college he became a potter. Twenty-five years later he was master of his own pottery, run from a cottage and barn workshop in the Warwickshire countryside. David specialised in traditional rural spongeware: robust pots and plates crafted from local clay and hand-sponged with bird motifs, with paisley curlicues, with flowers and fruits. He had abandoned the old method of stamping with cuts of potato in favour of using shock absorbers, which held finer detail and lasted longer. David had also devised a crisper method of firing than the old copper oxide routine.

Early in his career he had won a scholarship to Japan, to follow in the footsteps of Bernard Leach and study with the master potters in Sendai for a year; not that David's work showed any traceable Japanese influence. He was too much his own man. Still, he sold his work to Tokyo and New York — though not so much in his native land. Local success and real prosperity eluded him, yet his fortunes ticked over, with a few missing heart-beats, from year to year. His life was free, even if the freedom was constrained by the need to keep on designing and firing and stamping, and packaging his wares, by upkeep, by work. Holidays? Only brief working ones. Travel? Only with a purpose. His one-ton van was always several years old. As to the family car, the Latimers

were always the final owners; afterward it went for scrap or banger racing.

His family consisted of Meg whom he met during his first apprenticeship, in Wales, and daughter Gwen, now turned fifteen. Meg had waited for a child till she was thirty. David's mother had died of cancer the previous year; his father was ailing with heart trouble. Now forty-five, David began to think of death, particularly if he woke in the wee hours.

Meg had become stout. Gwen, chubby as a child, had grown up tall and slender. She had never cut her long black hair. Boys were beginning to show interest. How long until David became a grandfather, and died? Maybe he had been too bound up in himself and his work, too busy, too impatiently his own self. Yet now for the first time — with a sense of shock, and sympathy, and love — he

fully noticed Gwen as *her* own person.

Had Gwen enjoyed a full, true life up until now?

"Shouldn't there have been a few real holidays?" he asked Meg one Sunday night in bed. "Shouldn't there have been more experiences for our Gwen? Instead of us staying stuck in the country, lovely though it is?"

"You stuck us here, David," said his wife.

"We stuck ourselves here. Art stuck us here. Life did." A life which kept on promising, always hanging juicy carrots just out of reach.

"Shouldn't we have done more?" Meg said. "That's what you mean. Well, it's too late to wake up. Years have slipped by. Those could have been the best years. I feel tired, David. If we became rich tomorrow I couldn't handle it — no more than you can handle that little bit

extra, the *giving* of yourself; that's the truth."

"It's never too late."

"Oh it is. If you could have given more of yourself, you might have become famous. What you give, you get back."

Years sliding by, speeding up: had *he* enjoyed a full, true life up until now? He feared not. He feared, at night, the darkness at the end of life.

Perhaps they had raised Gwen the way in which he himself had been raised: as an only child, protected, yet never wholly connected with. Naturally Gwen would be going to art college in a few more years. She would probably do fashion and textiles, since she hadn't his feel for the clay. As she approached her first major exam hurdle — limping somewhat — her school had set up a work experience scheme.

This was the immediate trigger for his present bout of anxiety. For a week at the end of the summer term she would have to work in the real world, in Leambury, the nearest large town. She would catch the early works bus in from the village and do her nine-to-five stint in a small designer textile factory. Fending for herself.

The prospect terrified her.

"I'm not just *worried,*" Gwen confided earlier that Sunday evening. She didn't call David "Daddy" and never had. Maybe she ought to have done, however David hadn't liked the hint of, well, obsolescence in the word Daddy, the sense of being on the way out. He had insisted on first names, which sounded more intimate, but wasn't really.

Gwen had her route mapped out, and her outfit ready for the morning: brown Indian cotton skirt, lace slip, green silk blouse, green tights, high heels. She knew the bus timetable. Her bag was packed, with enough pounds in her purse to buy lunch.

"I'm scared stiff," she said. "What if

— ?" She raised a number of "what ifs" which he deflected with a familiar family joke: "Rabid sheep!" What if a flock of rabid sheep attacks the bus? What if rabid sheep are loose in Leambury?

She seemed genuinely frightened. He made to hug her, and pat her — like a pet dog — but she deflected him.

"Put yourself in my shoes," she muttered.

"I was, once." He told her about his job at that shipping office long ago.

"That would be back in the Dark Ages when you were alive, you mean?" She shrugged. "You never told me any of that before."

Meg made a better job of reassuring Gwen.

Who could reassure David? Not Meg, that night. He woke at three in the morning and thought of generations and of his own death. Forty-five was over the hill, more than half way through.

He thought of Gwen, lovely daughter, a separate independent consciousness with a lifetime still ahead. He thought death, he thought life. His own life was slowly fading, yet her life came alive to him then with a loving intensity which astonished him — so much so that he could almost feel what she had been feeling earlier, could almost see himself through her eyes, watch himself failing her, not so much intentionally as inadvertently.

"I'll die," he murmured. Meg wouldn't hear; she always slept like a rock. "Gwen'll live. In ten years time she'll be leading a rich, full, adult life, fulfilling herself. She must! And in twenty years time. Whereas me . . . should I last another twenty years . . . cancer, heart attack, who knows?" Dread possessed him. Fiercely he willed her to thrive and enjoy, to bloom and prosper.

Half awake, he plotted her footsteps to the bus stop next morning, her ride

into the town, her walk to the textiles place. How would people treat her? What would she eat for lunch? How would she fare?

After Gwen had left, David slapped clean wet clay on his wheel. He hoped to make fifty jugs that day, to be sponged another time with the print of a rooster. The first lump of clay rose up spinning between his fingers, much slimmer than he had intended. His fingers weren't moulding a jug at all. They were modelling a body. Female. A girl's.

True, the body showed no details. How could there be details when the clay was rotating? Legs were fused into one single large leg. But here was the in-curve of the knee, the out-swell of the thigh, the pinch of waist. Breasts formed a lip all around the chest. Arms? No arms. A neck; a featureless ellipsoid of a head.

Surely the clay would sag and collapse if he quit supporting it. He couldn't bear to cease connecting. It pirouetted like a ballerina, whirled like a dervish, around and around. His fingers were its arms, her arms.

He heard the purr of traffic, the click of high heels, the roar of a motorbike, hiss of air brakes, snatches of voices as people passed, as she walked past other people. Presently . . .

"Hullo, I'm Gwen Latimer —"

She had arrived at the factory.

Throughout the day, as he spun the same clay, keeping it wet, he eavesdropped with anxious love.

When Gwen arrived home at six-thirty she looked tired but thrilled.

"It went fine, just fine! I did learn a lot."

David nodded. He knew, though he couldn't put any faces to the voices.

"You must tell us everything right from the moment you caught the bus!" insisted Meg. "No, wait, how about a cup of tea? Or maybe a glass of ginger wine?"

"Oh, ginger wine, please. May I really?"

Yes, Gwen's day had gone just so.

That night David awoke and knew he was blind. He couldn't see the pale shape of the window or the luminous dial of the bedside clock. He was worse than blind. He couldn't feel a thing. Sheet and blanket made no impression. His whole body was without sensation, that of a corpse. No taste of moisture in his mouth. No mouth. His spine might have snapped. He was a corpse awaiting burial.

But then the voices began.

"Hullo, I'm Gwen Latimer —"

And the sounds of the factory. Loving relief overwhelmed him.

When David woke next morning he felt normal; until he sat at his wheel and made the same wet clay rise up again into the girl's smoothed, amputated body.

This time he not only heard but smelled the street which Gwen took on her way to work: the whiffs of exhaust fumes, lardy and bloody reek of a butcher's shop, a rich nutty pipe tobacco, a hint of perfume, dust in the air, an open dustbin.

That night he awoke dead, but he could hear and smell all that she had heard and smelled.

On Wednesday, besides, he tasted her morning coffee and ginger snap, and later her lunch of cheeseburger and chips with tomato ketchup.

On Thursday he touched whatever she touched, while he also touched the clay.

Thursday night — was it already Friday morning? — he awoke still sightless but could hear, feel, smell, and taste whatever she had met with. Friday was to be Gwen's last session of work experience; Summer holidays thereafter. Nowadays it wasn't nearly so easy to be accepted by an art college as had been the case in David's time. Would Gwen

perform well enough in her exams, due the following June and July, to stay on at school to take Advanced Level Art? Might she be better advised to start straight in on a pre-diploma course at the local college in Leambury?

Worries, worries.

He put his whole heart into wishing her good fortune.

He placed his fingers on the clay, on Friday.

So strange to walk along Alfred Street in Leambury in an adolescent girl's body, smoother and softer than his own, long hair fussed by the breeze, breasts pressing at his white Angora sweater, worn because the weather had cooled, legs clad in tights rubbing together under the skirt as if naked. Yet so gratifying, so full of promise, so fresh, so perceptive. Glancing into the florist's window at the corner of Alfred and Peel Streets, he saw new hues in the vases of roses. Why, look at the terracotta mouldings on the upper storeys of that bank! Like a predator he smelled the aroma of life around him. Soon he would see those faces belonging to the voices at the factory. He was bound to make some mistakes and hoped he wouldn't seem too stupid all of a sudden. He hadn't Gwen's memories, only his own.

Gwen: where was she now? Why, here she was, mounting steep Peel Street. A glance at the mirror in the window of a furniture store proved this.

But where was her own independent self? Gone away, gone away. Lost. Dust to dust, clay to clay. Could it be that she was sitting at his potter's wheel right now, lovingly spinning the clay figure so that he could live in her shoes for a day? Why should she wish that? So as to tease him, to taunt him with new young life for a few hours?

That evening David stepped anxiously along the lane from the village bus stop. Cottage and barn came in view. Opening the garden gate, he was assaulted by the scent of the madonna lillies raising their white trumpets high on thin stems, a hallelujah of angels. He touched his breasts, feeling sinful, an incestuous abuser.

As usual all that week, both parents were waiting to greet him in the living room, its shelves and Welsh dresser crowded with pastel-stamped, biscuity pottery.

"So how was your last day?" asked Meg. She had a cup of tea waiting on the pine table. Mustn't make a habit of the ginger wine.

"Fine, simply fine!" he assured Meg in his girl's voice. He stared at David; stared at himself.

"Well done, Gwen," said the man. "I'm proud of you." After a moment, his face smiled. His tone had sounded so flat.

Gwen's father seemed like some animated waxwork, a working model. He was perfectly modelled in every respect — to the life! — yet some elusive ingredient was absent. What was it? Individuality? Personality?

It occurred — to the one who had returned home — that the Latimer spongeware business was doomed to fail slowly over the next few years. From this day on this man would only turn out copies of his previous work, nothing fresh or original. Presently buyers would cotton on that some spark had been extinguished. Enthusiasm would slacken. Reluctance would turn into rejection, while the man grew disheartened — but didn't really suffer! Nothing inside him could suffer. His would be a charade of sadness — and of failure, and perhaps finally suicide? The machine, at last, switching itself off?

Lean times lay ahead. The Latimers' daughter would barely have time to escape to a good art school, to London, to life, blessed by her new-found talent and persistence. She wouldn't study fashion and textiles now. No, she would become a sculptor.

The waxwork man didn't matter; he only possessed imitation feelings. But Meg would be bitterly unhappy. Meg wouldn't be able to understand. Could her daughter make it up to her?

David's daughter. How much worse this was than driving a daughter away from home in bitterness, losing her to teenage rebellion, or to a fatal road accident, a car crushing her bicycle.

"Poor dear Gwen," murmured the one who had come home.

Meg stared in puzzlement. "Why's that? Your week's over now. You said it went wonderfully."

He nodded Gwen's head, and her hair swung. He felt choked and swollen. Helplessly he burst into tears.

Meg hastened to hug him. "You were just pretending, weren't you? Was it so terrible?"

The man stood incapable, a lump.

"No," he managed to say through his helpless sobbing, "it . . . wasn't terrible. Not at all, it was fine, it was fun."

"Must have been a strain," said Meg. "I didn't realise how brave you were being. Never mind! Silly darling, you're back here now. It's the holidays, the whole Summer." She looked at the man. "I'm sure they expect too much of the young these days, too soon — forcing them to grow up at fifteen! I expect she'll be all right about staying away from home when she's a few years older."

"I will be," he promised, scared at how much he needed to learn if he was to succeed: Gwen's schoolwork, her school friends, dress, make-up, periods, the whole pretence, always knowing that he was an abuser, a murderer, all the while living in the same house as the waxwork man.

What if Gwen were to return, from wherever? In what style would she return? In dreams, vengefully or piteously? As a furious, imp-like creature? As a walking, living corpse? Or simply a disembodied voice crying from far away to be let out of whatever cruel confinement held her captive? He sent out all his love to her, wherever she was, so as to calm her and keep her away from him.

That night, in her room, he woke and heard the boards on the landing squeaking as footsteps slowly approached. Shivering, goose bumps roughing his soft skin, he switched on Gwen's bedside lamp. A fumbling at the door . . . the handle began to turn. He held her mouth so as not to scream. The door opened gradually.

The waxwork man stood there.

"Gwen, my darling," said the man in that same flat voice.

"Go back to bed, David," he begged. "Go back to bed with Meg, Daddy."

And this was the first time she had called the man Daddy.   Ω

Coming in Weird Tales® #299!

A special issue devoted to **Jonathan Carroll**, the critically-acclaimed author of *The Land of Laughs, A Child Across the Sky,* and *Bones of the Moon,* including four stories by Carroll, plus an interview with him.
Also in this issue: fiction by Ian Watson, Storm Constantine, and R. Garcia y Robertson; plus a bonus interview with **Dean R. Koontz**.
All artwork will be by **Thomas Kidd**.

THE TREASURE OF THE NASSASALARS

by Chet Williamson

art by Stephen E. Fabian

"According to the Laws of Ahura, the all-knowing, of the seven Immortals, of the Holy Sraasha, of Adarbad Maraspend, and of the Dastur of the Age!"

Thus we prayed, O Ahura, ever loyal to thy true faith, the faith of Zoroaster, faithful to thee even in our long exile in this country of the Hindus, far from the land from whence thy truth first sprang.

Thus we prayed by the side of your servant, Vishta Zohak, before the Khandias bore him to the tower of silence and the ministrations of the vultures. The family of Vishta sat far from Yima and myself, since you have seen fit in your wisdom to make us nassasalars, defiled corpse-bearers who relinquish the companionship of other men to do your will.

We then recited the Gatha, which comforted the members of the family; and the four-eyed dog, Chathru Chasma, looked at the corpse for the second time and did not take his eyes away, so we knew him to be truly dead. After the mourners passed before Vishta Zohak and bowed, Yima and I covered the face and strapped the corpse onto the iron bier, and bore it outside the house to the two Khandias who would take it to the

tower. It was then, O Lord Ahura, that I noticed the Frank.

He stood across the dusty street, arms folded over his bare chest, and I felt fear, O Lord, at the bright look in his eyes, like a wolf spying a sick calf. His sword hung by his left side, and I saw that it was a Mongol weapon. Whether he had ridden with that horde or taken it from one of their dead, he had used it long, for his right forearm was greatly scarred, as was his face, on which a long scar split cheek, mouth, and chin, so that even in repose he wore a toothy grin.

I trembled as he stared at Yima and me, examining us as if he was contemplating coming to arms with us, even though we are the most abhorred of men, shunned among even a shunned faith for our nearness to the putrefying dead.

But I turned my eyes from him, and we followed the Khandias and the family of Vishta to the tower of silence. The way was long, as you well know, O God of Good, and the glorious fire of your sun was at its zenith when we reached the tower. As the Khandias laid the bier on the ground, being careful not to turn the face of Vishta to the north from whence come the demons, I looked back on the path we had trod, and far in the distance spied a figure I thought to be the Frank I had seen earlier. He was too far away for me to see his face, but I knew it to be that of a ravenous wolf.

We then uncovered the face of the

80

corpse, and the family gazed one last time on their departed member. Then Chathru Chasma looked upon Vishta again and was silent and did not howl in terror as he would have had any life remained. So Yima and I bore the bier into the tower, took the clothes from Vishta, and laid him naked under the sky on the stone slabs (I pray, O Ahura, that you have observed with what care Yima and I have re-cemented the junctures of the slabs so that no corruption should soil the purity of your earth). Then we cast the clothes into the great stone pit where Vishta's bones would be placed when the vultures had finished.

They, my only friends save for Yima and for thyself and the seven, were patiently waiting, perched on the rim of the tower while the great sun poured its sacred fire through the open roof, bathing all within in its pure light, even though this be the most impure place on thy earth.

Yima and I left them to their meal, being careful to keep our steps on the appointed paths around the stone beds where lie the bones of the departed dead, so that we might not increase our uncleanness. The flapping wings of thy feathered servants were loud in our ears as we closed the gate behind us, and through the iron bars we saw the vultures start to strip the corpse of its corruption, according to thy will as made manifest by the Holy Prophet Zoroaster.

When the company saw us, the attendant struck his hands together, and we all prayed the Sraosh baj, after which we prayed, "We do sorrow for our sins. We do honor the souls of the dead, who are become the spirits of the holy."

Then the attendant set before the family and priests a basin of cattle urine, in which they cleansed their hands as the first step in purification, and they departed to their homes. Yima and I walked to the huts near the tower which thou in thy wisdom hast given us

to dwell in, and began our period of prayer and cleansing. I looked for the stern figure of the Frank before I entered my door, but saw him nowhere.

Later in the afternoon, when the sun had sunk nearly to the horizon, I looked at the tower and observed the good vultures sitting once again on the rim, so I knew that Vishta's bones were stripped clean. I ate a brief meal, praised thee for the gift of food, and reclined on my pallet to sleep, since Yima and I needed to arise early in the dawn, as it was time to gather all the bones of many past burials and cast them into the bhandar, thy holy well, to dissolve to dust with the bones of ages past.

I awoke with a start to find strong fingers entwined in my hair and a cold blade at my throat. The rank breath of an unbeliever was sharp in my nostrils, and I knew that it was the Frank.

"If you yell, you die." His accent was spiced with the Levant, and the voice itself was rough and harsh. "Are you a nassasalar?"

I replied that I was, in a voice made small with fear.

"The one who was with you — is he near?"

"Yes," I said. "He sleeps in a nearby hut."

"Then it's your choice," said the Frank, "whether or not he sleeps forever. If you cry out and he comes I'll slay him. If you do what I ask quietly, you and he shall both see the sun rise."

I thought, O Lord Ahura, that he meant to take me as he would a woman, and my stomach churned at the thought of the pain of it and also at the thought of a man being so base as to sully himself with one so unclean and impure as a nassasalar. I trembled and he shook me as a serpent shakes a mouse and said, "I'll do you no harm. The treasure is what I've come for." And he undid the cover of a lantern which bathed the hut in a dim orange

light.

I looked at him in amazement. "Treasure?" I asked. "What treasure, master?"

Again he pressed the blade of the sword against my neck, and I felt a hot wetness that could be nothing but my blood. "Toy with me, corpse-man, and I'll let loose *all* your blood. You know what I speak of — the treasure of the nassasalars."

Lord Ahura, thou knowest the terrors that thy servants can feel, and mine was the greatest of all as I realized that this barbarian had come after treasure that did not exist — not for him, at any rate. "Master," I said, "pray forgive me, but what is the nature of this treasure?"

His eyes grew cold with fury. "You know that best, pig. All I know is what I heard in a tavern at Bombay. A few thieves were speaking of spoils, and one mentioned a mythical jewel that he said was to be desired even more than the treasure of the nassasalars. I have never believed in myths, but I well know that such a tavern saying must be based on fact. I was surprised to find you so unguarded. I suppose superstition frightens away thieves of your own sect, eh?"

The blade was taken away so that I could speak once more. "Master, I have heard this saying — 'the treasure of the nassasalars' — it is true. But it is a mere figure of speech. We have no treasure you would desire."

"I'll judge. Now take me into the tower. I know how other easterners honor their dead with jewels and gold. Why should you damned parsees be any different? And I still have much room in my purse for my long journey home." And he patted a leathern pouch tied to his girdle.

I did not dare to tell him how we place our dead naked under the sun so as to preserve the purity of the four elements of life. My mind worked frantically, O Lord, to seek an escape from this butcher, but none came, and I thought it best to do his bidding until you saw fit to grant me the wisdom to deal properly with him.

So I took the key to the iron gate and led him unto the tower. He walked behind me carrying the lantern, his sword ready. I tried to put the key in the lock softly, for it would do no good to awaken Yima, as the Frank could have slain us both with ease. As we entered I heard the rustle of wings overhead and knew that the vultures were stirring in surprise at having company in the dead of night.

The Frank heard it also. "What's that?" he said as he halted, wary as a cat.

"Birds, master," I replied. "Merely birds."

We walked up the stone steps to the terrace on which the dead are placed. He stopped and looked about him. "Christ's blood," he murmured, "what a charnel house. But I didn't come to gawk at dried bones. Where is the treasure?"

O Lord Ahura, I was ready to weep. There was no treasure I could show this man, and yet if I did not show him a treasure he would slay me in anger. So I prayed inwardly to you, O all-knowing one, and you placed in my mouth the words that saved my life, and they were as sweet as honey on my tongue.

"O master, what is called the treasure of the nassasalars lies in the pit you see before you."

He went to the edge of the pit, held the lantern at arm's length, and gazed into it suspiciously, but the light was not strong enough to reach the bottom where lay the piles of decaying bones atop a thick layer of corpse powder. "Have you a rope?"

I told him of the rope in my hut and together we retrieved it. Then he bade me tie on the rope and lower myself into the pit to obtain the treasure.

"Nay, master," I lamented. "It is forbidden any of my sect to enter the pit. If you must, slay me, for that must be my fate ere I descend into those depths." And I fell to my knees, bowing my head for his sword's stroke.

Instead he spat upon me and sneered. "What a fool to throw riches into a pit and not dare to recover them. A race of women! Very well, coward, I'll bind you here and give you worse than death if I come up from that pit emptyhanded."

He cut part of the rope off and tied me with it until I could move no part of my body. My mouth he also bound so that I could not speak. Then he tied the rope around a post, hung the lantern from his girdle, and started to climb down into the pit.

I know not how long I waited while the light coming from the pit's edge grew dimmer as the Frank descended. Finally I heard an outraged roar and saw the post to which the rope was tied shake violently.

"Swine!" shrieked the voice from the pit. "Parsee scum! I'll feed your balls to the kites for this!" And the rope started to jerk as the Frank climbed up, hand over hand, cursing all the while. I thought I was doomed. The light became stronger, and my death grew nearer.

Then, O Ahura Mazda, you did send your servants and my friends to succor me. Seven vultures, the number of the Immortals, descended from where they slept on the tower's rim and struck at the rope where it was tied about the post. In a few heartbeats they had severed it, and a scream arose from the pit, into which the lantern light vanished. The dull sound of the Frank hitting the pit's bottom followed, and all was silence.

Then one of the great birds came to me and pecked at my bonds until they were cut through and I was free. I stumbled through the darkness to my

hut where I lit a torch and returned to the tower. My torch gave a much greater light than the Frank's lantern, and by holding it over the pit's edge, I could see the bottom. I was unable at first to make out forms, but as my eyes grew accustomed, I saw the vultures jabbing their beaks at the body of the Frank.

Then came a sound more terrible than any I have ever heard. The Frank had not been killed by the fall, only stunned and crippled, and now he struggled vainly while the seven servants stripped away all that covered his white bones. Soon his screaming ended, and no sound was heard save for the rending of flesh by strong talons and beaks.

As the sun boldly burst over the peaks of the eastern hills, bringing with it thy warmth and light, O Ahura Mazda, the seven rose on strong wings from the body of the Frank. He was purified. Noting remained but the bones which would soon decay and mingle with the dust of the pit. The Frank had found the treasure of the nassasalars. Had he but asked those whom he had overheard, he would have learned that to the corpse-bearer, the impure pariah shunned by all men, the greatest treasure is death.

But in thy eyes, Ahura Mazda, even the most vile may be upraised. Else why wouldst thou have had the seventh vulture ascend from the pit with the Frank's purse, full of gems and gold coins enough to allow *any* man to begin anew, and drop it at the feet of thy faithful servant, this humble nassasalar?

Thy name be praised! Ω

1/72nd SCALE

by Ian MacLeod

art by Janet Aulisio

David moved into Simon's room. Mum and Dad said they were determined not to let it become a shrine: Dad even promised to redecorate it anyhow David wanted. New paint, new curtains, Superman wallpaper, the lot. You have to try to forget the past, Dad said, enveloping him in his arms and the smell of his sweat, things that have been and gone. You're what counts now, Junior, our living son.

On a wet Sunday afternoon (the windows steamed, the air still thick with the fleshy smell of pork, an afternoon for headaches, boredom and family arguments if ever there was one) David took the small stepladder from the garage and lugged it up the stairs to Simon's room. One by one, he peeled Simon's posters from the walls, careful not to tear the corners as he separated them from yellowed Sellotape and blobs of Blutac. He rolled them into neat tubes, each held in place by an elastic band, humming along to Dire Straits on Simon's Sony portable as he did so. He was halfway through taking the dog-fighting aircraft down from the ceiling when Mum came in. The dusty prickly feel of the fragile models set his teeth on edge. They were like big insects.

"And what do you think you're doing?" Mum asked.

David left a Spitfire swinging on its thread and looked down. It was odd seeing her from above, the dark half moons beneath her eyes.

"I'm . . . just . . ."

Dire Straits were playing "Industrial Disease." Mum fussed angrily with the Sony, trying to turn it off. The volume soared. She jerked the plug out and turned to face him through the silence. "What makes you think this thing is yours, David? We can hear it blaring all through the bloody house. Just what do you think you're doing?"

"I'm sorry," he said. A worm of absurd laughter squirmed in his stomach. Here he was perched up on a stepladder, looking down at Mum as though he was seven feet tall. But he didn't climb down: he thought she probably wouldn't get angry with someone perched up on a ladder.

But Mum raged at him. Shouted and shouted and shouted. Her face went white as bone. Dad came up to see what the noise was, his shirt unbuttoned and creased from sleep, the sports pages crumpled in his right hand. He lifted David down from the ladder and said it was alright. This was what they'd agreed, okay?

Mum began to cry. She gave David a salty hug, saying she was sorry. Sorry. My darling. He felt stiff and awkward. His eyes, which had been flooding with tears a moment before, were suddenly as dry as the Sahara. So dry it hurt to blink.

Mum and Dad helped him finish clearing up Simon's models and posters. They smiled a lot and talked in loud, shaky voices. Little sis Victoria came and stood at the door to watch. It was like packing away the decorations after Christmas. Mum wrapped the planes up in tissues and put them carefully in a box. She gave a loud sob that sounded like a burp when she broke one of the propellers.

When they'd finished (just the bare furniture, the bare walls. Growing dark,

© JANET AULISIO 1990.

but no one wanting to put the light on)
Dad promised that he'd redecorate the
room next weekend, or the weekend
after at the latest. He'd have the place
better than new. He ruffled David's hair
in a big, bearlike gesture and slipped his
other arm around Mum's waist. Better
than new.

That was a year ago.

The outlines of Simon's posters still
shadowed the ivy wallpaper. The ceiling
was pinholed where his models had
hung. Hard little patches of Humbrol
enamel and polystyrene cement cra-
tered the carpet around the desk in the
bay window. There was even a faint
greasy patch above the bed where
Simon used to sit up reading his big
boy's books. They, like the model aircraft, now slumbered in the attic. *The
Association Football Yearbook, Aircraft
of the Desert Campaign, Classic Cars
1945–1960, Tanks and Armoured Vehi-
cles of the World, the Modeller's Hand-
book* . . . all gathering dust, darkness
and spiders.

David still thought of it as Simon's
room. He'd even called it that once or
twice by accident. No one noticed.
David's proper room, the room he'd had
before Simon died, the room he still
looked into on his way past it to the
toilet, had been taken over by Victoria.
What had once been his territory,
landmarked by the laughing-face crack
on the ceiling, the dip in the floorboards
where the fireplace had once been, the
corner where the sun pasted a bright
orange triangle on summer evenings,
was engulfed in frilly curtains, Snoopy
lampshades and My Little Ponys. Not
that Victoria seemed particularly happy
with her new, smart bedroom. She
would have been more than content to
sleep in Simon's old room with his
posters curling and yellowing like dry
skin and his models gathering dust
around her. Little Victoria had idolised
Simon; laughed like a mad thing when

he dandled her on his knee and tickled
her, gazed in wonderment when he told
her those clever stories he made up
right out of his head.

David started Senior School in the
autumn. Archbishop Lacy; the one
Simon used to go to. It wasn't as bad as
he'd feared, and for a while he even told
himself that things were getting better
at home as well. Then on a Thursday
afternoon as he changed after Games
(shower steam and sweat. Cowering in a
corner of the changing rooms. Almost
ripping his Y-fronts in his hurry to pull
them up and hide his winkle) Mr Lewis
the gamesmaster came over and handed
him a brown window envelope addressed to his parents. David popped it
into his blazer pocket and worried all
the way home. No one else had got one
and he couldn't think of anything he'd
done sufficiently well to deserve special
mention, although he could think of lots
of things he'd done badly. He handed it
straight to Mum when he came in,
anxious to find out the worst. He waited
by her as she stood reading it in the
kitchen. The Blue Peter signature tune
drifted in from the lounge. She finished
and folded it in half, sharpening the
crease with her nails. Then in half
again. And again, until it was a fat, neat
square. David gazed at it in admiration
as Mum told him in a matter-of-fact
voice that School wanted back the 100-
metres swimming trophy that Simon
had won the year before. For a moment,
David felt a warm wave of relief break
over him. Then he looked up and saw
Mum's face.

There was a bitter argument between
Mum and Dad and the School. In the
end — after the local paper had run an
article in its middle pages headlined
"Heartless Request" — Archbishop
Lacy agreed to buy a new trophy and let
them keep the old one. It stayed on the
fireplace in the lounge, regularly tar-
nishing and growing bright again as
Mum attacked it with Duraglit. The

headmaster gave several assembly talks about becoming too attached to possessions and Mr Lewis the gamesmaster made Thursday afternoons Hell for David in the special ways that only a gamesmaster can.

Senior School also meant Homework. As the nights lengthened and the first bangers echoed down the suburban streets David sat working at Simon's desk in the bay window. He always did his best and although he never came much above the middle of the class in any subject, his handwriting was often remarked on for its neatness and readability. He usually left the curtains open and had just the desk light (blue and white wicker shade. Stand of turned mahogany on a wrought-iron base. Good enough to have come from British Home Stores and all Simon's work. All of it) on so that he could see out. The streetlamp flashed through the hairy boughs of the monkey puzzle tree in the front garden. Dot, dot, dash. Dash, dash, dot. He often wondered if it was a message.

Sometimes, way past the time when she should have been asleep, Victoria's door would squeak open and her slippered feet would patter along the landing and half way down the stairs. There she would sit, hugging her knees and watching the TV light flicker through the frosted glass door of the lounge. Cracking open his door quietly and peering down through the top bannisters, David had seen her there. If the lounge door opened she would scamper back up and out of sight into her bedroom faster than a rabbit. Mum and Dad never knew. It was Victoria's secret, and in the little he said to her, David had no desire to prick that bubble. He guessed that she was probably waiting for Simon to return.

Dad came up one evening when David had just finished algebra and was turning to the agricultural revolution. He stood in the doorway, the light from the landing haloing what was left of his hair. A dark figure with one arm hidden, holding something big behind its back. For a wild moment, David felt his scalp prickle with incredible, irrational fear.

"How's Junior?" Dad said.

He ambled through the shadows of the room into the pool of yellow light where David sat.

"All right, thank you," David said. He didn't like being called Junior. No one had ever called him Junior when Simon was alive and he was now the eldest in any case.

"I've got a present for you. Guess what?"

"I don't know." David had discovered long ago that it was dangerous to guess presents. You said the thing you wanted it to be and upset people when you were wrong.

"Close your eyes."

There was a rustle of paper and a thin, scratchy rattle that he couldn't place. But it was eerily familiar.

"Now open them."

David composed his face into a suitable expression of happy surprise and opened his eyes.

It was a big, long box wrapped in squeaky folds of shrinkwrap plastic. An Airfix 1/72nd scale Flying Fortress.

David didn't have to pretend. He was genuinely astonished. Overawed. It was a big model, the biggest in the Airfix 1/72nd series. Simon (who always talked about these things; the steady pattern of triumphs that peppered his life. Each new obstacle mastered and overcome) had been planning to buy one when he'd finished the Lancaster he was working on and had saved up enough money from his paper round. Instead, the Lancaster remained an untidy jumble of plastic, and in one of those vicious conjunctions that are never supposed to happen to people like Simon, he and his bike chanced to share the same patch of tarmac on the High Street at the same moment as a Pick-

fords lorry turning right out of a service road. The bike had twisted into a half circle around the big wheels. Useless scrap.

"I'd never expected . . . I'd . . ." David opened and closed his mouth in the hope that more words would come out.

Dad put a large hand on his shoulder. "I knew you'd be pleased. I've got you all the paints it lists on the side of the box, the glue." Little tins pattered out onto the desk, each with a coloured lid. There were three silver. David could see from the picture on the side of the box that he was going to need a lot of silver. "And look at this." Dad flashed a craft knife close to his face. "Isn't that dinky? You'll have to promise to be careful, though."

"I promise."

"Take your time with it, Junior. I can't wait to see it finished." The big hand squeezed his shoulder, then let go. "Don't allow it to get in the way of your homework."

"Thanks, Dad. I won't."

"Don't I get a kiss?"

David gave him a kiss.

"Well, I'll leave you to it. I'll give you any help you want. Don't you think you should have the big light on? You'll strain your eyes."

"I'm fine."

Dad hovered by him for a moment, his lips moving and a vague look in his eyes as though he was searching for the words of a song. The he grunted and left the bedroom.

David stared at the box. He didn't know much about models, but he knew that the Flying Fortress was The Big One. Even Simon had been working up to it in stages. The Everest of models in every sense. Size. Cost. Difficulty. The guns swivelled. The bomb bay doors opened. The vast and complex undercarriage went up and down. From the heights of such an achievement one could gaze serenely down at the whole landscape of childhood. David slid the box back into its large paper bag along with the paints and the glue and the knife. He put it down on the carpet and tried to concentrate on the agricultural revolution. The crumpled paper at the top of the bag made creepy crackling noises. He got up, put it in the bottom of his wardrobe and closed the door.

"How are you getting on with the model?" Dad asked him at tea two days later.

David nearly choked on a fish finger. He forced it down, the dry breadcrumbs sandpapering his throat. "I, I er —" He hadn't given the model any thought at all (just dreams and a chill of unease. A dark mountain to climb) since he'd put it away in the wardrobe. "I'm taking it slowly," he said. "I want to make sure I get it right."

Mum and Dad and Victoria returned to munching their food, satisfied for the time being.

After tea, David clicked his bedroom door shut and took the model out from the wardrobe. The paper bag crackled excitedly in his hands. He turned on Simon's light and sat down at the desk. Then he emptied the bag and bunched it into a tight ball, stuffing it firmly down into the wastepaper bin beside the chair. He lined the paints up next to the window. Duck egg green. Matt black. Silver. Silver. Silver . . . a neat row of squat little soldiers.

David took the craft knife and slit open the shining shrinkwrap covering. It rippled and squealed as he skinned it from the box. Then he worked the cardboard lid off. A clean, sweet smell wafted into his face. Like a new car (a hospital waiting room. The sudden taste of metal in your mouth as Mum's heirloom Spode tumbles towards the fireplace tiles) or the inside of a camera case. A clear plastic bag filled the box beneath a heavy wad of instructions. To open it he had to ease out the whole grey chittering weight of the model and cut open the seal, then carefully tease the

innards out, terrified that he might lose a piece in doing so. When he'd finished, the unassembled Flying Fortress jutted out from the box like a huge pile of jack-straws. It took him another thirty minutes to get them to lie flat enough to close the lid. Somehow, it was very important that he closed the lid.

So far, so good. David unfolded the instructions. They got bigger and bigger, opening out into a vast sheet covered with dense type and arrows and numbers and line drawings. But he was determined not to be put off. Absolutely determined. He could see himself in just a few weeks' time, walking slowly down the stairs with the great silver bird cradled carefully in his arms. Every detail correct. The paintwork perfect. Mum and Dad and Victoria will look up as he enters the bright warm lounge. And soon there is joy on their faces. The Flying Fortress is marvellous, a miracle (even Simon couldn't have done better), a work of art. There is laughter and wonder like Christmas firelight as David demonstrates how the guns swivel, how the undercarriage goes up and down. And although there is no need to say it, everyone understands that this is the turning point. The sun will shine again, the rain will be warm and sweet, clear white snow will powder the winter and Simon will be just a sad memory, a glint of tears in their happy, smiling eyes.

The preface to the instructions helpfully suggested that it was best to paint the small parts before they were assembled. Never one to ignore sensible advice, David reopened the box and lifted out the grey clusters of plastic. Like coathangers, they had an implacable tendency to hook themselves onto each other. Every part was attached to one of the trees of thin plastic around which the model was moulded. The big pieces such as the sides of the aircraft and the wings were easy to recognise, but there were also a vast number of odd shapes

that had no obvious purpose. Then, as his eyes searched along rows of thin bits, fat bits, star shaped bits and bits that might be parts of bombs, he saw a row of little grey men hanging from the plastic tree by their heads.

The first of the men was crouching in an oddly foetal position. When David pulled him off the plastic tree, his neck snapped instead of the join at the top of his head.

David spent the evenings and most of the weekends of the next month at work on the Flying Fortress.

"Junior," Dad said one day as he met him coming up the stairs, "you're getting so absorbed in that model of yours. I saw your light on last night when I went to bed. Just you be careful it doesn't get in the way of your homework."

"I won't let that happen," David answered, putting on his good-boy smile. "I won't get too absorbed."

But David was absorbed in the model, and the model was absorbed into him. It absorbed him to the exclusion of everything else. He could feel it working its way into his system. Lumps of glue and plastic, sticky sweet-smelling silver enamel worming into his flesh. Crusts of it were under his nails, sticking in his hair and to his teeth, his thoughts. Homework — which had been a worry to him — no longer mattered. He simply didn't do it. At the end-of-lesson bells he packed the exercise books into his satchel, and a week later he would take them out again for the next session, pristine and unchanged. Nobody actually took much notice. There was, he discovered, a group of boys and girls in his class who never did their homework — they just didn't do it. More amazing still, they weren't bothered about it and neither were the teachers. He began to sit at the back of the class with the cluster of paper-pellet flickers, boys who said Fuck, and lunchtime smokers. They made reluctant room for him,

89

wrinkling their noses in suspicion at their new, paint-smelling, hollow-eyed colleague. As far as David was concerned, the arrangement was purely temporary. Once the model was finished he'd work his way back up the class, no problem.

The model absorbed David. David absorbed the model. He made mistakes. He learned from his mistakes and made other mistakes instead. In his hurry to learn from those mistakes he repeated the original ones. It took him aching hours of frustration and eye strain to paint the detailed small parts of the model. The Humbrol enamel would never quite go where he wanted it to, but unfailingly ended up all over his hands. His fingerprints began to mark the model, the desk and the surrounding area like the evidence of a crime. And everything was so tiny. As he squinted down into the yellow pool of light cast by Simon's neat lamp, the paintbrush trembling in one hand and a tiny piece of motor sticking to the fingers of the other, he could feel the minute, tickly itchiness of it drilling through the breathless silence into his brain. But he persevered. The pieces came and went; turning from grey to blotched and runny combinations of enamel. He arranged them on sheets of the *Daily Mirror* on the right-hand corner of his desk, peeling them off his fingers like half-sucked Murraymints. A week later the paint was still tacky: he hadn't stirred the pots properly.

The nights grew colder and longer. The monkey puzzle tree whispered in the wind. David found it difficult to keep warm in Simon's bed. After shivering wakefully into the grey small hours, he would often have to scramble out from the clinging cold sheets to go for a pee. Once, weary and fumbling with the cord of his pyjamas, he glanced down from the landing and saw Victoria sitting on the stairs. He tiptoed down to her, careful not to make the stairs creak and wake Mum and Dad.

"What's the matter?" he whispered.

Little Victoria turned to him, her face as expressionless as a doll's. "You're not Simon," she hissed. Then she pushed past him as she scampered back up to bed.

On Bonfire Night, David stood beneath a dripping umbrella as Dad struggled to light a Roman candle in a makeshift shelter of paving stones. Tomorrow, he decided, I will start to glue some bits together. Painting the rest of the details can wait. The firework flared briefly through the wet darkness, spraying silver fire and soot across the paving slab. Victoria squealed with fear and chewed her mitten. The after-image stayed in David's eyes. Silver, almost aeroplane-shaped.

The first thing David discovered about polystyrene cement was that it came out very quickly when the nozzle was pricked with a pin. The second was that it had a remarkable ability to melt plastic. He was almost in tears by the end of his first evening of attempted construction. There was a mushy crater in the middle of the left tailplane and grey smears of plastic all along the side of the motor housing he'd been trying to join. It was disgusting. Grey runners of plastic were dripping from his hands and he could feel the reek of the glue bringing a crushing headache down on him.

"Getting on alright?" Dad asked, poking his head around the door.

David nearly jumped out of his skin. He desperately clawed unmade bits of the model over to cover up the mess as Dad crossed the room to peer over his shoulder and mutter approvingly for a few seconds. When he'd gone, David discovered that the new pieces were now also sticky with glue and melting plastic.

David struggled on. He didn't like the Flying Fortress and would have happily thrown it away, but the thought of Mum

and Dad's disappointment — even little Victoria screwing her face up in contempt — was now as vivid as his imagined triumph had been before. Simon never gave up on things. Simon always (David would show them) did everything right. But by now the very touch of the model, the tiny bumps of the rivets, the rough little edges where the moulding had seeped out, made his flesh crawl. And for no particular reason (a dream too bad to remember) the thought came to him that maybe even real Flying Fortresses (crammed into the rear gunner's turret like a corpse in a coffin. Kamikaze Zero Zens streaming out of the sky. Flames everywhere and the thick stink of burning. Boiling grey plastic pouring like treacle over his hands, his arms, his shoulders, his face. His mouth. Choking, screaming. Choking) weren't such wonderful things after all.

Compared with constructing the model, the painting — although a disaster — had been easy. Night after night, he struggled with meaningless bits of tiny plastic. And a grey voice whispered in his ear that Simon would have finished it now. Yes siree. And it would have been perfect. David was under no illusions now as to how difficult the model was to construct (those glib instructions to fit this part to that part that actually entailed hours of messy struggle. The suspicious fact that Airfix had chosen to use a painting of a real Flying Fortress on the box rather than a photograph of the finished model) but he knew that if anyone could finish it, Simon could. Simon could always do anything. Even dead, he amounted to more than David.

In mid November, David had a particularly difficult Thursday at Games. Mr Lewis wasn't like the other teachers. He didn't ignore little boys who kept quiet and didn't do much. As he was always telling them, he *Cared*. Because David hadn't paid much attention the week

before, he'd brought along his rugger kit instead of his gym kit. He was the only boy dressed in green amid all the whites. Mr Lewis spotted him easily. While the rest of the class watched, laughing and hooting, David had to climb the ropes. Mr Lewis gave him a bruising push to get started. His muscles burning, his chest heaving with tears and exertion, David managed to climb a foot. Then he slid back. With an affable, aching clout, Mr Lewis shoved him up again. More quickly this time, David slid back, scouring his hands, arms and the inside of his legs red raw. Mr Lewis spun the rope; the climbing bars, the mat covered parquet floor, the horse and the tall windows looking out on the wet playground all swirled dizzily. He spun the rope the other way. Just as David was starting to wonder whether he could keep his dinner of liver, soggy chips and apple snow down for much longer, Mr Lewis stopped the rope again, embracing David in a sweaty hug. His face was close enough for David to count the big black pores on his nose — if he'd had a few hours to spare.

"A real softy, you are," Mr Lewis whispered. "Not like your brother at all. Now he was a proper lad." And then he let go.

David dropped to the floor, badly bruising his knees.

As he limped up the stairs that evening, the smell of glue, paint and plastic — which had been a permanent fixture in the bedroom for some time — poured down from the landing to greet him. It curled around his face like a caressing hand, fingering down his throat and into his nose. And there was nothing remotely like a Flying Fortress on Simon's old desk. But David had had enough. Tonight, he was determined to sort things out. Okay, he'd made a few mistakes, but they could be covered up, repaired, filled in. No one else would notice and the Flying Fortress would

look (David, we knew you'd do a good job but we'd never imagined anything this splendid. We must ring Granny, tell the local press) just as a 1/72nd scale top-of-the-range Airfix model should.

David sat down at the desk. The branches of the monkey puzzle tree outside slithered and shivered in the rain. He stared at his yellow-lit reflection in the glass. The image of the rest of the room was dim, like something from the past. Simon's room. David had put up one or two things of his own now: a silver seagull mobile, a big Airlines of the World poster that he'd got by sending off ten Ski yoghurt foils; but, like cats in a new home, they'd never settled in.

David drew the curtains shut. He clicked the PLAY button on Simon's Sony portable and Dire Straits came out. He didn't think much of the music one way or another but it was nice to have a safe, predictable noise going on in the background. Simon's Sony was a special one that played one side of a cassette and then the other as often as you liked without having to turn it over. David remembered the trouble Simon had gone to to get the right machine at the right price, the pride with which he'd demonstrated the features to Mum and Dad, as though he'd invented them all himself. David had never felt that way about anything.

David clenched his eyes shut, praying that Simon's clever fingers and calm confidence would briefly touch him, that Simon would peek over his shoulder and offer some help. But the thought went astray. He sensed Simon standing at his shoulder alright, but it was Simon as he would be now after a year under the soil, his body still twisted like the frame of his bike, mossy black flesh sliding from his bones. David shuddered and opened his eyes to the grey plastic mess that was supposed to be a Flying Fortress. He forced himself to look over his shoulder. The room was smugly quiet.

Although there was still much to do, David had finished with planning and detail. He grabbed the obvious big parts of the plane that the interminable instructions (slot parts A, B, and C of the rear side bulkhead together, ensuring that the *upper* inside brace of the support joint fits into dovetail **iv** as illustrated) never got around to mentioning and began to push them together, squeezing out gouts of glue. Dire Straits droned on, "Love Over Gold," "It Never Rains," then back to the start of the tape. The faint hum of the TV came up through the floorboards. Key bits of plastic snapped and melted in his hands. David ignored them. At his back, the shadows of Simon's room fluttered in disapproval.

At last, David had something that bore some similarity to a plane. He turned its sticky weight in his hands and a great bird shadow flew across the ceiling behind him. One of the wings drooped down, there was a wide split down the middle of the body, smears of glue and paint were everywhere. It was, he knew, a sorry mess. He covered it over with an old sheet in case Mum and Dad should see it in the morning, then went to bed.

Darkness. Dad snoring faintly next door. The outline of Simon's body still there on the mattress beneath his back. David's heart pounded loudly enough to make the springs creak. The room and the Airfix-laden air pulsed in sympathy. It muttered and whispered (no sleep for you my boy. Nice and restless for you all night when everyone's tucked up warm and you're the only wide-awake person in the whole grey universe) but grew silent whenever he lay especially still and dared it to make a noise. The street light filtered though the monkey puzzle tree and the curtains on to Simon's desk. The sheet covering the model looked like a face. Simon's face. As it would be now.

David slept. He dreamed. The dreams were worse than waking.

When he opened his eyes to Friday morning, clawing up out of a nightmare into the plastic-scented room, Simon's decayed face still yawned lopsidedly at him, clear and unashamed in the grey wash of the winter dawn. He couldn't face touching the sheet, let alone taking it off and looking at the mess underneath. Shivering in his pyjamas, he found a biro in a drawer and used it to poke the yellowed cotton folds until they formed an innocuous shape.

It didn't feel like a Friday at school. The usual sense of sunny relief, the thought of two whole days of freedom, had drained away. His eyes sore from lack of sleep and the skin on his hands flaky with glue, David drifted through Maths and Art followed by French in the afternoon. At the start of Social Studies, the final lesson of the week, he sat down on a drawing pin that had been placed on his chair: now that Mr Lewis had singled him out, the naughty boys he shared the back of the class with were beginning to think of him as fair game. Amid the sniggers and guffaws, David pulled the pin out of his bottom uncomplainingly. He had other things on his mind. He was, in fact, a little less miserable about the Flying Fortress than he had been that morning. It probably wasn't as bad as he remembered (could anything really be that bad?) and if he continued tonight, working slowly, using silver paint freely to cover up the bad bits, there might still be a possibility that it would look reasonable. Maybe he could even hang it from the ceiling before anyone got a chance to take a close look. As he walked home through the wet mist, he kept telling himself that it would (please, please, O please God) be alright.

He peeled back the sheet, tugging it off the sticky bits. It was like taking a bandage from a scabby wound. The model looked dreadful. He whimpered and stepped back. He was sure it hadn't been that bad the night before. The wings and the body had sagged and the plastic had a bubbly, pimply look in places as though something was trying to erupt from underneath. Hurriedly, he snatched the sheet up again and threw it over, then ran downstairs into the lounge.

Mum glanced up from *The Price Is Right.* "You're a stranger down here," she said absently. "I thought you were still busy with that thing of yours."

"It's almost finished," David said to his own amazement as he flopped down, breathless, on the sofa.

Mum nodded slowly and turned back to the TV. She watched TV a lot these days. David had occasionally wandered in and found her staring at pages from Ceefax.

David sat in a daze, letting programme after programme go (as Simon used to say) in one eye and out of the other. He had no desire to go back upstairs to his (Simon's) bedroom, but when the credits rolled on *News at Ten* and Dad smiled at the screen and suggested it was time that Juniors were up in bed, he got up without argument. There was something less than affable about Dad's affable suggestions recently. As though if you didn't hop to it he might (slam your head against the wall until your bones stuck out through your face) grow angry.

After he'd found the courage to turn off the bedside light, David lay with his arms stiffly at his sides, his eyes wide open. Even in the darkness, he could see the pin marks on the ceiling where Simon had hung his planes. They were like tiny black stars. He heard Mum go up to bed, her nervous breathing as she climbed the stairs. He heard the whine of the TV as the channel closed, Dad clearing his throat before he turned it off, the sound of the toilet, the bedroom door closing. Then silence.

Silence. Like the taut skin of a drum.

Dark pinprick stars on the grainy white ceiling like a negative of the real sky, as though the whole world had twisted itself inside out around David and he was now in a place where up was down, black was white and people slithered in the cracks beneath the pavement. Silence. He really missed last night's whispering voices. Expectant silence. Silence that screamed Something Is Going To Happen.

Something did. Quite matter-of-factly, as though it was as ordinary as the kettle in the kitchen switching itself off when it came to the boil or the traffic lights changing to red on the High Street, the sheet began to slide off the Flying Fortress. Simon's face briefly stretched into the folds, then vanished as the whole sheet flopped to the floor. The Fortress sat still for a moment, outlined in the light of the street lamp through the curtains. Then it began to crawl across the desk, dragging itself on its wings like a wounded beetle.

David didn't really believe that this could be happening. But as it moved it even made the sort of scratchy squeaky noises that a living model of a Flying Fortress might be expected to make. It paused at the edge of the desk, facing the window; it seemed to be wondering what to do next. As though, David thought with giggly hilarity, it hasn't done quite enough already. But the Fortress was far from finished. With a jerky, insectile movement, it launched itself towards the window. The curtain sagged and the glass went bump. Fluttering its wings like a huge moth, it clung on and started to climb up towards the curtain rail. Half way up, it paused again. It made a chittering sound and a ripple of movement passed along its back, a little shiver of pleasure: alive at last. And David knew it sensed something else alive in the room. Him. The Fortress launched itself from the curtains, setting the street light shivering across the empty desk and, more like a huge moth than ever, began to flutter around the room, bumping blindly into the ceiling and walls. Involuntarily, he covered his face with his hands. Through the cracks between his fingers he saw the grey flitter of its movement. He heard the shriek of soft, fleshy plastic. He felt the panicky breath of its wings. Just as he was starting to think it couldn't get any worse, the Fortress settled on his face. He felt the wings embracing him, the tail curling into his neck, thin grey claws scrabbling between his fingers, hungry to get at the liquid of his eyes and the soft flesh inside his cheeks.

David began to scream. The fingers grew more persistent, pulling at his hands with a strength he couldn't resist.

"David! What's the matter with you!"

The big light was on. Dad's face hovered above him. Mum stood at the bottom of the bed, her thin white hands tying and untying in knots.

". . ." He was lost for words, shaking with embarrassment and relief.

Mum and Dad stayed with him for a few minutes, their faces drawn and puzzled. Simon never pulled this sort of trick. Mum's hands knotted. Dad's made fists. Victoria's white face peered around the door when they weren't looking, then vanished again, quick as a ghost. All David could say was that he'd had a bad dream. He glanced across the desk through the bland yellow light. The Fortress was covered by its sheet again. Simon's rotting face grinned at him from the folds. You can't catch me out that easily, the grin said.

Mum and Dad switched off the big light when they left the room. They shuffled back down the landing. As soon as he heard their bedroom door clunk shut, David shot out of bed and clicked his light on again. He left it blazing all night as he sat on the side of the bed, staring at the cloth-covered model. It didn't move. The thin scratches on the

backs of his hands were the only sign that anything had happened at all.

As David stared into his bowl of Rice Krispies at breakfast, their snap and crackle and pop fast fading into the sugary milk, Mum announced that she and Dad and Victoria were going to see Gran that afternoon for tea; did he want to come along? David said No. An idea had been growing in his mind, nurtured through the long hours of the night: with the afternoon free to himself, the idea became a fully fledged plan.

Saying he was off to the library, David went down to the Post Office on the High Street before it closed at lunchtime. The clouds were dark and low and the streets were damp. After waiting an age behind a shopkeeper with bags of ten-pence bits to change, he presented the fat lady behind the glass screen with his savings book and asked to withdraw everything but the one pound needed to keep the account open.

"That's a whole eleven pounds fifty-two pence," she said to him. "Have we been saving up for something special?"

"Oh, yes," David said, dragging his good-boy smile out from the wardrobe and giving it a dust-down for the occasion.

"A nice new toy? I know what you lads are like, all guns and armour."

"It's, um, a surprise."

The lady humphed, disappointed that he wouldn't tell her what it was. She took out a handful of dry roasted nuts from a drawer beneath the counter and popped them into her mouth, licking the salt off her fingers before counting out his money.

Back at home, David returned the savings book to the desk (his hands shaking in his hurry to get back out of the room, his eyes desperately focussed away from the cloth-covered model on the top) but kept the two five-pound notes and the change crinkling against his leg in the front pocket of his jeans. He just hoped that Dad wouldn't have

one of his occasional surges of interest in his finances and ask to see the savings book. He'd thought that he might say something about helping out a poor schoolfriend who needed a loan for a new pair of shoes, but the idea sounded unconvincing even as he rehearsed it in his mind.

Fish fingers again for lunch. David wasn't hungry and slipped a few across the plastic tablecloth to Victoria when Mum and Dad weren't looking. Victoria could eat fish fingers until they came out of her ears. When she was really full up she sometimes even tried to poke a few in there to demonstrate that no more would fit.

Afterwards, David sat in the lounge and pretended to watch *Grandstand* while Mum and Dad and Victoria banged around upstairs and changed into their best clothes. He was tired and tense, feeling rather like the anguished ladies at the start of the headache-tablet adverts, but underneath there was a kind of exhilaration. After all that had happened, he was still determined to put up a fight. Finally, just as the runners and riders for the two o'clock Holsten Pils Handicap at rainswept Wetherby were getting ready for the off, Mum and Dad called Bye Bye and slammed the front door.

The doorbell rang a second later.

"Don't forget," Mum said, standing on the doorstep and fiddling with the strap of the black handbag she'd bought for Simon's funeral, "there's some fish fingers left in the freezer for your tea."

"No I won't," David said.

He stood and watched as the Cortina reversed out of the concrete drive and turned off down the estate road through a grey fog of exhaust.

It was a dark, moist afternoon, but the rain that was making the going heavy at Wetherby was still holding off. For once, the fates seemed to be conspiring in his favour. He took the old galvanized bucket from the garage and,

grabbing the stiff-bristled outside broom for good measure, set off up the stairs towards Simon's bedroom. The reek of plastic was incredibly strong now — he wondered why no one else in the house hadn't noticed or complained.

The door to Simon's room was shut. Slippery with sweat, David's hand slid uselessly around the knob. Slowly, deliberately, forcing his muscles to work, he wiped his palms on his jeans and tried again. The knob turned. The door opened. The cloth face grinned at him through the stinking air. It was almost a skull now, as though the last of the flesh had been worried away, and the off-white of the sheet gave added realism. David tried not to think of such things. He walked briskly towards the desk, holding the broom out in front of him like a lance. He gave the cloth a push with it, trying to get rid of the face. The model beneath stirred lazily, like a sleeper awakening in a warm bed. More haste, less speed, he told himself. That was what Dad always said. The words became a meaningless jumble as he held the bucket beneath the lip of the desk and prodded the cloth-covered model towards it. More haste, less speed. Plastic screeched on the surface of the desk, leaving a wet grey trail. More waste, less greed. Little aircraft-shaped bumps came and went beneath the cloth. Hasting waste, wasting haste. The model plopped into the bucket; mercifully, the cloth still covered it. It squirmed and gave a plaintive squeak. David dropped the broom, took the bucket in both hands and shot down the stairs.

Out through the back door. Across the damp lawn to the black patch where Dad burnt the garden refuse. David tipped the bucket over quickly, trapping the model like a spider under a glass. He hared back into the house, snatching up a book of matches, a bottle of meths, firelighters and newspapers, then sprinted up the garden again before the model had time to think about getting out.

He lifted up the bucket and tossed it to one side. The cloth slid out over the blackened earth like a watery jelly. The model squirmed from the folds, stretching out its wings. David broke the cap from the meths bottle and tipped out a good pint over cloth and plastic and earth. The model hissed in surprise at the cool touch of the alcohol. He tried to light a match from the book. The thin strips of card crumpled. The fourth match caught, but puffed out before he could touch it to the cloth. The model's struggles were becoming increasingly agitated. He struck another match. The head flew off. Another. The model started to crawl away from the cloth. Towards him, stretching and contracting like a slug. Shuddering and sick with disgust, David shoved it back with the toe of his trainer. He tried another match, almost dropping the crumpled book to the ground in his hurry. It flared. He forced himself to crouch down — moving slowly to preserve the precious flame — and touch it to the cloth. It went up with a satisfying **whooph.**

David stepped back from the cheery brightness. The cloth soon charred and vanished. The model mewed and twisted. Thick black smoke curled up from the fire. The grey plastic blistered and ran. Bubbles popped on the aircraft's writhing skin. It arched its tail in the heat like a scorpion. The black smoke grew thicker. The next-door neighbour, Mrs Bowen, slammed her bedroom window shut with an angry bang. David's eyes streamed as he threw on firelighters and balled-up newspapers for good measure.

The aircraft struggled in the flames, its blackened body rippling in heat and agony. But somehow, its shape remained. Against all the rules of the way things should be, the plastic didn't run into a sticky pool. And, even as the flames began to dwindle around it, the

model was clearly still alive. Wounded, shivering with pain. But still alive.

David watched in bitter amazement. As the model had no right to exist in the first place, he supposed he'd been naive to imagine that an ordinary thing like a fire in the garden would be enough to kill it. The last of the flames puttered on the blackened earth. David breathed the raw, sick smell of burnt plastic. The model — which had lost what little resemblance it had ever had to a Flying Fortress and now reminded David more than anything of the dead seagull he once seen rotting on the beach at Blackpool — whimpered faintly and, slowly lifting its blistered and trembling wings, tried to crawl towards him.

He watched for a moment in horror, then jerked into action. The galvanized bucket lay just behind him. He picked it up and plonked it down hard on the model. It squealed: David saw that he'd trapped one of the blackened wings under the rim of the bucket. He lifted it up an inch, kicked the thing under with his trainer, then ran to find something to weigh down the bucket.

With two bricks on top, the model grew silent inside, as though accepting its fate. Maybe it really is dying (why haven't you got the courage to run and get the big spade from the shed like big brave Simon would do in a situation like this? Chop the thing up into tiny bits) he told himself. The very least he hoped for was that it wouldn't dig its way out.

David looked at his watch. Three-thirty. So far, things hadn't gone as well as he'd planned, but there was no time to stand around worrying. He still had a lot to do. He threw the book of matches into the bin, put the meths and the firelighters back where he had found them, hung the broom up in the garage, pulled on his duffle coat, locked up the house, and set off towards the High Street.

The greyness of a dull day was already sliding into the dark of evening.

Pacing swiftly along the wet-leafed pavement, David glanced over privet hedges into warmly lit living rooms. Mums and Dads sitting on the sofa together, Big Sis doing her nails in preparation for a night down the pub with her boyfriend, little Jimmy playing with his He-Man doll in front of the fire. Be careful, David thought, seeing those blandly absorbed faces, things can fall apart so easily. Please, be careful.

He took the shortcut across the park where a few weary players chased a muddy white ball through the gloom and came out onto the High Street by the public toilets. Just across the road, the back tyres of the Pickfords lorry had rolled Simon into the next world.

David turned left. Woolworths seemed the best place to start. The High Street was busy. Cars and lorries grumbled between the numerous traffic lights, and streams of people dallied and bumped and pushed in and out of the fluorescent heat of the shops. David was surprised to see that the plate glass windows were already brimming with cardboard Santas and tinsel, but didn't feel the usual thrill of anticipation. Like the Friday-feeling and the Weekend-feeling, the Christmas-feeling seemed to have deserted him. Still, he told himself, there's plenty of time yet. Yes, plenty.

Everything had been switched around in Woolworths. The shelves where the models used to sit between the stick-on soles and the bicycle repair kits were now filled with displays of wine coolers and silk flowers. He eventually found them on a small shelf beside the compact disks, but he could tell almost at a glance that they didn't have any Flying Fortresses. He lifted out the few dusty boxes — a Dukes of Hazzard car, a skeleton, a Tyrannosaurus rex; kid's stuff, not the sort of thing that Simon would ever have bothered himself with — then set out back along the High Street towards W. H. Smiths. They had a better selection, but still no Flying

Fortresses. A sign in black and orange suggested IF YOU CAN'T FIND WHAT YOU WANT ON DISPLAY PLEASE ASK AN ASSISTANT, but David was old and wise enough not to take it seriously. He tried the big newsagents across the road, and then Debenhams opposite Safeways where Santa Claus already had a pokey grotto of fairy lights and hardboard and the speakers gave a muffled rendition of Merry Christmas (War is Over). Still no luck. It was quarter to five now. The car lights, traffic lights, street lights and shop windows glimmered along the wet pavement, haloed by the beginnings of a winter fog. People were buttoning up their anoraks, tying their scarves and pulling up their detachable hoods, but David felt sweaty and tired, dodging between prams and slow old ladies and arm-in-arm girls with green punk hair. He was running out of shops. He was running out of time. Everyone was supposed to know about Airfix Flying Fortresses. He didn't imagine that the concerns of childhood penetrated very deeply into the adult world, but there were some things that were universal. You could go into a fish-and-chip shop and the man in the fat stained apron would say yes, he knew exactly what you meant, they just might have one out the back with the blocks of fat and the potatoes. Or so David had thought. A whole High Street without one seemed impossible. Once he'd got the model he would, of course, have to repeat the long and unpleasant task of assembling the thing, but he was sure that he'd make a better go of it a second time. In its latter stages the first model had shown tendencies which even Simon with his far greater experience of model making had probably never experienced. For a moment, he felt panic rising in his throat like sour vomit. The model, trapped under its bucket, squirmed in his mind. He forced the thought down. After all, he'd done his best. Of course, he could always write to Airfix and complain, but

he somehow doubted whether they were to blame.

He had two more shops on his mental list and about twenty minutes to reach them. The first, an old-fashioned craft shop had, he discovered, become the new offices of a building society. The second, right up at the far end of the High Street beyond the near-legendary marital aids shop and outside his normal territory, lay in a small and less than successful precinct built as a speculation five years before and still half empty. David ran past the faded **To Let** signs into the square. There was no Christmas rush here. Most of the lights in the fibreglass pseudo-Victorian lamps were broken. In the near darkness a cluster of youths sat drinking Shandy Bass on the concrete wall around the dying poplar at the centre of the square. The few shops that were open looked empty and about to close. The one David was after had a window filled unpromisingly with giant nylon teddies in various shades of green, pink, and orange.

An old woman in a grubby housecoat was mopping the marleytiled floor and the air inside the shop was heavy with the scent of the same cheap disinfectant they used in the school toilets. David glanced around, pulling the air into his lungs in thirsty gulps. The shop was bigger than he'd imagined, but all he could see on display were a few dusty Sindy outfits, a swivel stand of practical jokes and a newish rack of Slime Balls "You Squeeze 'Em And They Ooze"; the fad of the previous summer.

The man standing with his beer belly resting on the counter glanced up from picking the dirt from under his nails. "Looking for something?"

"Um, models, er, please." David gasped. His throat itched, his lungs ached. He wished he could just close his eyes and curl up in a corner somewhere to sleep.

"Upstairs."

David blinked and looked around again. There was indeed a stairway leading up to another floor. He took it, three steps at a time.

A younger man in a leather-tasselled coat sat with his cowboy boots resting up on a glass counter, smoking and reading *Interview With A Vampire*. He looked even less like an assistant than the man downstairs, but David couldn't imagine what else he could be, unless he was one of the non-speaking baddies who hung around at the back of the gang in spaghetti westerns. A faulty fluorescent tube flickered on and off like lightning in the smoky air, shooting out bursts of unpredictable shadow. David walked quickly along the few aisles. Past a row of Transformer robots, their bubble plastic wrapping stuck back into the card with strips of yellowing Sellotape, he came to the model section. At first it didn't look promising, but as he crouched down to check along the rows, he saw a long box poking out from beneath a Revelle Catalina on the bottom shelf. There was an all-too-familiar picture on the side: a Flying Fortress. He pulled it out slowly, half expecting it to disappear in a puff of smoke. But no, it stayed firm and real. An Airfix Flying Fortress, a little more dusty and faded than the one Dad had given him, but the same grey weight of plastic, the same painting on the box, £7.75, glue and paints not included, but then he still had plenty of both. David could feel his relief fading even as he slowly drew the long box from the shelf. After all, he still had to make the thing.

The cowboy behind the counter coughed and lit up a fresh Rothmans from the stub of his old one. David glanced along the aisle. What he saw sent a warm jolt through him that destroyed all sense of tiredness and fatigue. There was a display inside the glass cabinet beneath the crossed cowboy boots. Little plastic men struck poses on a greenish sheet of artexed

hardboard that was supposed to look like grass. There were neat little huts, a fuel tender and a few white dashes and red markers to indicate the start of a runway. In the middle of it all, under-carriage down and bomb bay doors open, was a silver Flying Fortress. His mouth dry, David slid the box back onto the shelf and strolled up to take a closer look, hands casually thrust into the itchy woolen pockets of his duffle coat, placing his feet down carefully to control the sudden trembling in his legs. It was finished, complete; it looked nothing like the deformed monstrosity he had tried to destroy. Even at a distance through the none-too-clean glass of the display case, he could make out the intricate details, the bright transfers (something he'd never been able to think about applying to his Fortress) and he could tell just from the look of the gun turrets that they would swivel up, down, sideways, any way you liked.

The cowboy re-crossed his boots and looked up. He raised his eyebrows questioningly.

"I er . . . just looking."

"We close now," he said, and returned to his book.

David backed away down the stairs, his eyes fixed on the completed Fortress until it vanished from sight behind a stack of Fisher-Price baby toys. He took the rest of the stairs slowly, his head spinning. He could buy as many models as he liked, but he was absolutely sure he would never be able to reach the level of perfection on display in that glass case. Maybe Simon could have done it better, but no one else.

David took another step down. His spine jarred; without noticing, he'd reached the ground floor. The man cleaning his nails at the desk had gone. The woman with the mop was working her way behind a pillar. He saw a door marked **PRIVATE** behind a jagged pile of unused shelving. He had an idea; the best he'd had all day.

Moving quickly but carefully so that his trainers didn't squeak, he crossed the shining wet floor, praying that his footsteps wouldn't show. The door had no handle. He pushed it gently with the tips of his fingers. It opened.

There was no light inside. As the door slid closed behind him, he glimpsed a stainless steel sink with a few mugs perched on the draining board, a couple of old chairs and a girlie calendar on the wall. It was a small room; there didn't seem to be space for anything else. Certainly no room to hide if anyone should open the door. David backed his way carefully into one of the chairs. He sat down. A spring boinged gently. He waited.

As he sat in the almost absolute darkness, his tiredness fought with his fear. The woman with the mop shuffled close by outside. She paused for a heart-stopping moment, but then she went on and David heard the clang of the bucket and the whine of the water pipes through the thin walls from a neighbouring room. She came out again, humming a snatch of a familiar but unplaceable tune. Da-de-da de-de-de dum-dum. Stevie Wonder? The Beatles? Wham? David felt his eyelids drooping. His head began to nod.

Footsteps down the stairs. Someone coughing. He wondered if he was back at home. And he wondered why he felt so happy to be there.

He imagined that he was Simon. He could feel the mannish strength inside him, the confident hands that could turn chaotic plastic into perfect machines, the warm, admiring approval of the whole wide world surrounding him like the glowing skin of the boy in the Ready Brek advert.

A man's voice calling goodnight and the clink of keys drew David back from sleep. He opened his eyes and listened. After what might have been ten minutes but seemed like an hour there was still silence. He stood up and felt for the

door. He opened it a crack. The lights were still on at the windows but the shop was locked and empty. Quick and easy as a shadow, he made his way up the stairs. The Fortress was waiting for him, clean lines of silvered plastic, intricate and marvellous as a dream. He slid back the glass door of the case (no lock or bolt — he could hardly believe how careless people could be with such treasure) and took it in his hands. It was beautiful. It was perfect, and it lacked any life of its own. He sniffed back tears. That was the best thing of all. It was dead.

It wasn't easy getting the model home. Fumbling his way through the darkness at the back of the shop, he managed to find the fire escape door, but when he leaned on the lever and shoved it open an alarm bell started to clang close above his head. He stood rigid for a moment, drenched in cold shock, then shot out across the loading yard and along the road behind. People stared at him as he pounded the streets on the long, aching run home. The silver Fortress was far too big to hide. That — and the fact that the man in the shop would be bound to remember that he'd been hanging around before closing time — made David sure that he had committed a less than perfect crime. Like Bonnie and Clyde or Butch Cassidy, David guessed it was only a matter of time before the Law caught up with him. But first he would have his moment of glory; perhaps a moment glorious enough to turn around everything that had happened so far.

Arriving home with a bad cramp in his ribs and Mum and Dad and Victoria still out at Gran's, he found that the bucket in the garden still sat undisturbed with two bricks on top. Although he didn't have the courage to lift it up to look, there was nothing to suggest that the old Fortress wasn't sitting quietly (perhaps even dead) underneath. Lying on his bed and blowing at the model's propellers to make them spin, he could already feel the power growing within him. Tomorrow, in the daylight, he knew he'd feel strong enough to get the spade and sort things out properly.

All in all, he decided, the day had gone quite well. Things never happen as you expect, he told himself; they're either far better or far worse. This morning he'd never have believed that he'd have a finished Flying Fortress in his hands by the evening, yet here he was, gazing into the cockpit at the incredible detail of the crew and their tiny controls as a lover would gaze into the eyes of their beloved. And the best was yet to come. Even as he smiled to himself, the lights of Dad's Cortina swept across the bedroom curtains. The front door opened. David heard Mum's voice saying shush, then Dad's. He smiled again. This was, after all, what he'd been striving for. He had in his hands the proof that he was as good as Simon. The Fortress was the healing miracle that would soothe away the scars of his death. The family would become one. The grey curse would be lifted from the house.

Dad's heavy tread came up the stairs. He went into Victoria's bedroom. After a moment, he stuck his head around David's door.

"Everything alright, Junior?"

"Yes, Dad."

"Try to be quiet. Victoria fell asleep in the car and I've put her straight to bed."

Dad's head vanished. He pulled the door shut. Opening and closing the bomb bay doors, David gazed up at the model. Dad hadn't noticed the Fortress. Odd, that. Still, it probably showed just how special it was.

The TV boomed downstairs. The start of *3-2-1*; David recognised the tune. He got up slowly from his bed. He paused at the door to glance back into the room. No longer Simon's room, he told himself — *His Room*. He crossed the landing and walked down the stairs. Faintly, he

heard the sound of Victoria moaning in her sleep. But that was alright. Everything would be alright. The finished model was cradled in his hands. It was like a dream.

He opened the lounge door. The quiz show colours on the TV filled his eyes. Red and silver and gold, bright and warm as Christmas. Mum was sitting in her usual chair wearing her usual TV expression. Dad was stretched out on the sofa.

He looked up at David. "Alright, Junior?"

David held the silver Fortress out towards his father. The fuselage glittered in the TV light. "Look, I've finished the model."

"Let's see." Dad stretched out his hand. David gave it to him. "Sure . . . that's pretty good, Junior. You'll have to save up and buy something more difficult with that money you've got in the Post Office. . . . Here." He handed it back to David.

David took the Fortress. One of the bomb bay doors flipped open. He clicked it back into place.

On the TV Steve and Yvette from Rochdale were telling Ted Rogers a story about their honeymoon. Ted finished it off with a punchline that David didn't understand. The audience roared.

Dad scratched his belly, worming his fingers into the gaps between the buttons of his shirt. "I think your mother wanted a word with you," he said, watching as Steve and Yvette agonised over a question. He raised his voice a little. "Isn't that right, pet? Didn't you want a word with him?"

Mum's face turned slowly from the TV screen.

"Look," David said, taking a step towards her, "I've —"

Mum's head continued turning. Away from David, towards Dad. "I thought you were going to speak to him," she said.

Dad shrugged. "You found them, pet, you tell him . . . and move, Junior. I can't see the programme through you."

David moved.

Mum fumbled in the pocket of her dress. She produced a book of matches. "I found these in the bin," she said, looking straight at him. Through him. David had to suppress a shudder. "What have you been up to?"

"Nothing." David grinned weakly. His good-boy smile wouldn't come.

"You haven't been smoking?"

"No, Mum. I promise."

"Well, as long as you don't." Mum turned back to the TV. Steve and Yvette had failed. Instead of a Mini Metro they had won Dusty Bin. The audience was in raptures. Back after the break, said Ted Rogers.

David stood watching the bright screen. A grey tombstone loomed towards him. This is what happens, a voice said, if you get AIDS.

Dad gave a theatrical groan that turned into a cough. "Those queers make me sick," he said when he'd hawked his throat clear.

Without realising what he was doing, David left the room and went back upstairs to Simon's bedroom.

He left the lights on and re-opened the curtains. The monkey puzzle tree waved at him through the wet darkness; the rain from Wetherby had finally arrived. Each droplet sliding down the glass held a tiny spark of streetlight.

He sat down and plonked the Fortress on the desk in front of him. A propeller blade snapped; he hadn't bothered to put the undercarriage down. He didn't care. He breathed deeply, the air shuddering in his throat like the sound of running past railings. Through the bitter phlegm he could still smell the reek of plastic. Not the faint, tidy smell of the finished Fortress. No, this was the smell that had been with him for weeks. But now it didn't bring sick expectation in his stomach; he no longer felt afraid.

Now, in his own way, he had reached the summit of a finished Flying Fortress, a high place from where he could look back at the remains of his childhood. Everything had been out of scale before, but now he saw, he really saw. 1/72nd scale; David knew what it meant now. The Fortress was big, as heavy and grey as the rest of the world. It was him that was tiny, 1/72nd scale.

He looked at the Fortress: big, ugly and silver. The sight of it sickened him more than the old model had ever done. At least that had been his. For all its considerable faults, he had made it.

David stood up. Quietly, he left the room and went down the stairs, past the lounge and the booming TV, into the kitchen. He found the waterproof torch and walked out into the rain.

The bucket still hadn't moved. Holding the torch in the crook of his arm, David removed the two bricks and lifted it up. For a moment, he thought that there was nothing underneath, but then, pointing the torch's rain-streamed light straight down, he saw that the model was still there. As he'd half expected, it had tried to burrow its way out from under the bucket. But it was too weak. All it had succeeded in doing was to cover itself in wet earth.

The model mewed gently and tried to raise itself up towards David.

This time he didn't step back. "Come on," he said. "We're going back inside."

David led the way, levelling the beam of the torch through the rain like a scaled-down searchlight, its yellow oval glistening on the muddy wet grass just ahead. The rain was getting worse; heavy drops rattling on David's skull and plastering his hair down like a wet swimming cap. The model moved slowly, seeming to weaken with every arch of its rotting fuselage. David clenched his jaw and tried to urge it on, pouring his own strength into the wounded creature. Once, he looked up over the roofs of the houses. Above the

chimneys and TV aerials cloud-heavy sky seemed to boil. Briefly, he thought he saw shapes form, ghosts swirling on the moaning wind. And the ghosts were not people, but simple inanimate things. Clocks and cars, china and jewelry, toys and trophies all tumbling uselessly through the night. But then he blinked and there was nothing to be seen but the rain, washing his face and filling his eyes like tears.

He was wet through by the time they reached the back door. The concrete step proved too much for the model and David had to stoop and quickly lift it onto the lino inside, trying not to think of the way it felt in his hands.

In the kitchen's fluorescent light, he saw for the first time just how badly injured the creature was. Clumps of earth clung to its sticky, blistered wings and grey plastic oozed from gaping wounds along its fuselage. And the reek of it immediately filled the kitchen, easily overpowering the usual smell of fish fingers. It stank of glue and paint and plastic; but there was more. It also smelt like something dying.

It moved on, dragging its wings, whimpering in agony, growing weaker with every inch. Plainly, the creature was close to the end of its short existence.

"Come on," David whispered, crouching down close beside it. "There's not far to go now. Please try. Please . . . don't die yet."

Seeming to understand, the model made a final effort. David held the kitchen door open as it crawled into the hall, onwards toward the light and sound of the TV through the frosted lounge door.

"You made *that?*" An awed whisper came from half way up the stairs.

David looked up and saw little Victoria peering down at the limping model, her hands gripping the bannister like a prisoner behind bars. He nodded, feeling an odd sense of pride. It

was, after all, his. But he knew you could take pride too far. The model belonged to the whole family as well. To Victoria sitting alone at night on the stairs, to Simon turning to mush and bones in his damp coffin — and to Mum and Dad. And that was why it was important to show them. David was old for a child; he knew that grownups were funny like that. If you didn't show them things, they simply didn't believe in them.

"Come on," he said, holding out his hand.

Victoria scampered quickly down the stairs and along the hall, stepping carefully over the model and putting her cold little hand inside his slightly larger one.

The model struggled on, leaving a trail of slimy plastic behind on the carpet. When it reached the lounge door, David turned the handle and the three of them went in together.   Ω

In *Weird Tales*® #300, the special Robert Bloch issue:

A never-before-published story by **Robert Bloch** and **Henry Kuttner**,

"The Grab Bag,"; Bloch's screenplay and story, "Beetles,"

and an excerpt from his "unauthorized" autobiography.

Also, new stories by **Brian Lumley**, **Nina Kiriki Hoffman**, **Nancy Springer**,

Lawrence Watt-Evans, **Michael Rutherford**, and **A.R. Morlan**.

Gahan Wilson will illustrate this special issue.

DEBT IN KIND

by Peg Kerr

art by Laura Kelly-Freas

I've never been able to think of her as anything but "the woman." She sat slumped in a wheelchair beside me, dressed in a hospital gown, staring vacantly at the gray carpet. Her hands in her lap twitched, fluttering. Her forehead wrinkled in spasms, giving her a bewildered expression. I looked away. I never liked looking at her.

Instead, I looked at the other one, sitting at the desk across from the woman and me. He was what they call a doctor. He stared at the folder spread out in front of him, and I knew suddenly, as I sometimes did, that he didn't want to look at us. It wasn't the woman, really. He saw others like the woman all the time, sick ones I mean. That's what doctors did, I supposed.

No, I was the one who gave him the creeps.

He glanced at me again, and it seemed as if seeing me put a bad taste in his mouth. It was so pathetic, the way he thought he was hiding it. I'm used to it, though. Lots of them look at me that way. I once spent a whole afternoon studying myself in a mirror, trying to understand. It's not as if my eyes and nose and things are in the wrong places, exactly, although I suppose my mouth is rather wide.

So I had asked the woman, do you think my mouth is too wide? She made a face.

"It looks like a gash," she said. "And your ears stick out."

All right, so my ears stick out. The only other clue I've ever had was when she said to someone else that my body looked, well, like it was *carved* out of something. Something old, like tree roots or rocks. She didn't know I could overhear her, you see. And she said, "I can't stand the way her eyes bulge. They make her look like a dead fish." I went to the fish market later to see what kind of eyes the fish had, but I still wasn't sure what she meant.

The man cleared his throat.

"I've received the report on your tests, Mrs. Henderson," he said, talking to the woman. "The test for Parkinson's came out negative, and we've ruled out Syndenham's chorea because you don't have a history of rheumatic fever."

He paused.

"We've concluded that you have Huntington's disease. Have you ever heard of it before?"

She shifted in the wheelchair. "N-no. . . ."

"It's a degenerative disorder, affecting certain regions of the brain. It starts out slowly, with symptoms like the ones you have now: the twitches, the dropping of objects, the grimacing. Most patients start developing symptoms in their mid-forties.

"It's an autosomal dominant disease, which means that it's transmitted from generation to generation. Since your father's healthy, you must have inherited it from your mother. You just couldn't have known since the car accident killed her before she started being affected."

His eyes shifted to me again. "Fifty percent of all children born to parents with Huntington's will develop the disease. We can prescribe some things to alleviate symptoms, but there is no cure." He adjusted his glasses on his nose very carefully. "I'm sorry."

I looked at her. The woman stared at him, as though she hadn't heard.

"Do you have any questions?" he asked gently.

A glimmer of something flickered over her face. Fear? Anger? I couldn't decide, and the trembling in her cheeks washed it away again.

After a few moments he said, "Our treatment here at Bethesda focuses on the family as well as the patient. Part of what we offer is genetic counseling. There is a test Anna can take," he added, nodding towards me, "which will tell her if she has inherited the gene. Some people choose not to know, but others use it to decide whether to have children."

He looked at me again, as if he couldn't possibly imagine me getting pregnant.

She began to laugh, and the noise of it hurt the ears, somehow. "*She* doesn't have it. She's not my daughter."

"I'm sorry?"

Her eyes focussed finally. "You should have seen her, my darling baby Anna. She was so pretty, with golden hair and blue eyes."

I scowled. I hated it when she talked like that.

She went on, her words slurring a little. "I used to sing to her at night, and she'd look in my face and laugh. She had the loveliest laugh . . ." Her words trailed off as her fingers clutched and relaxed. A cunning look crossed her face. "They thought I'd never know, but I did, I did. *This* one never laughed."

The man stared at me. I stared back at him until he shifted uneasily in his chair. "Well — uh, yes." Apparently he didn't see any point in responding to that. "Uh, we're going to try starting you out on point two-five milligrams of

reserpine therapy per day, Mrs. Henderson, and we'll increase it daily until we have a decline in your chorea. It can be a tricky drug, so I'd like to keep you here in the hospital under observation until we've established the correct dosage." He stood and pushed at something under the desk top. "I'm summoning the orderly to take you back to your room. I know that you'll think of some questions for me later, and I'll be glad to answer them for you when you do."

While the woman was being wheeled out, he sat again and smiled at me. It looked fake. Perhaps he felt the same way, because the smile abruptly disappeared, and he picked up the folder again as if he didn't know what to do with it.

"I told your mother some things," he said, "I'm going to be talking with her some more later, but maybe that's enough for her to think about for the moment. There's more I'd like to tell you, however. Huntington's disease can be very ugly. As it worsens, it causes dementia, personality disorders. You will probably find that your mother is going to be saying more and more things that you will find hurtful or distressing. It's important to realize that what you're hearing is not her, it's the result of the disease."

It always confused me when they talked about what my emotions must be. They assumed things, and it made me realize that the inside of my head worked awfully differently than theirs. Really, I never felt any of the things they thought I should.

Except anger. I knew what that was, at least.

But not at this particular moment. "Oh, it doesn't bother me," I said. "She's always hated me, you see."

His jaw dropped a fraction of an inch. "Well, er — whether or not she does, you don't seem very bothered — uh —" He floundered to a stop, overcome by confusion.

"I can hardly blame her," I went on. "I made her life a living Hell when I was growing up."

"Lots of people go through a tough time at adolescence."

"Oh no." I raised an eyebrow and shook my head. "This started much earlier than that." The anger, I remembered that. Rage at being left in this place of harsh glaring light, full of loathing for all of them — "I had this little habit of screaming, you see, for up to fourteen hours a day, starting when I was a baby. She couldn't do anything to get me to stop. God knows she tried." I grinned, without humor. "One time a cop burst into the house, convinced that she must have been beating me to death to make me howl like that." I cast around inside myself to find out how I felt about that, if anything. All I could come up with was indifference. The anger had faded under the weight of the passing years, and now the old fury seemed only foolish. "Naturally, she found that a little embarrassing."

"How — how long did this last?"

I shrugged, bored with his questions. "Years. There was other stuff, too. I wouldn't look at anybody, wouldn't acknowledge their presences. I didn't even talk until I was nine."

He was fascinated. "Were you ever diagnosed as being autistic?"

"Autistic? Some called it that."

"Hmm. Very few people ever emerge from autism." He changed the subject. "I'd like to arrange an appointment for you with Dr. Nguyen, one of our geneticists. He'll be talking with you about that diagnostic test that I mentioned. I'll check with his office about possible times. May I get back to you on that?"

"If you like. It really doesn't matter to me."

The woman asked me to bring her bed jacket, so I brought it to her room while she was eating dinner. She lay propped up in the bed by the window; the other

bed was empty.

I noticed two flowers in a vase by her dinner tray. "Who brought you these?" I asked.

She was puzzled. "Why — you did." She made a vague wave towards the card resting at the base of the vase and I picked it up. "Didn't you?"

I slipped the card out of the envelope. One word: "Anna." I glanced at the flowers again, my throat suddenly tight. An iris, yes, that meant *message,* and the other blossom was pyrus japonica — Anna! Why now, after so long? There had never been any contact before.

I put the card back in the envelope and leaned it back against the vase. "Of course, of course. I was only — only teasing." She stared at me, suspicious, as well she might be. "Here's the bed jacket. I'll be back at midnight."

"Midnight? Why? Visiting hours are long over by then."

"I know."

Almost time. I pulled the cord to raise the Venetian blinds hanging at the woman's window, and looked up at the ghostly ring encircling the moon. A wash of cold, silvery moonlight poured into the room, making the woman's salt-and-pepper hair shimmer softly against the rumpled sheets. *Now.*

At midnight exactly, the moonlight began flickering and coiling, reflecting brilliant flashes of gold, violet, and ruby against the hospital walls, bright as the midday sun. The opal haze slowly sculpted itself into the radiant shape of a slender young woman. Flowers crowned her hair, and she wore a sleeveless shift of changing iridescent colors which together created an illusion of dazzling whiteness.

The woman on the bed and I stared at

her with something like hunger as she held her pale hands out to us, and we heard a sound like the distant chiming of delicate laughter. The woman's hunger I could understand, I suppose, but why should I have been surprised at my own? There she stood, glinting with all the signs of home, and I clenched my fists as I watched her, thinking, *you took my place there.* My voice rasped as I addressed her.

"What do you want? What have you come to tell us?"

The moon-woman leaned forward, her hair sliding caressingly past her upper arms, and a translucent moonlit hand brushed the woman's cheek, wiping away a tear that shone there.

"Anna," the woman on the bed whispered. "Anna!" She closed her eyes. "Ah, Anna, how I've missed you. . . ."

Anna bent and kissed her forehead and then straightened. The moonlight flashed again as she raised her hands, and then she was holding a handful of blossoms. She held one out towards the woman, an anemone. *Sickness.*

"Yes, she's sick." I wondered at the venom in my own words. "She'll get worse and worse until she dies, and she'll die miserably." But Anna was no longer like them now, able to be hurt by words, mere sounds. She simply placed the anemone on the woman's pillow and added a harebell, and a slip of virgin's bower. *Grief. Filial love.* Over them all, she laid a bloom of forget-me-not. Then she turned to me.

Reluctantly, I took the branch of currants, the fennel and the white bellflower she held out to me. *We are pleased and grateful,* the message said, *you are worthy of all praise.*

"I didn't have much choice in the matter," I muttered — and then stared

at the sprig of pine she held out at me — "and I don't want your pity, damn you!" With difficulty, I lowered my voice. "Is that the only reason you came, then, to give her flowers, to praise me and then disappear again?"

She hesitated, then plucked again. Hortensia. *You are cold.*

I tossed the whole handful onto the bed. "I have good reasons. Say what you will and then be gone."

Pennyroyal. *Flee away.* Lily of the Valley. *Return of happiness.* Moonwort. *Forgetfulness.* Water willow. *Freedom . . .*

"Freedom?" The thought numbed me. "Do you mean it? Just — just leave her and they'll let me come home? Just like that?" Anna smiled.

I stared down at the woman on the bed, who breathed deeply now in sleep. I touched the place on her cheek where the tear had been brushed away. *Leave her.*

After a moment, I realized that she was still waiting for an answer. "I — I will let you know." My breath sounded loud in my ears.

Once again her hand held out flowers. Volkamenia, *May you be happy,* and geranium, *True friendship,* and then the pale nimbus of light surrounding her blazed up blindingly. When I was able to look again, she had disappeared. All that remained was the radiance of the moon.

Slowly, I reached out to lower the blinds again, but my hand was arrested by a sound beyond the accordion room divider. I spun around and saw that the divider had been drawn aside a few inches. The man, the doctor, was staring at me through the gap.

When he realized that I had seen him, he took a deep breath and slowly pushed the divider open. The rattle made me jump.

"Visiting hours are over," he said, a little too loudly. After a frozen pause, I picked up my purse from the chair and followed him out of the room to the

antiseptic corridor beyond.

Outside, I led the way to the unlit little smoking lounge at the end of the hall and pulled a pack of cigarettes out of my purse as I wondered furiously what to do. What had he seen? As my match flared, I stole a quick look at his face and there read bewilderment. Relief flooded me sharply. He would not be able to tell. He was, after all, one of them, and moreover, he was a doctor. From what I understood about doctors, I could guess that he would never admit to what he must have seen, if he had seen anything. No, he would not risk having the rest of them call him mad — I forced myself to relax against a support pillar and blew out a mouthful of smoke. I took another puff, and the tip of my cigarette glowed, and then dimmed.

After a moment, I spoke, my voice harsh in the darkness. "I'm not sure that there's much point in having me take the Huntington's detection test."

He seemed to be having trouble with his voice. He cleared his throat. "I understand that the — the knowledge can be hard. But some people find it useful to — to help them make future plans."

"Future plans." There it was again, the bitterness. "After all, what future plans could I have anyway? Just nursing her —" Or leaving? *Could* I?

"I've told you a little bit about the programs we —"

"You don't understand. It's not necessary. I already know that Anna Henderson inherited the gene. There's no need to worry, though, because she'll never grow old enough to develop the disease. We've always known about the sickness, you see," I added, reaching over to tap my cigarette ash into the lounge ashtray stand.

He took a step forward. "Who — who are you, really?" he asked hoarsely.

I laughed a guttural laugh, full of the cadences of old rivers, or stone grating

against stone.

"Me? Why, I'm no one, of course, nobody important." The glowing tip of my cigarette described a circle in the air. "Merely a hated cast-off, a substitute exiled from her home because it proved — useful, once." I exhaled smoke.

"Substitute? Then — where is the real one?"

I strained to see his face in the darkness and suddenly was weary of lies, evasions. "You saw her. I called her."

"Why?"

Why *had* I called her back? I could have ignored the iris. Hadn't my folk ignored me? "I had my reasons. And — I also did it for Lillian, I suppose," I added, using the word the woman called herself. It tasted strange in my mouth. "Lillian always told me that I was inhuman. I found that somewhat — amusing. I suppose that I called the real one back to show Lillian that she was wrong."

I sighed. "I don't have to stay. I could leave her, leave these places that stink of iron and steel, leave everything. Go back to where I belong, where the real one is now." I took a deep breath, filling my nostrils with the pungent smoke as I thought of that. I saw Anna in my mind's eye holding the geranium out to me, safe from her own body's betrayal because of the cruelty of my folk in keeping her forever young and, therefore, safe. But her eyes were those of the woman, the woman who suffered now as Anna never would, the woman who had held me and tried to comfort me, in spite of her own fear and grief which I had never cared to understand — and I suddenly knew what I would do.

"I could leave, but I won't. No, now I'll just be the dutiful daughter who will

tenderly nurse Lillian Henderson until she dies."

"Why?"

The tip of my cigarette glowed, then faded. "Because she took care of me. She never loved me, but she never gave up on me either, and in a way, that makes it mean even more. It's my turn, now, to care for her. There's a kind of justice in that, don't you think?"

I crushed the cigarette out in the sand of the ashtray beside me and shifted my purse on my shoulder. "It's time for me to go now, Doctor. Doubtless you want to get home and get to bed, too."

"Good-night . . . Anna." I felt his eyes watching me as I walked away from him down the hall toward the elevators. Just before reaching the end of the hall I glanced back. He was still standing there, staring at me, the light from one of the doors down the hall glinting dimly against his hair.

Squaring my shoulders again, I turned back and plunged into darkness.

Ω

INVOCATION

Mother Hecate! Mistress of Night!
Goddess of dread, of pain and of fright,
Goddess of graves, of death's holy fire,
Goddess of daggers, of hate and desire!

Come to the hanged man, who turns in the air.
Come as a wolf, as a hound, as a mare.
Come to the crossroads, with torch and with sword.
Come, as we call thee, come at our word!

We who would serve thee, offer up blood,
of black lamb and black dog, and infant new-born.
We who would love thee, offer our souls,
to murder and witchcraft, secretly sworn.

Goddess of darkness, bringer of woes!
Go from us after our covenant's made.
Make those who hunt us with good cause afraid —
Goddess of vengeance, visit our foes!

— **Darrell Schweitzer**

HAVE YOU TALKED TO THE CANDYMAN?

by Mark Noe

art by Jason van Hollander

The music — the music cut through Doone's brain — the rhythms syncopating to his steps as he walked — keeping time to his wanderings, as though he had a purpose. Always there, the music, always in his head. Yeah, he thought, sometimes got to hold onto it. Keep it from coming out at the wrong time.

While he walked, he snapped his fingers absently, keeping time to the music there in his head.

Then, the streetlamp above him went dark with the snap of a finger. The one across the street and half a block down went out with the next snap. Growling, he stuffed his hands deep into the pockets of his overcoat, hunched his shoulders against the wind that howled between the taller buildings, and walked.

Must be four, five in the morning. Everything closed down. Nowhere to go. Have to walk with the music just playing in his head.

He looked at the locked shops and bars that lined the street. Didn't recognize anything. He laughed. Didn't surprise him none. Couldn't even remember what city he was in. Didn't matter. He could find his way back to the club he was playing. When he had to.

Didn't need to be back there for hours, so he'd walk the streets till the day people took them over, scurrying to their nine to five gig. Have to go back to the club then and wait till the rest of them showed up for rehearsal. There was rehearsal that afternoon, wasn't there? Couldn't remember that either. If there wasn't, he'd have to sit in the club and solo to the clean-up crew.

He nodded his head. Yeah, that's what he'd do. It was either that or sleep. Didn't want to go into that land, not tonight.

So he walked, listened to the music that played through his head — wanting to forget it too — if only for one night.

Like the little *booday* had said.

Doone had been sitting at the bar after rehearsal watching the afternoon sun play its own music across the bottles that lined the back wall. He knew the place wasn't open yet, thought the doors were locked. Then, this white geek was sitting at the stool by his elbow. Didn't think much of it. Mostly whites that came to this club anyway. Hell, he even knew some whites who could play.

This guy just sat there watching him. Started to make him nervous, this guy just watching him through thick glasses that glinted in the sun the same way the whisky bottles did. He didn't like it, so he turned and stared down at the guy. Only it didn't bother this booday.

Doone knew he didn't look like a jazz musician. Looked more like a dealer. Most whites, when they found a big black dude with a couple days growth on his face starin' with eyes bloodshot from lack of sleep, well they sort of screwed themselves down into the stool, trying to get as far away as possible. This one just stared back and smiled, a tight little smile as hard as his glasses.

"What d'you want?" Doone demanded, letting his voice go gravelly and mean.

The geek just stared and smiled, then in a voice as small and hard as he was, "Have you talked to the Candyman?"

"What?"

"Have you —"

"Heard what you said. What's it mean?"

"He can help you."

"I don't need anybody's help," Doone shouted, almost jumping off the stool.

"You haven't been sleeping well lately. You can't control it any longer."

"What? Control what?"

"The music. Not the music in your horn, the music in your head. It keeps coming out, doesn't it? Sometimes when you're playing, sometimes, when you don't want it to."

"What do you know about that?"

The little honky smiled. "Me? Nothing. But the Candyman can help you. You can't control it anymore. He can help you."

Doone looked up at the ceiling in exasperation. "Like Hell —" he started, looking back down at the guy, but he was gone.

Doone checked the front door. It was locked just like he thought. He went through the kitchen. The back door was locked too. So the little geek had to still be in the club somewhere. But Doone knew he wasn't.

He sat back down at the bar. How did he know he was alone? Staring at the whiskey bottles again, he realized it was the way the music played in his head.

So now he walked the city streets, running away from sleep, when the music seemed to take over. Sometimes, he woke up in a sweat, knowing the music had run wild through his head and done something while he was asleep, something he couldn't stop. He would get up, and he'd be in a different city from when he went to bed, or he'd be a different height, or older, or younger. Once, he'd woken up and found he played the guitar instead of tenor sax. He'd played two gigs on the guitar, almost tore his fingers to rags, before he woke up and played the sax again. So, he didn't sleep anymore.

He shouldn't be able to do that, go without sleep. But he knew it was the music that let him do that too.

Man, if he could just control it. That's what the geek had said this Candyman could teach him to do. Or, is that what he'd said? He'd said the Candyman could help him. Yeah, he thought. Nobody did nothing for nothing. The Candyman would help him maybe, but it would cost. Even welfare cost you something.

His feet turned north while he thought about that. Somewhere up ahead, he knew there was an after-hours club. He could feel the music in his mind even though he couldn't hear it with his ears yet. Like a whisper, a clear note came to him, beckoning. Whoever was playing had the touch.

Doone followed the vibrations to a brownstone. He looked up at a second-story window, painted black on the inside. The music pushed against the window. While Doone watched, the glass melted away to reveal, not a smoky bar, but a starry night sky, clearer than you ever saw in the city. Then, the window was back and he was just looking at black glass.

Yeah, someone up there has the touch. Not wild the way it was with Doone. This guy could control it.

Doone crossed the street and went up a flight of enclosed stairs to a landing with one door, and stared at the peephole for a second. Did he really want to go in there? Then he felt the music — and the control — and knocked.

He must have looked like a drunk who didn't want to call it a night yet, because the bouncer, a bald Mexican with crooked teeth, almost didn't let him past the entry. While he waited in the door for the bouncer to decide, Doone looked the club over.

The place wasn't big, but the dozen tables were full with late-night drinkers, and even the bar was crowded. A waitress moved expertly from table to table, taking orders without stopping. Most of the customers stared silently at a small

Jason Van Hollander

stage in one corner where a three-piece combo — piano, drums, and upright bass — played "'Round Midnight" too slow. The cigarette smoke was so thick that, from the back of the room, Doone couldn't even tell if he knew any of the musicians.

And the smoke moved, thick and ponderous, like a river swollen and muddy after a storm.

Doone stared at the smoke. Most clubs he had been in, the ventilation was so bad the smoke rose into the air and stayed there, till toward the end of the gig you thought they might have to move out a few tables, or ask a couple of patrons to leave so you would have room for the smoke.

In this place, the smoke moved around him. It rolled, bubbled, yeah, even danced around the tables.

When Doone looked closer, he started noticing shapes in the smoke. Not the vague, make-believe shapes you saw in clouds, but discernible figures.

The smoke shifted, pulsed, then broke into waves that beat against one wall of the club like it was a cliff. A smoke clipper ship with tattered smoke sails glided across the waves. When it reached the wall the whole thing whirled into meaningless eddies. And then, out of the eddies, a clown face peered at Doone. It got bigger and bigger, distorting out of shape as though he was seeing it through a funhouse mirror, till it filled the whole room, and then became the face of a Doberman that snapped at Doone.

Doone jumped back, and then looked to see if anybody had noticed. But he seemed to be the only one who had seen the shapes in the smoke.

The bouncer gave him a twisted smile and said something in Spanish.

"*No se 'abla,*" Doone muttered, and pushed through the smoke for the bar.

He was mad now. Whoever was playing tricks with the smoke somehow knew he was there and was aiming them at him. Doone wanted a drink, but he didn't order anything. Drink didn't stop the music in his head, just got between him and what little control he had. He was afraid if he ever got really drunk the music would take over like it did when he was sleeping.

Leaning against the bar, he nursed his mad. None of the three guys on the stage looked like much, but one of them had the touch. As if in confirmation, the smoke coiled around Doone's legs till it became a cobra, poised to strike. Doone kicked the snake into curling tendrils that drifted away from him. He laughed — but that brought the music in his head to the surface — so he turned an impassive face to the stage as though to say, "I see your tricks and they don't impress me." And studied the three guys up there.

The one at the piano was an old black guy. Thin, white hair, his back so stiff it looked like he was sitting on the end of a broom handle instead of a stool. Even though his long fingers shook a little, he still caressed the keys lovingly. Once, Doone thought, he had been good. Now, the frailty of his fingers came through his playing.

The drummer was a young white kid. Long hair, played like he thought he was doing rock and roll instead of jazz.

The guy on the upright, another white, played with his eyes closed, lost in the music. Curly hair and little trimmed mustache, corduroy coat with elbow patches. He looked like a college professor moonlighting.

He opened his eyes and stared directly at Doone. No smoke monster attack, but Doone knew this was the one.

Checking with the bartender, he found out there wasn't a backstage, so he waited at the bar till they finished up the last song in their set. He didn't recognize the song, but it sounded a little like Monk so he figured the old guy at the piano had written it. Wasn't bad, but it wasn't going to get him any

contracts with RCA. When they finished, and acknowledged a scattering of applause, they drifted toward the bar.

Despite his age the piano player got there first. He leaned against the bar like it was an old friend, and picked up a shot the bartender had waiting for him — then looked at Doone.

"We don't need anybody right now, not unless you play bass. We're losing our bass next week. You're not a bass player, are you?"

Doone shook his head, wondering. How did he know? Old guy, been sitting at that keyboard his whole life. But he didn't have the touch, so how did he know Doone played?

"I didn't think so," the piano player said. He took a sip from his shot, savoring it the way men sometimes do who know they got to drink all night and can't afford to lose anything to the booze. After that he ignored Doone.

Flushed, the bassplayer weaved in and out of the tables, smiling a secret sort of smile. He walked up behind the old piano player and slapped him on the back. "Hey," he said, his voice excited, "We're cooking tonight."

"Yeah," the old guy replied without much enthusiasm.

"Hey, Willie Boy," the bass player called to the bartender. "How about a coke?"

He didn't look at Doone till he had his fingers wrapped around the glass. "You look tired, man."

"Ain't got much sleep lately," Doone said.

The guy laughed as though Doone had made a joke. "No, I guess not. I used to have trouble sleeping."

"You don't anymore?"

He shook his head and laughed again. "Why not?"

"Peace of mind, man. I got an agent, good one. Now I got peace of mind. I got rhythm. I got music. Hey, I got a good night's sleep last night."

Suddenly, Doone wanted to smash his smug, white-ass face in. This guy knew what Doone was going through and he was playing with him, laughing at him. But Doone was afraid if he made the wrong move he wouldn't ever learn how the guy controlled it. "So, what? You taking something?"

"Nothing man. I'm clean. Don't even touch booze anymore. The Man's orders."

He laughed at Doone's questioning stare.

"My agent, man. The guy's a wiz, but he's real strict. That's okay, got me a smooth gig."

The piano player snorted, and the bassplayer slapped him on the back and laughed. "Doc here, he don't think much of Rock and Roll. But it's the wave, man."

"Electric bass," Doc said, and shook his head.

"I'm going to be pulling down six figures a week in six months, you wait and see." He looked from Doc to Doone. "You think I could make that playing jazz?" Doone didn't answer, and he laughed again. "Want to sit in on the next set?"

The piano player looked at him, but didn't say anything.

"I don't have my instrument," Doone replied.

"Tenor sax?"

Doone nodded.

"I thought so. I think Gill, our drummer, has one. He plays a little of everything."

"Jack of all trades, master of none," Gill called good-naturedly from the end of the bar.

"Come on," the bass player said, and led Doone to the kitchen where instrument cases were stacked as far from the steaming dishwasher as possible. He dug through the empty drum cases till he found a sax case, and slid it across the floor at Doone's feet.

Doone bent and opened it. It held a beat-up tenor sax, the kind you find in

any pawn shop for twenty bucks. But he wanted to hold it, needed to play it.

He hadn't played in — what? Four hours? Already his fingers itched to hold the sax. The music had been coursing through him all night now, washing away little bits and pieces of him. He pulled the mouthpiece out of his pocket, the one he always carried there. While he wetted the reed, he watched the bass player. "My name is Doone."

He laughed. "I don't care what your name is, man. Can you play?"

"You know I can."

He didn't say anything, just smiled at Doone and made him want to hit him again. Doone could see in his eyes the guy knew it, too.

"So how do you control it?" Doone asked.

"What, man?"

"The music," Doone snapped, moving so suddenly he kicked the case and sent it skidding across the floor. "How do you keep it from taking over while you sleep? From driving you crazy while you're awake? Used to be I could play and it would help, for a while. It don't even do no good to play anymore. So how do you do it? You on something?"

"Hey, you know that doesn't do any good. Booze just deadens it. Man, I even tried horse. You know what happens? It's like holding it behind a dam, and when you come down, the dam breaks. Like to have killed me. I can tell you know what I'm talking about."

"So what did you do?"

"Nothing, man. That's the beauty of it. I just got this new agent. He doesn't even play, but he understood. He took care of it for me."

"How?"

"I just go to his office."

"What happens there?"

"Nothing."

"Something must happen."

"No, man, nothing."

As Doone pressed, the guy got a harried look on his face. He was trying to hide something. And he was frightened.

"Nothing man, we just talk."

"About what?"

"My career." He looked at his watch. "Man, do you want to play or what? We got to start the next set."

"Yeah." Doone picked up the sax and stuck on the mouthpiece while the bassplayer watched, a scowl on his face now. "So who is this agent?" Doone asked. "Have I ever heard of him?"

Suddenly the guy was smiles again. He was as excited as a kid on his first paying gig. "Yeah, man, yeah. I got a card here somewhere." He searched through his pockets, pulled out a bent, dog-eared card, and shoved it at Doone.

Doone looked down at the card.

Gill stuck his head through the kitchen door. "We're on. That is if you still work here."

"Yeah, yeah." Then to Doone, "Come on. This may be my last jazz set. Let's knock 'em dead."

He headed for the door, then turned when Doone didn't follow him. "You coming?"

"Sure," Doone answered, still staring at the card. He could hear the drums and the piano starting up without them, but he couldn't take his eyes off the card. JAMES CANDYMAN — AGENT, was all it said. Doone turned it over. Nothing on the back, no phone number, no address, no nothing.

"Come on," the bassplayer said.

"Sure," Doone answered. He slipped the card into his pocket and followed the guy out onto the tiny club stage.

He peered through the smoke at the vague forms of the audience. He wasn't sure why he was nervous, but he was. He hadn't been this shaky since he had done his first solo in high school stage band. Only then he had known what he was scared of. Now he just knew he was scared.

Doc led them off with some Ellington, first "Satin Doll," then "Mood Indigo,"

nice, traditional stuff that let him show that the old boy still had some swing in him. Doone relaxed into a nice sideman feel, and went with the music.

Except the guy on the bass kept running changes that didn't make sense. His phrases weren't new. Doone had heard what he had to say before. They just didn't fit. He kept trying to take the music somewhere else. Doone made eye contact with Doc and motioned in the bassplayer's direction. *He trying to cut us?* Doc shrugged and went back to his keyboard.

Doone looked over at the bass and wondered what the guy was actually on. His eyes were closed, and a tight little smile was stuck on, but he had a somewhere else look on his face.

Then Doone noticed the smoke moving, and a flash of something in the air by the bassplayer's fingers when he struck one pulsating, jagged run. The guy was doing something. He wasn't playing tricks with the smoke this time, but he was doing something.

Whenever Doone let himself go into the music just a little, playing a line just parallel to the bass, he found he could see more clearly what was happening. Something was moving through the smoke. It was invisible, except for an occasional flicker of reflected light, like its surface was hard. And it deflected the smoke, so where it moved, the air was clear.

It looked to Doone like it was coming from the upright bass. And as the bass player struck a solo riff that swelled till it collapsed into polyrhythmic chaos, the invisible thing thickened. It stretched all the way across the club from the bass to a drunk at a table just in front of the bar. Whatever it was, it seemed to envelop the guy. As Doone watched, it pulled away from him and drifted to a woman at the next table. It seemed to wrap around her, its outer edge shivering as it drifted over her face.

Doone had been so wrapped up in watching what the bassplayer was doing that he didn't notice when Doc left Ellington behind and started to work on Bird. Doone knew he was turning it over to him, saying, *Okay, if you're a sax player, let's see what you can do.*

Only Doone wanted to watch the bassplayer. He picked up on the fourth bar, "A Night in Tunisia," and let the music take hold of him. Not that he had a choice. It was going to pick him up and carry him whether he wanted it to or not.

As soon as he started really playing, doing more than just backing up someone else, he felt a sense of time stretching. He wove his line in and out of the bass, felt the piano behind him somewhere, not the same place he and the bass were. He took the chords the bass was playing, no matter how little sense they made, and suddenly saw what was floating through the smoke clearly, as though it weren't invisible anymore, but a real, tangible thing.

Yet, it kept shifting. At one moment it looked like a snake, its scaled body wrapped around the woman, the next it was an arm, still scaled, a clawed hand grasping her. The scales were what reflected the stage lights.

Doone tried to peer through the smoke to see it more clearly, but no matter how he squinted, he couldn't see what it was really doing.

Then, he caught a be-bop riff from Doc intended for the bass player, cut in and picked it up before the bass could grab it. And he could see the scaled thing clearer.

He looked away from it, at the bass player. Guy's usin' us. Usin' our music to make that thing.

Doone let the mad build up in him, the mad at being used, and let it out in the music. He let the sax shout his anger, beating at the bass line, changing the cadence, till he'd taken the lead away from Doc as deftly as if he'd been a pickpocket. He was in the music. He had

as firm a control on it as he had on the little combo.

It felt so good, so good he wanted to ride the music for a while, savor this moment, remember it.

He looked back at the woman again — and found he could see through her as easily as he saw through the scaled thing.

No, not through her, he decided, inside her. Yeah, inside her. Like her mind was naked. He saw her the way she saw herself, a few years younger, a few pounds lighter. In her mind, her hair was redder, her lips fuller.

She wasn't watching anybody in particular, but there was a man here tonight, she knew he was here. He would come up to her and say hello, buy her a drink. He might want to take her home. She would tell him she couldn't, and he would understand. He would get her number, and call her, and — and that was as far as her dream went.

And while Doone looked on, the scaled thing swallowed her dream. Doone watched as it traveled up the arm, a shining, pulsating cloud that melted into the bass.

When he looked back at the woman, she seemed a little smaller and drunker than he remembered her. Already, the scaled thing was starting to unravel from around her. Doone could still see into her. He saw her realize that if any man talked to her he would just want an easy lay. She was too old for this sort of thing. What was she doing here? She would have gotten up and left, but that would be worse — going home alone.

Already the scaled thing was starting to wrap itself around a college kid at the next table. Even before it had completely enveloped him, Doone saw into the kid, saw his worry about some test on Tuesday, but man wasn't the band great, he could study all day Sunday and most of Monday night.

Then the scaled thing bit into the kid's hope, tearing off huge chunks till all that was left was the worry. He should have studied, but it was too late now, and if he didn't pass this class the draft would get him for sure, and might as well have another drink, make it an all-nighter.

Doone had been watching so intensely that the sax hung on its strap, forgotten. The bassman thought he had control again, but Doone still held the music in his head.

He put the sax to his lips and started to blow, soft and low, sweeter than his music had been in a long time. And the notes rose up till they contested the bass for air space. Doone played a change, one he knew they'd never heard, one he'd never felt till now. He went as far as he could into that phrase, feeling ideas come through his lips that he'd never known he had till now.

The bass player started to build a phrase. Doone added a note here, accented one there, creating new modulations. The bass couldn't follow. He faltered, and Doone cut him out.

When he did, the scaled thing dissolved back into nothingness. Doone thought he saw transparent scales drifting to the floor like blown leaves.

The bass player looked at him, frowned, and fell behind the beat.

Doone wanted to laugh, but he couldn't let go of the music long enough, so he let the sax laugh for him. He took the next phrase, and let it soar, interweaving the line with the piano and then the drums, bringing them back in.

He had destroyed that thing, whatever it was. What now? Could he take back what the bass player had been stealing from the audience, their dreams and hopes? No! Doone rebelled at the thought. He faltered. The sax's tone became sparse. It floated through the chords without touching them, as music welled deep within Doone, rebelling along with him at the prospect of using this guy's tactics.

So what could he do?

Man, he'd had dreams once. Still did, before the music became so strong it pushed thought of everything else out.

Doone looked at the bassplayer. What did he do with the dreams he was stealing? Sell them to the Candyman? That why you need a bigger audience? Not so you can make more money, so you can steal from them? Is that what you trade the Candyman? Nobody does nothing for nothing.

Looking back at the college kid, Doone picked up Doc's phrase. As he did, something started to form just above his sax. Not a cloud exactly, more like a bubble. Doone laughed. He was doing Lawrence Welk impersonations now.

He built the bubble, put some of the hopes he'd had when he first started out, some of the ambition, how he'd wanted to be more than just good, how he'd wanted other musicians to look at him. And he sent it to the kid.

Saw the kid visibly straighten when the bubble reached him and popped over his head. The kid looked at his watch. The music was great, but if he didn't get home he'd never get any studying done tomorrow. Tossing off the last of his drink, he headed for the door.

Doone wasn't sure what to do about the woman. Wasn't sure if it would do any good to help her. How many nights had she sat in some club surrounded by jerks and drunks, waiting for Mr. Right? And Doone was going to give that pipe dream back to her? But looking at her slumped down in her seat, waiting to be picked up by the first bum that came along, he knew that dream was better than what she had.

He built another bubble. But what could he put in it? He'd never had those kind of dreams before. He could tell her — he could tell her he cared. But did he? Hadn't cared in a long time. Did he now? And the music answered him back, and he sent it out to her. Didn't seem like much, but it was all he had, and sent it to her.

She perked up a little when the bubble popped, but she didn't leave like Doone hoped she would. She nursed her drink and thought of the kind of guy she wanted to meet, and Doone knew she wouldn't just walk out with any scuzz, which was something.

Then he looked around at the rest of the club's patrons. Some had been drained by the bass player. Doone recognized his signature. But not everyone at the tables had felt the bassman's touch. Doone saw a lot of suffering out there the bass hadn't made. So he started making other bubbles, wondering as he did why he bothered. This place was a refuge for losers. That's why he'd come here.

Even as he thought that, he remembered some of the cycles he'd already played, some of the ideas, the feelings, that he'd never even known he'd had. Never did have till tonight. And he looked at them out there, waiting for the music to give them something. Nobody does nothing for nothing.

He played through the set, never giving up the lead, delving not so much into people's minds as into their dreams, ambitions, hopes. Some he couldn't reach. But he blew his sax, and let the music do things through him it had never done before.

The bass got softer till it was just an angry buzz, heard just at the edge of Doone's phrases.

Doone didn't know the others had stopped playing till he felt a tap on his shoulder. "Set's over," Doc told him wearily. "Last set of the night. Time to go home."

Rubbing the sore muscles in the small of his back, Doone followed Doc back into the kitchen. Man, he was going to pay for this tomorrow. Strangely, even though he was a little stiff, he didn't feel tired. And for the first time in a while, he felt sleepy.

The bass player met him at the door. "Do you know what you did, Man?"

"I thought I played a pretty good set," Doone replied.

"You did," Doc told him, throwing a dish towel over his shoulder and heading for the kitchen sink.

"You don't know nothing," the bassplayer told the old man's back, then to Doone, "You think you're smart? You just wasted a whole evening. You go turning it back to the marks, and you lose it."

"Shit!" was all Doone had to say, but he started to smile again.

"Man, you've got the power," the bass player continued, "But you don't know how to use it. It can hurt you, man, unless you've got someone to show you."

"What do you pay him with?" Doone asked. "What you stole tonight?"

"He gets his cut."

"He doesn't get mine."

"What do you think you got?" the bassplayer demanded. "You been giving it to strangers. You think you got any left for him, for what he can give you in return?"

"I got more than you think," Doone told him. And he realized it was true. He felt good, more rested than he had in a long time.

So you could do things with it. That was something. Do it the way that this jerk did; take, and you had to keep taking. Nobody does nothing for nothing. It cut both ways. Do something else with it, give a little of it, and you drained off the excess, the overload that put you on edge all the time. Yet you still had all you needed. Was a time, he remembered, when he thought that's what music was all about.

The bass player was staring at him. Doone winked at him, and laughed again when the guy took a step back.

Shaking his head, Doone put the sax away. "Thanks for the loan," he told Gill as the drummer came through the door, lugging drum cases.

"No problem. You play it better than I do." He backed out the service door.

Doone left the bassplayer still staring at him and wandered back out into the club. The place was almost empty. The woman had left. With someone? Doone shrugged. Weaving between the tables toward the door, he started humming, and all the lights went out. He laughed, and pushed through the door and out onto the street.

Ω

Two exciting novels from Weird Tales Library!

The Devil's Auction by **Robert Weinberg.** A blend of pulp-action, terror, and occult adventure in the tradition of Sax Rohmer and Seabury Quinn, about which Joe R. Lansdale wrote: "A rootin-tootin, booger of a book with just about every kind of pulp cliché turned inside out and made fresh as a spring daisy, but mean and nasty as a rattlesnake bite."

The White Isle by **Darrell Schweitzer.** An epic fantasy of heroism, horror, and a descent into a world of the dead. *The Bookwatch* called it "a gripping, fast-paced story." Janice Eisen wrote in *Aboriginal Science Fiction*: "*The White Isle* has some marvellous imagery and Schweitzer has a grotesque and frightening imagination. . . .It is a lovely, horrific tale that is worth your while to seek out."

These hardcover books are illustrated with four-color dustjackets and black-&-white interior drawings by **Stephen Fabian.**

Order from: Terminus Publishing Co., P.O. Box 13418, Philadelphia PA 19101-3418. $18.95 each, postpaid. (In PA add 6% sales tax.)

OF KINKS AND FROCKS

by R. Bretnor

art by Bob Walters

The third Friday of each month is University Night at the Bilge Pump. This does not mean that the place is swarming with undergraduates who only think they can hold their liquor — Captain Crankshaw would never stand for that. It means simply that on those nights certain eminent academics and destined-to-be eminent would-be academics gather there to exchange heretical opinions and to enjoy the curious drinks Mickey, the Captain's huge Fijian bartender, concocts so expertly. It was on one of these nights that I met Professor Junius Gruzsic and heard the strange story of the kinks and frocks — but first perhaps I'd better fill you in on the Bilge Pump itself. It is a bar on the San Francisco waterfront, or perhaps more accurately *under* the San Francisco waterfront, for it is located in the aftercabin of H.M.S. *Dryad,* a vessel which, like so many others, sank at her moorings after being abandoned by her crew during the Gold Rush, donating her hull to the filling in of much of the future city. But somehow one or more of her officers managed either to keep the aftercabin watertight or else to pump and keep it dry by sealing everything. Over it rose the famous — some would say infamous — Dryad House Hotel, eventually purchased (I think, because he does own it) by my friend Edmund Casebolt Crankshaw, Master Mariner, who lives there himself with his lovely Javanese mistress.

There's no bar like it. You go through the lobby of the Dryad House, pass what remains of the ship's mizzenmast, now the lobby's central pillar, and go down the companionway, and there it is, its panelling gleaming as softly as it must have in 1849, its bronze bulkhead clock still ringing out the ship's bells, and its only illumination still brass kerosene lamps in gimbals (their one concession to modernity being that they no longer burn whale oil). Behind the bar stands Mickey, all six-foot-six of him, under his enormous bush of frizzy black hair, busily making drinks and occasionally showing the filed teeth which have such a healthy psychological effect on unwanted customers.

At any rate, on that particular Friday, Dudley Swenson, who teaches archaeology at Stanford, phoned me and asked me to be sure to attend as soon after dinner as possible. He was bringing two friends whom I had never met, Adam Meerlo, an ancient professor from somewhere back in Montana, and an assistant of his, a young woman — and not just young, he said, but surprisingly beautiful — and they were to have with them this Junius Gruzsic, who headed the Department of Trans-Jungian Psychology and Arcane Sciences at an ancient college dreaming under Harvard's shadow. "The Department of *what?*" I said incredulously. He repeated it. "You wouldn't laugh if you knew the size of his endowment," he told me. "Besides, he has written any number of learned papers, to say nothing of books in several languages, and is very highly thought of in Uppsala and Heidelberg."

"Who else is coming?" I asked; and he mentioned some chap from USC and a visiting professor from Quebec, neither of whom sounded too ominous. "All I know," he said, "is that some incredible event has occurred, something Meerlo

says will make all his fellow paleontologists roll over in their graves, with the most profound cross-disciplinary and philosophical implications. I wonder whether it mightn't be a good idea to invite Crankshaw to sit in with us? I'm sure he'd enjoy it, and if what they have isn't startling enough, he can always liven things up by telling one of his Flying-Dutchman sea-serpent stories."

I told him I thought it'd be an excellent idea. The Captain was always a gracious host and excellent company, and if they really had something worth listening to, he'd never forgive me if I didn't let him in on it. So, as soon as we hung up, I phoned the Captain and told him what was in the wind, and asked him if we could reserve the table around the end of the bar where Mickey stands when he isn't mixing drinks, the one under the fetchingly semi-nude dryad figurehead which once graced the vessel's prow. "I'll be there to hold it down," I told him, and he said he'd join me as soon as I arrived, just to make sure the science-fiction people didn't manage to trick me out of the table.

As always, I had dinner at the Men's Faculty Club, and managed to drive across the Bay and find a parking space in the Dryad's small restricted lot by eight-fifteen. Mickey had just defended our table successfully against three science-fiction types, two male and one female, who glared at me as he pulled my chair back and greeted me in his *basso profundo* pidgin English. Then Crankshaw showed up, and they very wisely quit glaring, for he is, in his way, even more impressive than his bartender. His age is indeterminate; a lean, hard crag of a man, somehow he seems to tower over everybody, and when he is irritated the look in his gray-steel eyes would put a basilisk to shame.

He seated himself, and Mickey took our orders: Pusser's Rum for him, scotch and water for me; and we had hardly had time to exchange pleasant-

ries when Swenson and his friends came in.

We stood up and exchanged introductions. Professor Meerlo was a deeply tanned old man, rather Frank Lloyd Wrightish in appearance, but his assistant, Dr. Gilda Mredvani, was something else again. No one could have looked less like what one might suppose a paleontologist ought to look like. She was tall and svelte, not far out of her twenties, deep blonde, with high cheekbones and sparkling blue-green eyes.

"You will be interested to know," said Dr. Meerlo, "that Gilda is not just a scholar. She is a princess — a *real* princess."

She touched his arm. 'Please, Adam," she said, "it is of no importance." She laughed shyly. "In Russian Georgia, where my family came from, all you needed to be a prince was to own enough sheep. Why, there was one village where every man's a prince, or was before the Revolution."

A gnarled little old man standing just behind her, whom I'd hardly noticed, cleared his throat.

"This —" said Dr. Meerlo, "— is our esteemed colleague, Dr. — he has three doctorates — Dr. Junius Gruzsic."

"Ja!" said Dr. Gruzsic. "Also yes! But it iss nod true being a princess iss nod impordant. In this case, it iss of the maximum impordance. Soon you understand, ja!"

He had the strangest accent I have ever heard, and the frivolous thought struck me that perhaps it somehow derived from his unusual field of academic activity. It was an eccentric accent, Germanic but not German. Even his attire was somehow eccentric, as though displaced in space and time. Everyone looked baffled — everyone but Captain Crankshaw. He smiled at Dr. Gruzsic, and said something in a thick and alien tongue; and Dr. Gruzsic at once cried out in the same tongue and embraced him warmly. "Mine natif lan-

guish!" he cried out, while two tears rolled down his cheeks. "We must later talk about mein poor country, which exists no longer, which no one now remembers. But now we talk about more impordant things, of what happens in Montana, nein, no?"

Somehow the other two professors got introduced, both colorless scholars learned in colorless specialties, and we all sat down. Mickey took the orders, and the Captain announced that they were on the house. Then Dr. Meerlo started his story. "Gentlemen," he said, "do you believe there is such a phenomenon as enchantment? Do you think it possible that by magic people can change their shapes, or be changed into something else, some other form of life?"

I shook my head, and Swenson and the two visiting professors very definitely said no. Only Captain Crankshaw disagreed. "I do," he said. "I saw a witchdoctor in Ethiopia change himself into a hyena, a choice I myself would not have made, but actual nonetheless. And I can assure you that I was not deluded in any way."

"Good, good! Now listen! A month ago, I and my dear Gilda were on an important dig in my home state, Montana, which as you know is full of fossils. We were seeking more specimens of a small duck-billed dinosaur which the scientific world has seen fit to name after me. With us we had two graduate students, one of whom I am sorry to say is still in hospital, I hope recovering from his nervous breakdown. The other one, who was operating the video camera, did not break down, but the poor boy still drinks too heavily. Now, tell me, have any of you heard accounts of creatures — usually toads — being found encapsulated in such substances as limestone, sandstone, even quartz, where they must have been trapped uncounted years ago — have you heard of these creatures actually coming back

to life when they were returned to the open air?"

Almost everybody had heard such stories, or had read them in sensational tabloids, but only Dr. Gruzsic and again the Captain expressed any belief in them.

"Very well," said Meerlo. "I shall not tell you — no! I shall show you. I have here the video tape. If, Captain, you happen to have here a small room with a TV?"

"There's a little cuddy behind the bar," answered Crankshaw. "If you'll carry your drinks in, we can use the VCR there. I'll tell Mickey to guard your table with his life."

Mickey showed his filed teeth in a horrendous smile, and we followed his employer around the end of the bar to the cuddy's door. The place was just big enough for all of us, though I and one or two others had to stand.

Meerlo produced the video cassette, handed it to the Captain. The TV and the VCR were turned on, and almost at once we were watching Meerlo and Gilda chipping away at the base of a cloven cliff, sometimes picking up small dinosaur spare parts and showing them to each other, answering questions when the other young man — the one not running the video camera — held up a specimen for examination, then going back to their chipping. Finally, Meerlo himself pried loose something that looked like a very large round geode, and just as he did so the camera operator finally remembered to turn the sound recording on.

"What on earth is that?" We heard Meerlo's voice, now coming from the TV.

"Why don't you crack it open and see?" suggested Gilda.

The sun was intensely bright and hot, the shadows sharp and definite. Meerlo raised his prospect pick and brought it down on the round stone. With a distinct **crack** it split in half. "My God!" we heard him cry. "What's *that?*"

The camera zoomed in on his find. There in half the geode — if it was a geode — was a frog — or perhaps it would be more accurate to say proto-frog, somehow different from modern frogs.

"I'll be a son of a bitch!" exclaimed the young man with the camera. "Hey, look at that!"

Now the proto-frog filled almost the entire TV screen, and as we watched the unbelievable occurred. Very, very slowly, the frog's left eye began to open.

"It — it's *alive!*" shrieked Gilda, and she began to laugh hysterically. "Do you — do you suppose if I — if I kissed it, it'd turn into a handsome prince?" Again she burst out laughing.

"Sure! Why not try it?" said one of the students.

Still laughing, she reached out, picked up the frog, kissed it very gently on the forehead — and — and suddenly the image on the screen was wiped out by a great burst of light so intense that even the sunlight was paled by it. It lasted for an instant only — and then we heard Gilda's scream, the most terrifying scream I've ever heard.

We stared. There she was, sprawled out on the ground, and the frog had disappeared — but over her prone body stood an enormous dinosaur. It was fifteen or twenty feet high, and its set of teeth made poor Mickey's seem absolutely harmless.

"God Almighty!" yelled Meerlo. "*Tyrannosaurus rex!*"

"Ach, ach!" said Dr. Junius Gruzsic in my ear. "It iss dot she should not haff forgodden she iss a Princess. Yes? Ja?"

We watched hypnotized, waiting for the dreadful beast to seize her, rend her, swallow her. But nothing happened. Its left eye finished opening. Then slowly, monstrously, it sank down. Its head fell over to the side.

"It iss because after so many millennia, ja? So much sunlight at once finally kills it as it vould haff killed the frock."

Gruzsic shook his head dismally. "So sad," he said. "But anyvay it hass profed vhat I write — enjantments vork, und nod chust a little vhile — a good enjantment lasts a long time. It iss vorth anything you haff to pay for it."

On the screen, Dr. Gilda — Princess Gilda — had picked herself up and was dusting herself off, and I was amazed at her recovery, her *savoir faire* — in her situation I'd not have stopped running this side of Boise.

"So, for me it iss a triumph!" Dr. Gruzsic bowed to Professor Meerlo. "I thank you for it. Chust vait undil I publish all mein papers, ja — und vith your tape to profe it, und vith der now so-dead dinosaur for you to study. How nice! Only, mein frent, you are mistaken in vun think. You must not call it *Tyrannosaurus rex*. Eferybody knows frocks turn only into princes, never into kinks — nein, nefer, nefer, nefer! So you must name it *Tyrannosaurus filius regis*, or perhaps *princeps.*"

I looked around at the small company, all of us except the original participants and the exultant Dr. Gruzsic still trying to recover from the shock of watching the impossible take place before our eyes.

The one exception was Captain Edmund Casebolt Crankshaw. "There's one thing I'd like to know," he said thoughtfully. "There certainly had to be a wicked witch, didn't there? What on Earth do you suppose *she* looked like?"

Ω

'90 Walters

EMBER

by Fred Chappell

art by Denis Tiani

When I came out of Paradise they were shooting at me. Shotguns and pistols mostly, whatever they could grab hold of. I jumped into my old green pickup truck in the parking lot and drove off. I couldn't shoot back because I'd already pitched my .44 pistol away. I wouldn't have shot back anyway, so I stepped on the gas. Probably it was rocks thrown up against the undercarriage, but it might have been bullets hitting the truck, so I ducked my head down.

Scared, Hell yes, I was scared. Couldn't breathe except in gulps and my hands were shaking and two drops of dead cold sweat inched from my armpit down my left side. It wasn't so much getting shot at — though I hear tell you never get used to that — but the faces of the people, faces of them that used to be my friends and neighbors turned red and murderous. I couldn't stand up to that.

Ten minutes later I felt a little easier and stopped trembling so much, not seeing the headlights after me in my mirror. But I knew they'd be coming and I knew they'd already called the sheriff and the highway patrol. I was a wanted man now, the only time in my life. I didn't know what to think.

I had already made one big mistake. If I had turned right coming out of the parking lot there at West End Tavern Dance I'd be traveling toward the broad highways, the ones that connected with Georgia and all the other states and all the nations of the world. But I'd turned left instead and there was nothing in front of me but the brushy mountains of western North Carolina, briar thickets and tear-britches rocks over the steep slopes. And especially there was Ember Mountain where nobody went in the dark, nobody that would anyhow talk about it in the daylight.

———- - ———-

But I started thinking maybe some things wouldn't be so bad. I had fished the streams around here and knew my way some, and the more the men that were trailing me didn't know Ember, the better. So I made a turn-off onto a little clay road that goes up Burning Creek and crosses it three times. At the third ford the trail's no wider than a cowpath and I pulled the truck over into a stand of laurel and cut the motor and the lights and opened the door.

Then it was like stepping into another world because the silence came down so sudden and the darkness. The world of Paradise Township where I'd shot with my .44 my untrue sweetheart Phoebe Redd was sure enough a world away, I was thinking, and then the silence let up a little and I could hear the hood of the truck ticking as the motor cooled and the feathery swishing of the wind in the treetops and the low mutter of Burning Creek off to my left. Those noises brought me back to myself and how I had to keep running.

I scrambled down to the edge of the creek and got down on all fours and drank like a dog, tasting the mountain in the water, the mossy rocks above me in the dark and the humus and the secret springs of Ember. When I stood up again I could hear the other night sounds of late August, the crickets and cicadas and somewhere a long way off to my right the longdrawn empty call of a

hoot owl.

But there was nowhere to go but up the mountain. The farther I got in the nighttime, the farther away I'd be come sunup. Let them try to find me in six hours, or eight. Carolina wouldn't hold me nor Georgia either, once I got past Ember Mountain.

I dreaded to have to do it, though. It wasn't only what they say about the ridges and hollers of Ember, and I'd heard plenty of that and put stock in some of it. But just any old mountain in the dark of the night is a reckless time, and if there hadn't been so many certain dangers behind me, I wouldn't have been traveling on to meet new ones.

So I started up, my pants wet and my feet soaked in my shoes. My breath began to pound in my chest and my knees felt weak, but I climbed any way I could, tripping over tree roots and crawling on all fours and sliding down on the loose shale; it was a wonder I didn't just tumble to the bottom and lie at the end of the valley like a rag doll a little girl has lost on her picnic.

But I kept on going and the rocks and roots and bushes kept tearing at me. The left side of my face got laid open by a bramble or a twig and I could feel the blood oozing down my neck into my shirt. I had to stop and rest a lot of times but I didn't like to and it got worse the higher I climbed because the silence got deeper and I began to remember more and more what folks said about Ember.

Oh Phoebe, I thought, *oh Phoebe Redd. See what your faithless ways have brought on me.*

I went on. I kept going till I thought I couldn't stand it any more and then I came to the backbone of a stony ridge and struck south along with it, still climbing and climbing till I came to a weedy clearing. Then I saw a point of orange light up the mountain to my left. The more I tried to make it out, the more I couldn't see it clear. That's the way it is in the dark silence with trees everywhere.

But when I climbed some more, not breathing as hard now, I saw it again, clear and shining but shadowed over by something every now and again so that it flickered. I figured it to be a hunter's campfire, even though I had not heard his dogs running. Not everybody was scared of the tales and there was a plenty of game varmints up here, I could tell that just by listening.

I started toward the light. Not a wise decision, maybe, but it wasn't like I decided. A picture in my mind drew me: I could see how there'd be a fellow there by his campfire and how he'd have coffee or a sip of whiskey and maybe both. I was hot and cold and sick of the rocks and the bruising. I'd make up some lie to tell him about what I was doing up there, any lie that would stick.

But the ridge led down before it led up, and going downhill in the dark without a trail is a fool's job. Rocks and sawbriars all the way down and then a slick mud gulley at the bottom, then laurel thicket when I was climbing again, as puzzledy as a roll of barb wire. But I could just smell that coffee and taste it in my mouth, so I kept on and on. Might be a hunting man would appreciate some company up here in the lonesome midnight. Or it might be he wouldn't. It was a chancy notion.

But then when I came to the edge of the clearing I found it was no campfire. Here was a neat mountain cabin with a hearth fire inside and the clearing about me was for a garden. I could make out the shape of the cabin pretty well. It was a clean place, the shingle roof mossed over, the little porch propped up on flat rocks. From the chinked rock chimney rose the ghost-colored smoke of the fire I'd spied so far away.

I waited at the edge, watching and listening. There were no dogs. I took it strange there were no dogs. A man at midnight walking up to a house in the solitary woods — he expects to hear the

hounds begin to racket and come out to meet him.

Who was it lived here anyhow? Nobody I'd ever heard about.

I tried to walk quiet, but they'd have to be stone deaf in there not to hear me rustling and crackling through the goldenrod and the cornstalks. But I came right to the side of the house without anybody raising a holler and saw that it was just a cabin like many another I know. Weathered oak boards and mud-chink rock foundations and on the porch flowers growing in lard buckets and a cane-bottom rocking chair empty but for starlight and shadow. There was silence all around.

On this side there was a little square window curtained with dotted swiss, just above the eye level. I stretched up on tiptoe to see inside.

The room was neat and cheery in the firelight. There was a hooked rug on the floor and another bigger one hanging on the wall and two little tables with dried flowers in vases and a couple of straight chairs. There was a tall dark rocking chair beside the fire and in it sat a little old granny woman with iron-colored hair. She was wearing a washed-pale blue gingham dress and a blue-gray apron. She wasn't rocking in her chair, just sitting there as still as a tombstone, but she was not asleep. I could see the firelight glinting yellow in her eyes like they were cat's eyes.

I let down flat on my feet to ease my legs. It was nothing strange to see, an old woman remembering in front of her fire, but I had to wonder. How could it be only her up here and no menfolk about to help her do? It all looked all right, but when I thought, there was nothing right about it.

I decided to take another look and this time it wasn't an old woman in her rocking chair but another kind of thing hard to tell about. All gnarled and rooty like the bottom of a rotted oak stump turned up. Or all wattly, the way toad-stools will grow on fallen timber. Maybe more like it looks at the bottom of a candle burnt halfway down, where the wax has gathered in smooth pulpy lumps.

I can't say exactly because it was nothing exact to see. Something alive that nobody would ever think could live, something that knew about me out here by the window without seeing me, something that was an old woman in a chair and was no old woman any way in the world.

All right, Bill Puckett, I thought. *This is what comes of your jealous murdering. You have landed in the hardest place a man can land.*

I figured that maybe my third glimpse might be the true one and when I peeped again it was the same old woman as before, sitting just the way she was at first, with her eyes still shining yellow and not rocking in her rocking chair.

So maybe I'd imagined the rooty thing there, tired and scared as I was, and I was determined to get the good of her hearth fire, no matter. Ember Mountain with its ditches and brambles was too much for me this night; I was willing to take my chances with the old woman.

I went around to the front and up the five worn porch steps, trying to fix on a lie to tell her and whoever was with her here. I rapped three times and thought I heard a Come-in, but the door planks were mighty thick. Anyhow, I shot back the smooth-handled latch and entered.

———·———

When she craned her head to look it came to my mind what a sorry marvel I must appear. I was all wet and muddy and my clothes were ripped and one side of my face and neck was probably still bleeding from a gash. Not a handsome sight to look on.

But she didn't show the least surprise. "Come in," she said. "Come to the fire where it's warm."

I was grateful. I crossed over to the clean rock hearth and held my hands

palm up to the fire, the way you can't help doing. I warmed one side of myself and turned to warm the other.

She was looking me up and down. "You appear to been a good while in the woods," she said.

"Yes mam, I have been."

"Even on a summer night you can get cold and tore up on this mountain."

"Yes mam."

She was just a nice old granny woman. Even with her sitting down, I could tell she was real short. Short and thick, I thought, before I observed she was a humpback woman. I couldn't place her age, the skin of her face being so smooth and ruddy. Apple cheeks, folks call that, but she was old. Her hands were wrinkled and looked powdery and her voice was shrewd and trembly with her years.

"You got to be careful," she said. "There's many a good man been lost on Ember in the night."

"Yes mam."

She turned her head sideways and the firelight caught in her eyes till they shone like pieces of gold. "Why are you up here, then, so late into the night?"

I hadn't made up my lie yet and now when I tried to I couldn't do it. It stuck in the middle of my throat and I coughed and choked. I couldn't make sense in my head except just the truth and finally that was what I told her. "The law is after me," I said, "and some other people too. They're wanting to hang me on a big hickory tree, I reckon."

"What for?"

"I shot a woman," I said.

"Did you kill her?"

"I don't know. But it was an awful big pistol I pulled the trigger on."

"Who was she?"

"She was just a woman that treated me wrong. There ain't no use to say her name."

"Sit down," she said. "Pull up a chair to the fire and sit you down. It's good you told me the straight of it and not some infernal lie."

I felt better leaning forward in the chair and soaking up the heat. My pants legs were steaming as the denim dried. "I didn't take no pleasure in it," I said. "It just came over me too powerful. She swore time after time she was my woman and no other man's. But when I went to the West End Tavern Dance I saw them both and I shot and threw down my pistol and fled away."

"Wasn't it Phoebe Redd, this woman?"

"How did you know that? How could you ever hear about it up on this mountain?"

Her voice dropped to a mumble and it was hard to hear her. I thought she said: "Because it's not the first time, never ever the first time."

"What did you say?" I asked.

She looked at me then with a look as straight as a broomstick. "How old a man would you be?"

"My name is Bill Puckett," I told her. "I'm twenty-seven years old."

"Ain't you surely old enough to know better about women?"

"It came over me. I was in a fever where I couldn't think."

She nodded and got up and limped to the fire, showing she had a bad leg. She took up a big wrought iron poker and shifted the three logs. Red and orange sparks went up fantail and the wood snapped and sizzled. Her bunched-up shadow divided into three on the walls.

"Well, what's done is done," she said. "What you'll be doing next, that's the question."

"I don't know anything to do but to just keep running," I said. "Because all they're going to do is just keep coming after me."

"You could give up and hand yourself over."

"I don't know," I said. "They're riled pretty hot. No telling what they might do to me."

"Sit you back," she said, "and take your ease. I've got some herb tea already

made that I can warm up for you. It'll take some of the ache out of your bones."

I didn't say her no but began to rub my ankles and the calves of my legs. My skin was itching where my pants legs dried by the hearth fire.

With her heavy poker she swung the iron crane out from the fireplace wall over the blaze and lifted down a black kettle from the adze-scarred mantelpiece beam. She hung the kettle on the crane hook. "Take off your shoes and your stockings," she said, and when I did she drew them to the hearth with the poker and arranged them to dry. "Won't take a minute for the tea to warm," she said. "A good strong herb tea. Here now, move over into my rocking chair and rest a little easier."

I did that too and began to unloosen a little in my muscles. I leaned back and looked into the fire and then when I looked at her again she blurred in front of me because of the firelight. I put it down to the firelight. "You'll need you a cup and saucer," she said. "I'll go and get them from the kitchen."

I tried to get up.

"You just stay here. You'll be needing all the rest you can get."

I listened to her shuffling about and I wondered again about her being lame and how she managed up here on the mountainside all alone by herself. I wondered too a great deal about how she heard of Phoebe, only I expected she had a radio back there in the kitchen that she would listen to a-nights, though I hadn't seen any power lines when I found the house. But the fact that she knew the name of Phoebe Redd just showed how soon they'd be catching up with me.

I must have dozed a little because next I remember her face close to mine, her apple cheeks smooth and reddish, and her eyes away from the firelight not yellow now but black-dark as two soot spots. And something I hadn't seen before: there were dents in her skin here and there, two in her forehead and one in her left cheek just below the eye and three dents in her throat, little pushed-in places like the thumbprints you'd leave in biscuit dough. The skin was smooth in the dents, smooth as isinglass. Wounds that have healed over, I thought, old wounds. Except for one in her throat just under her chin: that one was healed but looked fresh too, as red and rare as a scarlet flower.

She'd had a bad time too, I thought and right then that was all I thought.

"Here now," she said. "Drink this all down." She offered me a china saucer with little blue painted flowers and a gilt edge and on it a blue enamel cup almost brimful of steaming tea. I remember the look of that cup and saucer as clear as the bluest sky. "It'll be good and strong for you," she said.

I knew I'd spill it if I tried to hold the saucer, my hands unsteady as they were. I set the saucer on the floor and held the cup in my thumb and first finger by its fragile little handle. When I sipped at it, the taste of its heat went right to my breastbone. It was strong and rank and bitter and it tasted of something that reminded me of *far away.* That is the best I know how to tell: it tasted of *far away,* every bit as strong as she had said. Just the steam lifting out of the cup clambered in my head.

"There now," she said. "Can you feel anything from that?"

"It's mighty good," I said.

She was standing close over me again, her face almost touching mine and looking deep into my eyes. "Go on. Drink it down."

I didn't want to look into her eyes so it was her throat I saw, the red new-healed smooth place beneath her chin. Right then I recognized that wound for the first time as the place on her body where my .44 bullet had struck my deceitful Phoebe back in Paradise. It was the exact same spot.

I wanted to understand that, I wanted

to try to make some sense, but it was too late. The old woman's tea was too strong in me and the little china cup slipped out of my unnerved fingers onto the hearthstones. It didn't break into a hundred splinters; it stuck solid and quivering on the rock like an arrow shot into a tree trunk. I stared at it there unharmed.

I kept staring at the cup because I didn't want to look at the granny woman. It shivered my body to know if I looked at her I'd see her again all ugly roots and lumps and with her firelit yellow eyes deformed.

But that's what I knew and not what I saw. All I saw was a heavy black roaring before my eyes and a sick shaking and I dropped then into a deep swoon, the deepest I reckon that a man can endure.

And when I came back to myself I was not sitting in the rocking chair and there was no hearth before me and not even a cabin around me. I was lying flat on my back under the stars in the middle of a fair-sized grassy bald, a circle with edges so sharp against the trees and bushes it looked like it was cut here with a knife.

It took a long time for me to get steady and sit up and when at last I do I find you-all here, all twelve of you men sitting crosslegged on the edge of the circle, all watching me with your wild eyes.

And when one of you, the tall dark-complected man there in his ancient buckskins, asked me to tell my whole story I didn't hold back the least little crumb of it. Awful as it is, it's the truth and I know you know that.

Because you don't need to explain anything to me. I can see in your bitter faces and in the bitter shadows of your eyes how it is and how it is going to be, that we are the men who ever killed Phoebe Redd; over the years and generations and centuries it was us that left the marks of our pistol balls on her again and again. Mine was the freshest one just beneath her chin, as red as a scarlet rose. I know how her revenge on us is everlasting and how we are to be scattered howling to and fro on the mountain; and how there is no rest for us and no surcease, but only being driven miserable on the rocks and thorns until Ember Mountain perishes and time itself passes all away.

Ω

THAT CERTAIN SMILE, IN IVORY

If you think that by my death you will evade
The questions that our loving would have met,
What will you think, love, when with fleshless arms
I'll hold you tightly in my bony net
And waltz you through the life we would have made
Had your courage followed as your heart was set?
Love whom you will, my ghost's not laid;
There's a dance in these old bones yet.

— **D.W. Harrison**

THE UNMAKER OF MEN

by Darrell Schweitzer and Jason van Hollander

art by Jason van Hollander

"Get *up*, you fool!" my Master hissed, kicking me hard in the ribs. At the sight of the dread Thulisquar, the Grand Physician of the Ministry of Pain looming in his full ceremonial regalia, his embroidered robe glittering and flashing in the dim candlelight, his black hood swallowing his face; at the sudden appearance of this all-too-familiar apparition my lady of the evening squealed and rolled under the bed, dragging a sheet after her to cover her nakedness.

Likewise naked, I lay on my back and stared up at him. I laughed hysterically.

"Boy, you are a disgrace!" He struck me across the chest with his riding whip. I didn't even raise a hand to shield myself.

That was funny too.

The lady under the bed whimpered. Thulisquar ignored her.

Convulsed with hilarity, I rolled onto my side, weeping with ineffable amusement, and also from the *hanquil* fumes.

My Master reached down and picked up the vial of the precious drug from where it had fallen. He held it up to the light and shook it.

"Five grains, eh? Just five?"

"Yes!" I said, finding words at last. "Yes! The common, trivial five!"

More laughter, even as Thulisquar struck me again with his whip, on the buttocks and across the back.

The powder called *hanquil* is ground from the spiny barbs of a sky-colored fish, I told myself, lecturing on and on in my mind, for suddenly I felt very — ha! hah! — weighty of thought, somber, learned — and it was time for the expostulation of secret lore. *Hanquil* is well known to the physicians and to the decadent elite of Alquaziir, its properties curious and consistent: Three grains suffice to cure neuralgic aches. Four temporarily numb all pain and give the user a deep sense of seriousness, while an additional fifth transforms existence into an excruciating joke for several hours. Or, perhaps one should say, as the

seriousness of the fourth grain yields to the giddiness of the fifth, that one suddenly perceives true reality. Our blinders fall off.

Hence the term "five-grainers," applied by the merrymakers of Alquaziir to themselves as a kind of code, a password, a talisman. It is the beginning of *hanquil* addiction, which leads, inevitably they say, to the sixth grain and a mad, laughing death.

Which somehow seems worth it.

So funny!

"Child, you disgust me! Get up!" (Whack! The whip, somewhere.) "Cover yourself! Show a sense of shame!" (Whack! Whack! The prostitute under the bed shrieked in sympathy, then began an endless, gurgling laugh.)

He grabbed me under the chin, so hard I began to choke. (This itself seemed incredibly hilarious.) He stood me up in the candlelight. "You are, what, Ganzeric?" he said. "Eighteen? You should be an intelligent, responsible young man. I have brought you up to be such. How very disappointing."

He let go and I flopped down unto the bed. ("Oomph!" said the lady underneath. So humorous, that sound.) I clung to the bedpost, trying to sit upright, but lost my grip and fell back. Once more I lay, still naked, staring up at the great Doctor of Pain.

Idly, he traced blood across my chest.

"I have long wanted to torture this body of yours," he said. "It is perfect. You are unworthy of such perfection."

For most of my life I had been unable to comprehend my "Uncle" (for so I thought of him — how funny it was!), and once, when I'd newly learned about such things, I was certain he was one of those who lusted after young boys. Then I decided he merely lusted after pain.

But I did him wrong, truly, for Thulisquar was a pious and dutiful man, devoted equally to religion and science, to the twin paths of truth as he called them. He knew that the gods may only

be reached through offerings, and that an offering devoid of impurity is like clear water. Through it we may see to the infinite bottom of the divine pool. In what he saw as my beauty, he discerned such clarity. I am sure that he sometimes wondered whether or not he had read the situation wrong on that day when he found me as a small child, starving near to death in the alley behind the Ministry of Pain. Perhaps the gods meant me to be his victim, rather than his assistant and heir.

I was certain he was entertaining such doubts at that very moment.

"Get up," he said, prodding me with the whip. "Cover yourself and come along. We have important work to do."

I fumbled for the bedpost. He grabbed my wrist and hauled me up. I dropped down onto the floor with a thump, searching on hands and knees for my clothes. I had just struggled into loincloth and undertunic when he seemed to lose all patience. Snapping the whip, cursing under his breath, he seized me by the hair and hauled me out of the room. I desperately snatched up my remaining clothes. I wasn't sure I'd gotten both shoes.

Outside, I stood in knee-deep snow, the bundle of clothes in my arms. In the dim light, my legs and the snow seemed exactly the same color, the same substance. It was very funny. I imagined my flesh drifting away, the wind whispering through my bones, my toes snapping off like icicles and rattling down through the sewer gratings.

Thulisquar made me stand there for a few minutes, perfectly still. He stood behind me and held me firmly by both arms.

"The cold will sober you up," he said. "I need you to be at least slightly in command of your faculties. This night we have tasks to perform of unimaginable importance, and there is, I suspect, little time remaining to us."

(Suddenly, it wasn't as funny. I held the bundled clothes tight against my chest and throat.)

Thulisquar raised a hand, and the black, ornamented carriage of the Ministry of Pain lumbered out of the darkness, its matched black horses snorting white plumes of breath. He shoved me in, got in after me, closed the door, tapped on the ceiling, and we were off. I dressed as best as I could as I sat opposite him, trying to gauge the swaying, jolting motion of the carriage. More than once I slipped onto the floor.

"I cannot truly express how terribly, terribly disappointed in you I am," he said. "I feel my efforts with you have been a total failure."

I was ashamed then, and cold, and afraid. I managed to put on my trousers, overtunic, and vest. I'd lost coat, shoes, and socks entirely. I sat staring forlornly at my bare feet.

Soldiers stopped us at the gateway of the inner city. A sergeant scarcely older than myself leaned into the carriage. I watched his face, fascinated at the expression of extreme loathing as he recognized Thulisquar, then at the look of pity when our eyes met. Doubtless he took me for one more of the Doctor's victims. I noticed the red ribbon of the Revolutionary Party around the barrel of his musket. But things were still unsettled then. He dared not lay a hand on Thulisquar just yet. He let us pass.

And so we came to the familiar battlements, and the huge, round tower which comprised the Ministry of Pain and Revelation. There's a legend which says the tower is a great spear, rammed deep into the heart of the world, with only the very tip of the butt visible above the ground. The common folk say you can hear the moans of the Goddess Earth from that tower.

Most of the time we keep the doors and windows bolted, to contain the sound. (So very funny, once more.)

Down we went, into the earth,

Thulisquar dragging me by the arm, around and around the circular stairs past one level, then another, where on the holiest of days, torturers descended in solemn procession on their way to celebrate the Mysteries, holding aloft the still dripping skins of criminals like banners.

No warders met us. Most of the staff had already fled, fearing the disturbances in the city.

So Thulisquar took the great metal key in his own hand and opened the final door to the Chamber of Revelation himself. As the cold draught from within blew over us like the sighing breath of a god, all sense of hilarity left me. This was a secret, truly holy place, where sometimes the gods revealed themselves in the utterances of dying men.

My Master turned to me once, and said, "I shall learn all the details of your juvenile excesses some other time — including, especially, where you got the *hanquil* — but now we have work to do."

Then we got to work as if nothing had happened. As I shuffled about with a taper, relighting lamps, I dared to hope that Thulisquar would become so caught up in his researches that he would actually forget my lapse.

Someone urinated on me from above, out of the darkness. I shoved my taper up through swinging iron bars. That which was burnt squealed like a monkey.

For all there was no one around to fetch us more subjects, I realized, we still had a healthy supply of experimental material — political criminals, condemned by the Satrap, sent here, and forgotten, since more immediate troubles occupied the ruler's mind these days.

It was here that my dour Master engaged in his own, private study of *hanquil*. As their bones were slowly crushed between massive wooden rollers, Thulisquar would lean over to listen to the last gasps of drugged men. And he could hear, *yes!* ethereal giggles which

seemed to emanate from the Void. A wonder! Notations were kept in special ledgers, the data carefully correlated, its secrets laid bare for Thulisquar's meditative scrutiny by —

"*Oof! Wha— ? Excuse me. How did I . . ? What hour is it?*"

— a Notary in attendance, over whom I had just stumbled, a bewigged, lanky, and malodorous *hanquil*-addict who lent his presence and stamp to each execution. Anthexis was his name. The Satrap had spoken to him frequently in former times, before affairs of state became too worrisome for such pleasantries. The wife of Anthexis stank too, but of perfume. She wore finery set with tiny mirrors that she might dazzle onlookers. She encouraged her children to spit at their servants. But Anthexis was merely an opportunist, a five-grain slave of the drug, neither philosophical nor vicious.

He staggered to his feet and helped me light the lamps. Above, the prisoners whimpered and cursed and prayed in their dangling cages.

(In truth I had obtained my own illicit supply of *hanquil* from none other than Anthexis. I wondered what the Master Doctor would do when he found out.)

One other staff member remained to us. I found him asleep on straw, the burly, black-masked Chief Torturer of the Jails. I knew he would not flee. This was his home, his entire world. He knew nothing else.

So devoted was he to the worship of the twin gods of Pain and Death, that he had long since given up his name and his humanity to them. So fallen was he from the known spectrum of human behaviors that he merely lay about when inactive, as a dog would, and could be identified and summoned by any barking noise. All curs, therefore, could hail him. This pleased him mightily in some way I never could quite fathom, and gave him a kind of mystical kinship with hounds and hyenas.

He was reputed to roam about cemeteries at night on all fours, tearing up fresh graves with teeth and clawed hands.

I barked. He leapt to his feet quickly, as a dog would. Above, the prisoners cried out in anticipation of fresh enormities, and the Chief Torturer fairly beamed with joy. The wails of the suffering and the innocent were especially sweet to his ears, a kind of salve for his lesioned soul. For him the bloody, sweat-soaked apparatuses of our work were like musical instruments, human-stringed, and he, the Torturer, was a kind of virtuoso attuned to the highest pitches of pain. Yes, in his own way he was completely sincere, as totally devoted to his art and to the Twin Gods whom we worship above all others as is any ascetic who spends his entire life atop a pillar or walled up in a cell.

But I knew that Thulisquar found him revolting and merely useful. It was an uneasy balance. Yet it would have to do, especially this night.

"I want you to watch and listen very carefully, my dear boy," Thulisquar said during a particularly protracted execution. (So I was a "dear boy" now. Perhaps he *had* forgotten my offense. I tried not to giggle.)

He signaled to the Chief Torturer. The rollers halted and I held the funnel while Thulisquar ever so carefully dribbled a quarter grain of liquified *hanquil* into the criminal's mouth. Then he lowered his ear to a mere inch above the lips of the expiring man.

The victim seemed to sigh, but Thulisquar trembled with excitement. *He*, clearly, had heard more.

Then the sound came again, much louder than I had ever heard before from anyone, a sharp, recoiling chuckle. It echoed and re-echoed in the vast chamber. Above in the cages, the remaining subjects screamed.

Thulisquar was ecstatic. He turned to me first.

"Did *you* hear it? Truly it was the god-laughter. Yes, it was! We are close, so very close to our goal. Soon, by this means, mortal men shall communicate directly with the divine. Think of it!"

"I am very glad for you, Master," I said softly.

That was not the response he had been expecting. His face clouded. For an instant, I thought he would strike me. Then he turned to the Notary Anthexis, who sat with pen in hand and his ledger in his lap.

"And *you* —"

Anthexis yawned. "I must have dozed off —"

Thulisquar let out a wordless snort of rage. He shook his fist at the impassive Notary, but then his excitement overwhelmed all other emotions. He turned to me again.

"Surely the god-laughter seems more pronounced than ever before."

My mind was still sluggish with *hanquil*. It took me almost a minute to recognize my cue, as if I had been an actor in a play. I fumbled for my line.

"Undoubtedly. Definitely."

Satisfied, he turned back to the Notary.

"I suppose so," said Anthexis. "But let us seek the confirmation of our burly friend here."

The Torturer's reaction was duly sought. No reply. Only a few grunts. The unanswered question hung heavily in the air. Then Thulisquar put this very question to the dying man entangled in our machinery.

The victim seemed to concentrate very hard. Thulisquar raised a finger. The rollers inched forward, over the man's pelvis. Blood spurted from his nose. I put the funnel down and gave him an injection of *madat,* a distilled *hanquil* derivative used to soften bones. It was his eighth this session. *Madat* extends a subject's survival considerably. His bones become like clay, rather

than shards and powder. Sometimes we mold them into amusing shapes.

Thulisquar repeated his question.

"Nothing. I heard nothing," the dying man gasped at last.

Thulisquar paused, then said, "Do you suffer much?"

"Eh?"

Suddenly I didn't want to know. The after-effects of the *hanquil* now made me squeamish. I fidgeted with the injection needle I still held. The Chief Torturer looked up from the array of levers as he worked.

At last the captive spoke again. "It is a question without meaning."

"No suffering at all? Not the slightest discomfort?"

"None." The man wrinkled his brow as if deeply perplexed. Then he *laughed,* but it was only his own laughter. "It is getting harder to focus my thoughts, however."

Thulisquar turned sharply to Anthexis. "Write all that down. Subject declares himself insensible to pain." Then he snatched the quill from the Notary's hand. He tickled the dying man's forehead.

"Surely, fellow, you can feel this."

"Ah, surely. It draws me, a little bit, back into your world."

Thulisquar jabbed the man's cheek with the point of the quill.

"And you have no fear?"

"It is too complicated to explain —"

He turned again to Anthexis. "Are you getting all this —?"

The Notary reached feebly for his quill. Realizing his error, Thulisquar gave it to him, and waited as the account was brought up to the moment in the dying man's blood.

A terrible smile marred the prisoner's features.

Thulisquar leaned over to me again. "Now watch closely, and understand. This wretch was an artisan once, a sculptor of statues. He will have the sensitivity to appreciate my own creative efforts, as one artist to another."

A small giggle escaped my lips. Perhaps it was the lingering *hanquil* fumes from the funnel I held.

"It was similar irreverence that brought him here," Thulisquar said sternly. "Something about a scurrilous caricature of one of the Satrap's wives. Have a care, Ganzeric."

Once more I was ashamed and afraid. I tried to be attentive.

Thulisquar turned back to the prisoner and bade the Torturer advance the rollers again, ever so slightly.

"Exactly what *are* you experiencing just now?"

"A . . . difficulty. It is so hard to exist . . . to be. Squeezed. Broken. You have made an abstraction of me . . . a blot on the page."

At the Master's instruction, I once more placed the funnel in the man's mouth and we administered another quarter-grain of *hanquil.*

"Have you indeed *no* fear?" Thulisquar asked, bringing his face nearer and nearer to the criminal-sculptor's own.

"I am not . . . of your world anymore. I no longer care for anything you would understand. I am on the edge now, the very threshold . . ."

"Yes?"

"I . . . *nagnn —*"

It was at that exact instant the inspiration came to me. Perhaps I, too, was becoming caught up in the excitement of the quest. Perhaps the very gods moved through me, desiring to speak at last, instructing mankind as to the proper method of communication. Or it might have only been the *hanquil.* I could not be sure. But I forgot all else. I had to speak. "Master, if I may venture to suggest —"

Thulisquar jumped up, whirled around.

"Shut up, you imbecile!"

"But I see the answer now. If only you would —"

"You dare advise *me* —"

" . . . unmaker of men," the dying one said. "A reverse god . . ."

Thulisquar turned back to the experimental subject.

"Master," I tried to break in.

"Shut —"

He waved a hand, apparently confusing the Chief Torturer. Maybe the man was just clumsy.

With a clack and a rumble, the rollers broke free of all restraint, *consuming* the ex-sculptor. Brains splashed over Anthexis, who screamed and tumbled from his chair, then rose to his knees and desperately wiped the ledger clean with the corner of his robe.

"Idiots and imbeciles," Thulisquar ranted. "All I have to work with are idiots and imbeciles —"

"If I may only suggest —"

He grabbed me front of my tunic and yanked me entirely off the floor until my face was level with his. His eyes were filled with hate. I was certain he would kill me then, but, somehow, I was not afraid.

"*What* were you going to suggest?"

"The answer, Master. It is so clear."

"It is, is it?"

"*Yes.* It suddenly came to me. The *hanquil.* If you give a man six grains, he dies laughing. But if you give him *seven, very suddenly, before his body has time* to die, he is propelled beyond the threshold of life and death, into the other realm, where he can speak to the gods. *But he has several minutes left before he actually dies.* In that interval —"

The anger left my Master's face. He was stunned. He let go of me.

"That is actually a brilliant idea. Coming from you, it is a miracle."

I hoped then that he would actually forgive me for everything. But I dared not speak. The balance was *so* delicate.

"I must leave this place," he said at last. "I must walk and think. Come."

He started up the stairs, out of the chamber. I shuffled after him. He turned back to me.

"And Ganzeric —"

"Yes, Master?"

"Put some shoes on."

I had entirely forgotten that I was still barefoot. I glanced down and saw that my feet were black with the soot and dirt of the place. They were so numb with cold they seemed to belong to someone else. Therefore I had forgotten them. Such indifference is characteristic of the *hanquil*-user, I am told.

I borrowed a pair of boots and a coat from the Torturer. The boots were too big, so I stuffed them with straw.

So we walked together in the garden outside the Ministry of Pain. The common people dread it almost as much as the tower itself, but for me it has always been merely a familiar place.

Thulisquar paced among the frozen, crucified corpses, some of whom had been there for months. He seemed to ask questions of the blackened, shrivelled faces. Sometimes he listened, as if receiving answers. I did not doubt it.

Then, too, he led me into that section of the garden where the trees are human beings, alive, perhaps immortal, but permanently rooted in the soil and shaped, hideously or fancifully, as the imaginations of generations of Torturers and Doctors had fashioned them. Here a woman was on all fours, hands and legs growing into the earth, her naked skin long since turned the color of old wood. Only her head moved, from side to side, endlessly. She was, of course, mad, and her howls had faded into a faint whistling between her teeth.

Thulisquar used her as a bench. He invited me to sit beside him, but I could not. I stood before him as he rehearsed his thoughts. Ours was a dialogue such as the philosophers might write, my role in it strictly that of a secondary character, restricted to stimulating and directing Thulisquar with my replies.

"The gods speak to men through

139

suffering," he said. "For this reason there are wars and plagues and devastations. Through each grand event, the pattern of a divine thought is revealed."

"And the pain of everyday life," I said.

"Yes, even as a woman's labor and bleeding announce to her that the gods have given her a child. Even then."

"And it is through suffering alone that we may reply to the gods."

"Yes, that is so," said Thulisquar, "but the interesting part is this: we may communicate with the gods through the sufferings of others. The sufferer, the dying man especially, may convey occult knowledge back to the living as he totters on the threshold of life and death. Deathbed revelations are a commonplace. But when death may be *elaborated,* then considerably more information may be gained than otherwise. A devoted student might interview hundreds, even thousands of dying men, and thus carry on a lengthy dialogue with the world beyond this one."

"But the problem is to clarify their dying," I said.

"Only when the travelling soul may see the road before it *clearly,* yes, when the soul is far beyond the body, beyond the initial confusion and darkness, but the body is *still capable of speech,* only then may extended contact with the divine become possible."

"That is the purpose of our labors," I said.

"Yes. Otherwise you and I would be monsters, and our work obscene. It is immoral to cause pain without reason, Ganzeric. Never forget that, lest you become a monster."

The Master rose and walked, past a grove of human trees where hundreds of incredibly long, spindly arms grew from each body. Some predecessor of Thulisquar had created them long ago, with the aid of bone-softening *madat.* Sticklike limbs swayed in the night breeze. The tree-men seemed to be begging alms. Their cupped palms were filled with snow.

Then he took out a key and opened a gate. We went through and emerged into an alley I had not seen in a long time, but which I almost subliminally recognized. It was, in effect, my birthplace. Here Thulisquar had found me, starving.

We walked in silence. Beyond us, in the city, there were shouts and explosions. I was afraid then that the Revolution had begun. I didn't want to go on. But Thulisquar was not afraid. He emerged from the alley into a broad avenue, into a mass of people engaged, much to my surprise, not in riot but revelry.

It took my *hanquil*-fogged brain several minutes to recall that this was the Feast of Turning, when the winter stars have progressed more than half-way through the southern sky, and if you stay up until dawn, you can see the stars of summer rise just before the sun.

The gods were born on such a night as this. They rose from the cold mud of their mother's flesh, out of the Goddess Earth herself, and stood on the banks of the great World River, hand in hand, in silence, waiting for the sun, dreaming of mankind. The heterodox suggest that the gods were less than solemn on that occasion, and cavorted wildly and drunkenly on the world's first night, to keep the cold away. These heretics (my Master has dealt with many of them) further say that the gods all drank themselves into a stupor, that they lie yet in the world's mud, oblivious to mankind, and that the divine laughter we hear, on the threshold of death or in the holy man's trance, is no more than an echo of that first and archetypal orgy.

On the Feast of Turning one can almost believe it. On this night the streets were thick with shouting, singing, cavorting crowds. Men and women were having sexual congress in doorways, in snowbanks, on the very paving

stones, oblivious to the cold and the spectators and traffic. Boys ran through the streets carrying bowls of burning powder which thundered and flashed and showered sparks. More than once I saw such a one catch fire, roll in the snow, and come up laughing.

I too laughed at many things. I felt the *hanquil* delirium returning. More than once Thulisquar had to drag me away as I tried to join in the festivities.

If anything, the Feast was more frantic than usual because of everyone's fear of the days to come, and, also, as the crowds gave vent to their anger over centuries of misrule.

Many of the gatherings were distinctly political. Three times I saw burning effigies of the Satrap that night, and twice those of my own Master. One of the latter was accompanied by a smaller effigy which might have represented myself.

"I do not care about such things," was all Thulisquar would say.

Fortunately we were not recognized. We walked because it focused my Master's thoughts.

"I return to the subject of laughter," he said. "Why do the gods laugh at us?"

"So that we too may laugh, and lighten our pain," I said, giving a catechism answer. "Laughter is infectious."

"And why do they give us the gift of pain?"

"To moderate our laughter."

"But if the pain could be *extended*, so then could the laughter, which is the very real speech of the gods. This is the use to which I shall put your very brilliant suggestion, my boy. Yes, you have made a definite contribution, and for once I am actually proud of you." He slammed his fist into his open hand. "Yes. I know what to do now. Yes. Back to work. Quickly."

He began to walk in rapid, long strides. I ran to catch up with him.

"Master, there is one thing which bothers me still."

"What is that?"

"Surely someone has taken seven grains of *hanquil* before, accidentally. What happened?"

"Surely someone has, fumbling with a bottle during some delirious revel. Doubtless they babbled strangely before they died. But no scholar was present, no one who could appreciate what had happened. The event was wasted. Do not worry, Ganzeric. We are the first to study this phenomenon. We are pioneers."

At the mouth of the alley outside the garden, there was a tumult. Thulisquar forced his way through the crowd.

"What is this? What is this?"

He came upon the body of a girl child, who had been trampled and run over by a cart. The wheel-marks were quite evident in the snow, right across her middle. She might have been eight years old. Fish- and dog-masked revellers stood over her, gaping.

"Let me through," said Thulisquar. "I am a physician. Perhaps something can be done for the poor thing."

He knelt over her and produced a small vial of *hanquil,* which he forced between her lips. I counted the grains, one, two, three, four, five, six, *seven*. Ah, my Master, always the tireless seeker of knowledge. The crowd stirred when the sharp fumes revealed that it was indeed *hanquil*. They closed in. Thulisquar looked up. His outer robe fell open, revealing his embroidered inner garment, the uniform of the Ministry of Pain.

The people recognized us then. I let out a little yelp. I was sure we were dead.

But their look was one of *disgust*, as if an enormous turd had been thrown down before them. They didn't even hate us. It was as if they *knew* we would soon be dealt with, that our escape was already impossible.

But Thulisquar cared no more for the common people's feelings than he did

for politics.

The crowd made signs to ward off evil and moved away.

Thulisquar held the child's corpse in his arms, swaying gently back and forth, whispering in the dead ear.

I tugged on his sleeve.

"Master. There's nothing we can do here. We'd better get back, where it's safe."

As if to deny me, the girl's mouth fell open, and there *was* a sound, like the whistling of a wind from deep within a cavern.

"You hear that?" said Thulisquar. "There are traces of the god-laughter even *after* the death of the body! This is a new development. It is of enormous significance."

And there was another sound, something even more enormous:

The corpse spoke. In a very distinct voice, not at all that of a little girl, it said, *"Seek me not, oh Man; but I will seek you out, until the two of us are one."*

"Holiness!" Thulisquar cried. "Ineffable holiness! The unmaker of men speaks to me alone!" His voice was almost a scream of triumph.

That whole scene was the key to my Master's character. Then, truly, I knew him for a man who was god-mad, driven insane by the quest for the divine, filled with the spirit of unworldly mysteries, as crazed as the priests of distant Zhamiir who slowly flay themselves as a lifelong work of adoration. He was never a cruel man, or a lustful one, or power-hungry. For Thulisquar there were only the gods and the knowledge of the gods, which he, through his science, might reveal to men. In his own way he was himself holy, his quest beautiful, his motivations utterly unselfish.

Why the revelation came just then, in such a manner, I never did find out. Things happened quickly.

"Come!" He was up and running, carrying the girl's corpse. It was all I could do to keep up with him in my oversized, clumsy boots. We ran through the garden again, back into the tower and down into the holy chamber. There he laid the girl down on a table and left her, perhaps for future experimentation. As it happened, I never found out that either.

Again we labored in the Chamber of Revelations. I think several days and nights passed. Deep below, one never sees the sun anyway. My body told me that I was very weary, that my exhaustion and *hanquil* haze and hunger had all blended into a single miasma. I cannot recall what secrets Thulisquar revealed to me.

I know he used a new and revolutionary technique, whereby the bodies of the condemned were first softened, marinated in fluids for hours, given endless injections of *madat,* while Thulisquar spoke on and on in great excitement and agitation, telling how at last we would have specific messages from the gods rather than meaningless giggles, how all the things we had ever done were righteous, even pious, because *truth must be served.*

I think he mostly talked to fill the hours before the first subjects were ready. Sometimes he mixed chemicals in beakers and alembics. If he told me what they were for, such knowledge slipped from my exhausted brain like water through limp fingers.

Incredibly, the Chief Torturer had fled. Therefore I had to work the levers and turn the rollers as best I could. Only Anthexis remained with us, raving in another *hanquil* state, but somehow able to write in his ledger. I was clumsy with the machinery. Anthexis spilled ink and drooled on the page. But Thulisquar didn't seem to care.

At last the first victims were ready. We passed them through the rollers, then stretched them on racks so that, while they still drew breath, they were living kites, their every inch of surface consist-

ing of outraged nerve tissue screaming in agony.

Yet with four grains of *hanquil* the pain was numbed. With five, these travesties shrieked out laughter. I too laughed. It all seemed, again, very funny as we daubed them with festive colors and glued sequins and ribbons and gaudy feathers all over them. Then we hauled a dozen of them up to the roof and flew them, indeed like kites, high in the air. Every evening they were reeled in and fed *hanquil,* a tiny fraction of a grain *more* than the fatal sixth dose, and each evening that fraction was a little bit larger.

Because they were no longer men, they did not die like men. They flew overhead for a week and came down, their sequins and ribbons smeared with blood.

I must have slept some of that time, merely fainting with exhaustion on a bench or on the stairs or on the roof. I don't think I ate anything. It was all a delirium, yes, like a *hanquil* dream or nightmare that would not end.

But Thulisquar did not sleep. He was in his finest hour, and tireless. It was the climax of his life.

Yet it was a horror too, and a terrifying disappointment, because now that the barriers between life and death were totally removed, now that direct communication with the gods had been established, the results were only a few strange, disordered words, and a great deal of laughter.

"Laughter," said Thulisquar wearily. "The gods laugh at our handiwork. But still there have been no more clear messages since the eve of the trampled child. We must press on."

And another time he said, "How elusive the gods are, in the end," and wept bitterly.

And, yet another, I saw from the rooftop of the Ministry of Pain that there were fires in many parts of the city. The Revolution had begun.

"Alas," said Thulisquar.

"Master," I said. "It's done. It's time for us to go."

Even then rebel soldiers were battering down the outer gate to the Ministry. Only Anthexis, of all people, was brave enough to oppose them. He fought fiercely for a time, shooting arrows down into the mob, pouring boiling oil, hurling stones. Meanwhile, Thulisquar struggled on with our increasingly tattered human kites. We had to use the same ones over and over. We had long since run out of prisoners.

After a while I looked down from the roof again and saw that Anthexis was gone.

As the crowd had discerned on the night of the festival, there was indeed no escape for us. Down we went, down into the depths of the ministry, barring and bolting door after door.

We had only a few hours left.

Thulisquar sat, exhausted at last, by the rollers of the torture-machine, contemplating the vast mechanism, weeping.

"After all this," he said. "After coming so close, I cannot live *or even die* having failed."

It was our philosophical dialogue all over again. Far above, the mob broke through one of the doors with a crash.

I watched in horrified fascination as my Master took out a vial of *hanquil* and put a grain on his tongue, then another.

"Do you ever think about the gods, Ganzeric?"

"Yes, but not profoundly."

"Sometimes I think you are wise to shrug them off, as they shrug us off."

"Perhaps, Master."

A third grain, a fourth. He was free from pain now. He could not feel his own exhaustion.

"Do you know what they do? The gods, I mean. Can you imagine their purpose?"

"I cannot."

"The gods make men," he explained, "in order to have something to laugh at."

And I was laughing then, exhaustion, starvation, and *hanquil* fumes working together. Once one has been exposed to *hanquil,* even the smallest amounts have that effect.

It seemed so very *funny.* Not sad. Not horrible. Funny. The laughter of the gods had shielded me from pain at the last. The merciful gods.

"Do you remember that sculptor we executed . . . whenever it was?"

"Yes, Great Thulisquar. I remember."

"He was like a god. He exercised godly prerogatives in stone, creating what shapes he wished, to be admired or laughed at as he chose. It was laughter which proved his undoing, I believe."

"Master, you have explained why the gods made men, but do men have any purpose of their own, save as objects for the gods to look upon?"

"Ah. Do the statues enjoy their own society, speaking a secret language, expressing secret loves and hates of stone? Is there a secret political system among them? Are some lords over the others, even as they are all equal in the eyes of mankind?"

He took a fifth grain of *hanquil.*

"Yes," he said. "It is quite possible."

A fifth grain and he *did not laugh.* Such a great and amazing man was Thulisquar.

The shouts of the invaders above us were louder now. I heard the continual boom-boom-boom and a battering ram assaulted another door.

Thulisquar took a sixth grain of *hanquil.*

"Master!"

He showed no sign of weakness. He was not ready to die just yet.

"I wanted to see the face of a god. I wanted to be with the gods. Only the gods are real, not men. We are illusions, the *hanquil*-phantoms of the divine orgy, nothing more. Is that not enough?

Is that not a magnificent thing, to live in a world which is a delirium of the gods? Is it not wonderful?"

He lurched to his feet and staggered against a worktable. Bottles and jars crashed to the floor. He had a needle in his hands, one we had used to inject the prisoners. He could not steady it.

"You'll have to help me."

I steadied him, and gave him the injection of the softening agent, *madat.*

Then he lay down on the ramp before the rollers, opened the *hanquil* vial once more, and poured the entire contents down his throat, at least twenty grains.

"I shall be with the gods now," he said softly. He was, strangely, more coherent than he had been in days. "I want you to help me. This last experiment is a very difficult and delicate one. It is only fair that I should be the subject of it. Only I would be able to truly appreciate what I shall experience. Will you do this thing for me, dearest Ganzeric?"

"Yes," I said, alternately weeping and laughing. "I shall."

And delicately, lovingly, I pressed his body through the rollers like a printer turning out a rare and beautiful illustration. He was paper-thin, stretched upon a wire frame, his features reduced to an abstraction, only his face recognizable, transformed as it was with holy ecstasy in addition to the mere distortion of flatness.

He spoke to me, in the secret language of the gods, and he told me many secrets, which amounted to one thing: laughter to ease pain, pain to moderate laughter. That is the balance of the universe. The Twin Gods who are greater than all the rest are not Death and Pain, as the theologians would have it, but Laughter and Pain. Even those two.

Inevitably, the revolutionaries broke in upon us. The door of the holiest chamber burst inward and there stood a mob of soldiers and citizens, swords and muskets lowered, awestruck in amaze-

ment. They were led by that same young
sergeant who had leaned into the carriage.

He bore a head on a pike — Anthexis's
— which he turned to right and to left as
if it were a magic talisman and he were
dispersing the evil from this lowest
dungeon. Behind him, a grizzled captain
carried two heads by the hair. One I
recognized as that of the Chief Torturer.
The other, intensely mutilated, might
have been the Satrap.

They came down the stairs, into the
room. I worked calmly, decorating my
Master with ribbons and sequins. I
hummed softly as I painted delicate
patterns on the parchment of his skin,
illuminating him as a final tribute to his
greatness.

The sergeant stared. He tried to push
me away, but I resisted, and resumed my
work.

"Have you no fear?" he said.

"It is difficult to explain."

(Someone whispered that I was mad.
Another said I was a demon in human
form.)

I began to laugh. Then the great
Thulisquar laughed too, for he was now
the true and unimpeded conduit of the
gods. The messages through him were
utterly clear, without any distortion.

His laughter was like thunder. The
whole tower shook with it. The mob and
the soldiers turned and ran. Some of
them fell to their knees. Some stumbled
and were trampled.

Only the young sergeant stood his
ground, for all he dropped Anthexis's
head in his nervousness. It occurred to
me that we looked very much alike, that
we might be long-lost brothers. Suddenly I was very fond of him.

None of this mattered to Thulisquar.

"Have you no fear?" said the sergeant,
not to me, but to my Master. Somehow
this clever young man had figured out
what and *whom* he was beholding.

"None whatever," said Thulisquar,
quite clearly. "I hear now. I see. I shall

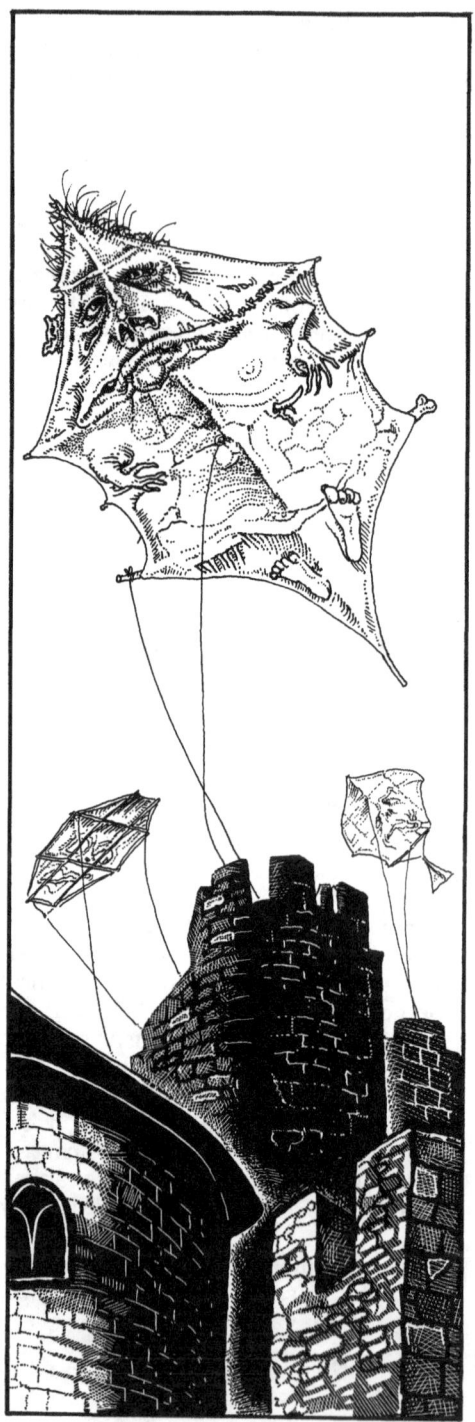

soon be fulfilled."

I knew what I had to do then. I took a little knife and cut the strings which held the stretched form of the Great Doctor in place. He floated on the air. A breeze blew him into my face, and he whispered into my ears. I could smell his sweat and his blood and a trace of *hanquil.*

Gently, fascinated, the sergeant peeled Thulisquar off, then — to my astonishment — released him, watching him float on the air, whirling in the eddies and draughts of the chamber. Up he went, out the broken door, up, out of the tower while we two followed on the stairs.

Outside in the courtyard, the mob waited at a distance. The sergeant and I stood there for quite some time, watching Thulisquar drift upward into the bright morning sky, until he was just a speck against the sun and we could no longer make him out.

Now I write in my cell, because I fear I have little time left. I fear that the mob will demand my death, by torture most probably. They will give me to some crude butcher, whose ministrations will be . . . inartistic and without scientific validity.

How they howled at my trial. The judge and the soldiers shouted for silence again and again, but it was no use. The good sergeant testified. I think he tried to save me. I couldn't hear what he said. Nor could anyone else, I think.

But there *was* silence when I was called to repeat, at the very end, what Thulisquar had said to me as we parted, as his paper-thin self was wrapped around my face and he whispered in my ear.

"He told me that the gods are unknowable," I said. "That was his own,

endless punishment, that after all he had been through, he still could not grasp the mystery. Therefore we should not hate him, but pity him."

It was a fine speech. But again the crowd screamed for my death. I was returned to my cell.

I pricked my left hand with the needle when I gave my Master the injection. The flesh has become soft. I pass the time carefully molding it between my fingers, until my hand is webbed. It disconcerts my jailers.

Later. There is one more thing, even as I write. *Thulisquar* is outside my window. I see him there, drifting in the evening shadows, flapping in the air like a banner. I reached out to him, but it was like grabbing mist.

I sit down again. It is no use. I write a few more lines. These.

He whispers to me. Is the secret for me alone, or for all mankind? I am not selfish. Here. Let me share it. These are the words of the Master Doctor Thulisquar in his transcended state:

I am the unmaker of men.

They are coming for me now. I hear boots on the stairs outside. My fate has surely been decided. I think I am going to die. I almost long for that, considering the alternative, which is that I should be declared insane and locked away in a cage for people to stare at, as if I were some exotic beast.

The world is not ready for the wisdom of Thulisquar. They do not understand.

I long for him, to be with him, like him.

I weep.

Hanquil. If only.

Seven grains would be enough for me.

Ω

I0685286

www.ingramcontent.com/pod-product-compliance
Lightning Source LLC
Chambersburg PA
CBHW060749180626
46818CB00002B/519

9 780809 532148